*Neffatira's First Challenge:*
*The Light Guardian Series Book One*

by Tom Xavier

© Copyright 2019 Tom Xavier

ISBN 978-1-63393-842-7

Published by

 köehlerbooks™

210 60th Street
Virginia Beach, VA 23451
800–435–4811
www.koehlerbooks.com

# NEFFATIRA'S
# FIRST CHALLENGE

THE LIGHT GUARDIAN SERIES BOOK ONE

# TOM XAVIER

VIRGINIA BEACH
CAPE CHARLES

# CHAPTER 1

# CLIMBING THE SPINE

"C'mon, hurry up."

"Shut up, I'm coming."

"Then hurry. Stop being a chicken."

Eyes alert, Jessica stood waiting for Cassie. Morning dew had plastered her blond, blue-tipped bangs against her forehead, a drip beaded her eyebrow. Neffie stood not more than an arm's length behind Jessica, the girl she had always wanted to be. Naturally, the misty air made Jessica's hair glisten, while Neffie's had erupted into a frizzy, unattractive mess.

*Figures,* thought Neffie gloomily.

Clumped in a group behind them were the other girls of Jessica's gang, all of them waiting for stout Cassie to catch up. Cassie was barely visible in the heavy fog down the trail, but Neffie heard her out-of-breath friend panting.

"I'm hurrying," shouted Cassie as she struggled to catch up. "And I'm not chicken."

"If you say so."

Jessica's ridicule caused some of the girls behind Neffie to snicker. Feeling sorry for Cassie, Neffie kept quiet while the other girls had their fun. *Go ahead,* she thought, *pretend you're not just as scared.*

Of course, they all had good reason to be scared: the Spine, that tall hill infamous for deadly fogs causing many climbers to get lost and fall to their deaths. Ascending it was not a smart thing to do—not smart at all.

Neffie couldn't believe she had agreed to be part of this newest adventure concocted by Jessica, who was notorious for coming up with crazy-dangerous stunts. Sure, Jessica was the coolest, most popular girl in Neffie's school. But was this one chance to hang with Jessica and her gang of girls really a good reason to risk everything, as she was obviously doing?

*You're a total idiot,* thought Neffie.

Of course, none of the other girls knew why Neffie had every right to be ten times more scared. How could they? Always careful when others were around, Neffie kept her most embarrassing secret to herself. Only her mother and her stepfather knew anything about it, and even they didn't know the full extent of Neffie's embarrassment.

"C'mon," Jessica shouted to Cassie. "Pick up your feet. We're already later than I want."

This last barb was aimed at Neffie, who had arrived late for their meet-up at Jessica's house, delaying the group's start by twenty minutes. Neffie clenched her teeth, feeling the sting of Jessica's criticism but saying nothing. She had no illusions about today. Jessica was not her friend, and today's adventure was in no way a first step into Jessica's gang.

Nor was Neffie a member of any of the other tight little cliques of girls that formed the social fabric of ninth-grade life at the Millard Fillmore Junior-Senior Consolidated High School in Windmere, Iowa. Sighing, she shook her head to get rid of the thought, but it was like one of those nightmares that stayed with you after you woke up.

"Forget it," she muttered under her breath.

When Cassie finally caught up, Jessica gave the girl her famed put-down stare, a look with such a crushing mix of impatience, annoyance and disapproval that it could shatter the spirit of even the most confident girl. Cassie withered visibly.

After smashing Cassie with her look, Jessica called to the others. "All right, let's get going. And everyone keep up or you'll get left permanently behind. I mean it—permanently behind."

This obviously meant being dropped from Jessica's gang—at least for the day. Neffie saw Cassie's lips tighten. The other girls nodded nervously. There would be no slackers from this point forward.

Jessica set a brisk pace, hiking nimbly up the steep trail on her long, athletic legs. Tall, agile Sarah, Jessica's first lieutenant, fell in line behind Jessica and had no trouble matching steps. The rest of the girls fell into their natural places in line with Cassie next to last and Neffie bringing up the rear.

Some of the other girls were quite a bit shorter or less athletic than the two leaders. Neffie soon heard their hard breathing as they struggled to keep up. Cassie was outright gasping as she chugged up the hill. With her long, muscular legs, Neffie walked effortlessly, even while she shivered from the cold dampness and the knot of fear in her stomach.

After about a quarter mile or so of hiking, the girls reached the end of the trail, and Jessica stopped on a small piece of flat ground in front of a tall gate. The city council of Windmere had erected the gate after the last and worst hiking accident on the Spine a few years earlier. The incident so shocked everyone in Windmere that the council closed the hill's trails forever. Gradually, the rest of the girls gathered in front of Jessica. Leaning back against the giant gate for effect, the leader surveyed her gang. From her place in the back, Neffie could easily see over the others. Jessica flashed her an eager smile.

"Come here, tall one," she called to Neffie.

Neffie moved to the front. She felt a bird fluttering its wings in her chest. It was her old friend, the woodpecker who awoke whenever there was danger to tap out a sharp warning on her sternum.

*This is it, Neff,* she thought as the woodpecker tapped away. *Your one chance to be cool.*

Neffie knew only bad stuff could follow this one moment of coolness. But she was not going to let anyone see her fear. Tightening her fists, she walked over to Jessica.

"What's up?" she asked, trying to sound nonchalant.

"Time to open the gate to adventure," Jessica replied with a wink. Neffie had no idea what this meant and shrugged. "Okay. Fine."

Pointing behind her, Jessica directed, "Take a look over there."

Tall pillars flanked both sides of the gate, forming a massive structure as tall as a basketball rim and impenetrable-looking. Along the top of the gate stretched a lethal coil of razor wire. Equally ominous wire crowned both pillars, and a high, chain-link fence topped with barbed wire extended along the hillside in both directions as far as Neffie could see.

There was an old metal sign attached to the gate and similar signs attached to the fence every ten feet or so. Each sign had the same dire warning etched in tall, red letters on a white background. The warning was emphatic.

*No Admittance*
*Extreme Danger*
*Trespassers Will Be Prosecuted*

Shifting her gaze from the sign on the gate to Jessica, Neffie said nothing. The other girls were obviously intimidated and remained silent, too. Fog swirled around them as Jessica reached to brush her fingers lightly over the warning sign. There was a long, uncomfortable silence before she spoke. At last, she gave a dry chuckle.

"Geez, they sound serious, don't they?" When no one reacted she said, "No one is chickening out, right?"

To Neffie's surprise, Jessica gave her an almost friendly smile while fishing around in her jacket pocket and pulling something out.

"A wire cutter," she explained, holding the tool in the air for Neffie to see. "I swiped it from my dad's truck."

"Okay," Neffie said. "Cool."

"It's time, tall one," continued Jessica, pointing at one of the gate's pillars. "You go stand over there and get ready."

The oddness of this command threw Neffie off balance.

"Um, do what?" she asked.

Neffie instantly regretted saying this. To question a command from Jessica was to invite a reprimand. Neffie sucked in her breath and waited nervously for Jessie to react. To Neffie's surprise, Jessica ignored her blunder.

"The plan is, you're going to lean your back against that brick thingy and make a step with your hands. Then I'm going to climb onto your shoulders and cut the wires so everyone can climb over you. Got it?"

*So that's why Jessica invited me?* "That's it?" Neffie huffed. "I'm here to be a human ladder?"

Jessica gave her a sharp look. "Exactly right. If you must know," she replied curtly, "cuz it would've been ridiculously hard to bike here with a ladder. Besides, what if we were spotted on the way? We'd be sunk . . . Plus, who the heck are you to question my plan? You got a problem with it?"

Neffie could only mumble a simple, "Nope."

"Good. Then let's get going. You know the plan."

As instructed, Neffie moved over and leaned back against the pillar. Bending at the knees, she laced her fingers to form a makeshift step for Jessica. Jessica placed her right foot into Neffie's clasped fingers and was about to lunge up when she stepped back and gave Neffie a curious look.

"Don't you have a question for me?" she sneered.

"Nope," mumbled Neffie, vowing this time to keep her mouth shut even though she did have a question—an important one.

Grinning a bit, Jessica pressed her. "Tell me you aren't wondering how you're going to get over after we're all on the other side and you're left standing here all by your lonesome."

Neffie wasn't about to cross Jessica again, so she shook her head and answered, "No, not really."

Jessica grinned.

"Good girl," she said. Then she pointed to her first lieutenant. "So, here's the deal. Sarah's going over last. When she gets to the top, she'll reach down for you to grab her hands." Glancing over her shoulder, Jessica called, "You hear, Sarah?"

"I hear," Sarah answered.

Looking Neffie in the eyes, Jessica whispered in a low voice meant only for her, "You'll need to be strong enough to pull yourself up and over because we're going to need you on the other side to get back. You can't mess up, okay?"

Neffie nodded, and Jessica signaled for her to get ready. Jessica slipped a foot into Neffie's clasped hands and launched herself. Nimbly, the girl worked her way up until she was standing on Neffie's bony shoulders. Gritting her teeth, Neffie braced against the brick pillar, head lowered, muscles working hard to support Jessica.

Jessica panted as she struggled with the razor wire. After a bunch of snips, she thrust her feet against Neffie's shoulders, and a second later Jessica's weight was gone.

"Okay, everyone," Jessica called from the top of the pillar, "let's move. Hannah, you're next. All the rest of you follow one at a time. Cassie, you go next to last and finally Sarah."

One by one, the other girls climbed up and over Neffie, none as smoothly and agilely as Jessica had done. Just as Jessica commanded, pudgy Cassie went next to last. She nervously placed her foot in Neffie's hands and thrust. Once off the ground, she tottered and would have fallen had Sarah not put a hand on her butt to keep her steady.

"Careful," Sarah warned. "Cassie, you mess up and you're not getting another chance."

Struggling to keep her balance, Cassie grabbed a hunk of Neffie's hair.

"Ow!" Neffie cried. "Careful."

Tottering precariously, Cassie grunted, "I'm trying."

"Try harder."

Sarah grabbed Cassie's hips to steady her and then added her own words of encouragement, exhorting, "Come on, Cassie, climb."

With Sarah's help, Cassie slowly stood on Neffie's shoulders.

"Now over," cried Sarah.

Neffie's back and shoulders trembled under Cassie's weight. *Oh my gosh,* she thought. *I can't do this.* After a second attempt, Cassie, huffing and groaning, hauled herself to the top.

"I made it," she announced.

*Thank goodness.* As Cassie dropped to the ground on the other side, Sarah moved to take her turn. Neffie's body was still shaking from the strain of bearing Cassie's weight for so long.

"You all right?" asked Sarah.

"I'm fine," answered Neffie through clenched teeth. "Just be quick."

Fortunately, Sarah was nearly as agile as Jessica.

"Here," she soon called from the top of the pillar, "take my hands."

Turning and sucking in a deep breath, Neffie jumped and grabbed Sarah's dangling hands. Sarah had a strong grip. Although her muscles ached, Neffie arched her powerful back, and with her eyes closed to keep from looking down, she walked her body up the side of the brick pillar.

Once she was safely on top, Neffie opened her eyes just long enough to catch the look of surprise on Sarah's face. Neffie felt a little spark of pride as she slid past Sarah and dropped to the ground on the other side.

*Finally,* Neffie thought, *someone knows.*

Neffie was gracefully athletic. But she never allowed anyone—not classmates, nor teachers—to see how strong and agile she was. Neffie's only desire in school was to blend, never to stand out. Unfortunately, among the all-white, nearly all-blond student body of Millard Fillmore, it was impossible for an abnormally tall, black-skinned, pink-freckled, frizzy-haired girl not to stand out.

Neffie glanced around. She stood on the edge of a rocky clearing inside a grove of stunted cedars. Jessica and the other girls were waiting a dozen feet or so up a well-worn trail that rose through the trees. Sarah dropped to the ground beside her, and Neffie instinctively gave her a friendly smile. To her surprise, the girl smiled back. Then the two of them hurried up the trail to join the others.

The instant they arrived, Jessica called to everyone, "All right, let's go."

Jessica took the lead with the other girls falling into their usual places. Neffie again brought up the rear. With the heavy fog hanging all around them, Neffie had no doubt everyone was thinking about the last and most terrible incident on the Spine, which ended tragically with two violent falls to the razor-sharp rocks below, resulting in one instant death and the other long and lingering. Still, everyone pushed on, and as they climbed Neffie heard the occasional cry of a girl whose toe caught on a rock or whose foot slipped in the greasy mud between rocks. Even Neffie stumbled hard at one point but regained her balance.

"Careful," Cassie warned, turning her head to give Neffie a weak smile meant to be encouraging. The fear in Cassie's eyes was clear.

"Thanks," answered Neffie, forcing herself to smile back. "You be careful, too."

"You betcha," agreed Cassie, her answer coming too quickly to sound confident.

Neffie kept quiet as the group trudged up the hillside. For the next quarter mile or so, the trail's incline wasn't too terrible. But then they reached a sharp turn, and the trail steepened significantly. Soon they were all breathing noisily as they struggled up a rocky path that grew more treacherous with every step.

Neffie paused to peer uphill, hoping to see through the fog but unable to make out anything. Shuddering, she couldn't help but feel as gloomy as the fog itself. But they kept climbing, slowly working their way toward the hill's most prominent feature, a jagged ridgeline of sharp-edged rocks that looked eerily like a human spine.

At last, there was an excited shout from Jessica at the front of the group.

"We're here!"

One by one, the girls reached the small area of relatively flat, gravelly ground on which Jessica stood. Nervously, they gathered in a circle around her.

"Is this really it?" Cassie asked with a hint of disbelief.

"Course this is it," Jessica answered.

"Really?" asked Erika, a pale-skinned girl who always reminded Neffie of a mouse. "How can you tell?"

"This is definitely it," affirmed Jessica. "Damn! We've come all this way and we can't see crap. This sucks."

"Um, which way's the river?" Sarah asked.

"Over there," answered Jessica, pointing. "Take maybe ten steps in that direction and you go, like, over the cliff and instantly you're dead. Even worse, the Spine is just over there. Just think, we can't see either, but we're smack in the middle between the cliff and the edge of the Spine, probably on the most dangerous spot on this whole hill. How's that for cool?"

Jessica grinned while her girls fidgeted and exchanged uncomfortable glances. Neffie was way too scared to look. She closed her eyes and waited, hoping the thick fog might cause Jessica to announce they were leaving.

"Come on," Jessica cried, "let's get closer. Maybe we can see down the cliff."

Neffie couldn't believe her ears. *Is Jessica crazy?*

Apparently she was because she had already started moving toward the cliff.

"This way," she called. "Make sure you spread out," she added as she inched forward. "No one bump anyone."

Nervously, the girls spread out and took tiny steps toward the cliff's edge. Lingering behind, Neffie found she couldn't move her feet. She was just too frightened. Somehow, Jessica noticed.

"You too, tall one," she called. "We're all in this together."

Taking a deep breath, Neffie forced one foot to move, then the other. The woodpecker in her chest immediately reawakened and pounded a warning, telling her to stop, to go back. But there was no going back.

*Here's where it all ends,* she thought.

Steeling her nerves, Neffie did her best to console herself as she inched inevitably toward her doom. *At least you're finally doing something,* she told herself. It was small consolation. After a dozen or so tiny steps, she finally made out the cliff's edge a few feet in front of her. Beyond the edge, there was nothing.

"I can't see a thing in this fog," Neffie called to no one in particular, secretly relieved. "Nada."

"This is, like, really annoying," Jessica complained. "If it doesn't clear soon, we'll have to leave without seeing crap. We're already super late for school, I bet."

Pulling her smartphone out of her back pocket, Jessica switched it on, and the blue light from its screen cast an eerie glow in the mist. Neffie glanced from side to side, and instead of seeing Jessica's gang, she saw only a wavy line of pale, terrified ghost faces. Jessica studied her phone briefly and then shoved it back in her pocket.

"Oh man!" she cried. "We're totally late. C'mon, everyone. Time to go."

Hardly disguising their relief, the other girls instantly turned from the cliff to head back downhill. Well, almost everyone did. For some reason, Neffie didn't turn right away. She should have—that's for sure. But Neffie had never been this high, and so she paused to take one last, stupidly dangerous look over the high edge of the cliff into the swirling fog below.

As Neffie peered over the edge, a sudden gust of strong wind broke the fog apart, clearing a view all the way to the river's bottom, far down the steep face of the cliff. Instantly, the old, familiar blackness started crawling over Neffie. Her eyes rolled back in their sockets, and she shuddered. Then she felt her body lift, and as it floated into the air, her torso and limbs began elongating as if she were some funny, stretchable rubber doll.

Directly above Neffie, the mist cleared; her body stretched even more as it floated up toward a patch of blue sky. Neffie grew groggy. She was about to be lost forever when there was a giant shuddering sound as if lightning were being ripped from a thundercloud by some wild, cosmic force.

Moaning, Neffie blacked out.

# CHAPTER 2

# BACK IN SCHOOL

Sometime later, through a blur of fluttering eyelids, Jessica's smooth, pretty face came into focus. The blond girl's eyes probed hers in a way that made Neffie want to look away, but she forced herself to return Jessica's gaze. She couldn't keep her eyelids from fluttering, however, and she still felt dizzy.

Slowly, her mind cleared, and as it did, Neffie discovered she was on her back on a gently sloping hillside. The ground beneath her was rocky but tolerably comfortable except where a sharp little stone dug painfully into her left shoulder blade. Even though she was stretched along the ground, Neffie felt surprisingly warm. It took her a second or two to realize someone had spread a coat over her chest. Adding to the warmth was a bright sun shining down on her from a clear sky, heating both her exposed skin and the dark material of the coat.

Neffie steadied her eyelids and was about to say something to Jessica when one of the girls gawking over her said, "Man, that was, like, totally weird."

"Yeah, the way her eyeballs rolled back in her head, that was crazy," another girl remarked.

"And what was that sound?" someone else added. "We all heard it, right? It was like an explosion. What the heck was that?"

"Yeah, it was big," someone agreed, "and I don't think it was natural. Definitely not thunder."

"I thought she was floating. Anyone else see the way she went into the air?"

The chatter suddenly spilled all around her, an emotional waterfall of words. In the chatter, Neffie heard the girls' nervousness, their fear and their confusion, all of which totally bummed her out. Her secret *thing* had obviously happened again. Only, this time, everyone had seen it. Neffie kept her eyes locked on Jessica's, holding her mouth tightly closed, suffering her embarrassment in silence. Inside, her stomach churned and she felt nauseous.

"When she stopped moving, I swear she was dead," said a voice. "I mean, she looked, like, totally dead."

"And how would you know what dead looks like, Hannah?" Jessica snapped. "Have you ever seen a dead person?"

There was an awkward silence before the girl answered cautiously, "No, but she looked dead to me."

"Well, if you've never seen a dead person, shut up," Jessica scolded before turning her gaze back to Neffie. "Are you strong enough to move?" she asked, her voice gentle. "We're, like, totally late for school."

Nodding, Neffie answered, "How long have I . . . been like this?"

"Don't know."

Neffie eyed the sun. "What time is it?"

Jessica fished her phone out of her jeans pocket. Giving its bright screen a quick glance, she opened her mouth to speak but then closed it. For a brief moment, she looked oddly unsure of herself, but quickly she regained her composure, and Neffie doubted any of the others saw her confusion.

"I have to say . . ." Jessica's voice trailed off, and she hesitated before continuing in a stronger voice, "Um, forget it. Like, I can't believe how late for school we are."

"So what time is it?" Sarah asked.

"Who cares?" Jessica said, shoving her phone back into her pocket. "We're so totally late, we're getting absences for sure for first and second periods. I already have four this semester, so let's get our butts moving. There's no way I'm getting put on mandatory attendance."

"Me neither," Sarah agreed.

Jessica whisked the coat off Neffie and tossed it to Sarah.

"Up you get," she called to Neffie.

Neffie had no desire to face life back in school, but she knew she didn't have a choice. Sucking in a deep breath, she struggled to her feet, her bones creaking. Straightening, she kept her gaze fixed on the ground. No way was she going to look out and have another attack.

As soon as Neffie was up, Jessica ordered, "Come on, let's go. And listen, everyone—mouths shut about today, you hear me?"

When no one answered, Jessica repeated her warning, and this time she received some timid yeses. Nodding, Jessica started downhill with her girls following in their usual line behind her. Now that they were leaving the Spine under a sunny sky, the hiking was a lot easier, and sooner than Neffie would have guessed possible, they reached the gate and scaled the pillar. For Neffie, again the last to go, the drop to the other side felt momentarily like she was leaving some dark, zombie-filled cave and emerging on a sunlit Mexican beach. *Only I'm not on some happy vacation*, she quickly reminded herself. No, she was with a bunch of her fellow ninth-graders who had just witnessed one of her weird attacks. The thought depressed her.

None of Jessica's gang talked while they pedaled their bikes to school, and all of them remained equally silent while they stashed their bikes on the metal racks in front of the entrance. Hurrying up the main stairs and through the front door, the girls split up, heading for class or to get stuff out of their lockers. Swallowing hard, Neffie headed for her third-period English class.

○◉●

Entering the classroom in the middle of class was bad enough for Neffie; having to face thirty pairs of curious eyes was pure misery. Crying would only have made everyone more curious, so she fought back her tears. Still, the undisguised looks she got made it obvious there'd be gossip once class was over. And gossip led to careless words.

The school day was one of Neffie's worst. Despite Jessica's warning to her girls to keep their mouths shut, one or more obviously found it impossible to stay quiet. Walking down the hallway between her last two classes of the morning, Neffie was painfully aware of the stares and whispers.

Apparently, the school's biggest freak had just gotten freakier.

Neffie hated the attention, hated how she stood out. Lunch was agony, and afternoon classes took forever. Time crawled at a snail's pace, only it was not your ordinary snail doing the crawling. No, it was a small-town, nothing-ever-happens-in-Windmere kind of snail, the kind that fed on gossip.

The worst incident of the day came after the last period. Neffie was crouched in front of her locker. In her current emotional state, she had no intention of doing any homework that night, and so she was pulling her books out of her backpack and stashing them in the bottom of her locker. Behind her, she heard a hushed voice.

"Hey, Neff," a girl called quietly. "You all right?"

To Neffie's relief, it was her friend Darcy, smiling. Neffie smiled back. Although the two of them didn't hang together all that often, Darcy was probably Neffie's best friend and the one most likely to be on her side on this terrible day.

All of a sudden, there was the sound of laughter as three girls breezed around the corner from the main hallway. Hannah was in the lead, followed by two other girls from Jessica's gang. Darcy immediately froze and lowered her head to stare at some invisible spot on the floor. As the girls drew near, Hannah gave a disapproving cluck of her tongue. Darcy's face reddened.

Giving Neffie a quick, uncomfortable glance, Darcy muttered, "Gotta go."

Before Neffie could say a word, she turned and hurried away toward the main hallway. Hannah and the others walked past Neffie without looking at her or saying a word. Once they were safely away, they broke into laughter. Neffie thought she heard a racial slur from Hannah. Something about a monkey.

*Guess I'm jungle poison*, she thought bitterly.

Desperate now to escape, Neffie quickly stuffed her still half-full backpack into her locker. Closing the padlock, she turned and literally ran through the hallways and out the front door. Leaving her bike in the rack, she raced down the street and ran home. By the time she reached her family's small, white-shingled cottage more than a mile away on quiet County Road 115 near the outskirts of Windmere, Neffie's chest was heaving and her eyes were wet with tears.

Skipping her usual wrestling match with the stubborn, rusted clasp of her front gate, Neffie hopped the picket fence, hurried to the side porch and shoved through the bright-red door into her family's house. Normally, getting home was a happy event for Neffie, but she didn't feel happy today. How could she? Her life was pretty much ruined.

# CHAPTER 3

# A STRANGER'S VISIT

As usual, Neffie found her mother in the kitchen making supper, back from her half-day job at the supermarket. Neffie's first instinct was to make a beeline to her bedroom without a word to her mother, but her emotions quickly got the better of her.

"It happened again," she called out, tears now streaming down her cheeks. "Oh my gosh, do you have any idea how embarrassing it is? This time, it was in front of Jessica and her girls, and now everyone at school knows. Everyone."

Before her mother could speak, Neffie turned and rushed through the kitchen, speeding down the back hall past her parents' room to her own little bedroom where she threw herself onto her bed and buried her face in her pillow, sobbing uncontrollably.

It took a long time for her crying to stop, but when it did, a new flood of emotions washed over her. There was frustration. Embarrassment. And worst of all, a terrible anger for letting temptation get the better of her. What an idiot she had been to accept Jessica's invitation to join them on their adventure up the Spine. And how incredibly stupid she had been to look down the cliff when all she had to do was turn and follow Jessica back down the hill.

*You stupid girl,* she scolded silently. *Stupid, stupid!*

A knock at the door interrupted Neffie's self-loathing.

"May I come in?" When there was no response, Katie Anderson let herself in and sat on the edge of the bed beside her daughter.

"Hey, Pumpkin. I know you probably don't want to talk, and I'm not sure I can say anything that would help but . . ." Katie paused. When her daughter didn't say anything, she continued, "There's one thing I can do for you if you'll allow me."

Rolling over and clutching her pillow to her chest, Neffie sighed. "What?" she said, her voice cold. "Can you, like, make this thing go away? That's what I really want, you know. For it to go away."

"I know, Neff, I know."

Katie Anderson's voice was gentle, which did nothing to comfort her daughter.

"I'm freak enough already. The giant, black girl with pink freckles." Neffie gave her mother a pained look before continuing. "But on top of everything else, there's my thing. I mean, I can't even go up a few stairs without having one of my fits."

"Baby, I know—"

Neffie interrupted, "Mom, you have no idea. If we're climbing ropes in gym class, I have to pretend I have a stomachache. I can't use the diving board. I can't walk over the bridge when the kids go swimming. I can't do anything normal and it's totally unfair."

Neffie's tears flowed again. Katie Anderson's only response was to stroke Neffie's braided hair until she was done speaking, her emotions spent and her words used up. Then her mother finally answered, soothing and sympathetic.

"Pumpkin, believe me, I know how hard it is for you to live with this. And I cannot make it go away. But I think the time has finally come for you to know a little about what it really is."

These words took Neffie by surprise. Eying her mother, she asked,

"What do you mean, know what it is? Are you saying you suddenly know what's wrong with me?" Neffie had seen several doctors over the years, and while all of them had ideas and suggestions, none of them ever labeled her condition.

"I know a little," her mother replied.

"You're kidding me, right?" Neffie muttered.

Putting a hand on Neffie's shoulder, her mother answered, "Pumpkin, I've had to wait until you were old enough to hear it. That's the truth. I know it's hard—"

Interrupting, Neffie cried, "Truth? Old enough? What the heck does that mean?"

"Listen, Pumpkin—"

"Don't Pumpkin me. I've needed the truth since I was, like, five."

Katie Anderson stiffened, and her voice lost some of its warmth. "You will have to believe I was duty-bound to wait."

There was something strained and unnatural about the way her mother answered that led Neffie to relent a little. Sighing, she muttered, "Okay, then tell me what you know."

Nodding, her mother chose her words carefully. "The thing is, if I try to say it, it will come out wrong. Luckily, there's someone who can say it better. I just called your dad at work and he is sending a message to . . . this person. He'll give you some answers."

This new and unexpected bit of information was too weird for Neffie, whose emotions were already stretched to the breaking point by her terrible day.

"All I hear you saying," she remarked, "is Dad and you have known all along what is wrong with me. That's totally unfair, and I don't need some new stranger. I need you to tell me right now everything you know."

Shaking her head gently, Neffie's mother resisted. "I can't. I mean, your dad and I are still duty-bound. You really need to talk to this other person."

Neffie gave her mother a cold stare. "I still don't get it. If there's some guy with all the answers, why didn't he come before?"

"I know it's been hard for you, really hard," Katie said, "but we needed to wait until you were old enough. That's all I can say. When you talk to this person, he can explain."

Neffie had no idea how to respond to this. Sighing, she closed her eyes, shutting out her mother and putting up a wall between them to stop the bad feelings. Her day had been painful enough that she didn't need any more right now, especially from her mother, who should be on her side, not against her.

"All I can say," Neffie muttered, "is I can't believe you and Dad have been keeping things from me."

"We had no choice. Soon you'll hear why and I hope you'll understand."

Neffie rolled over and shoved her face into her pillow.

"Leave me alone," she grumbled. "I just want to sleep."

"All right; you sleep." Katie carefully closed the door behind her.

Neffie quickly fell into a deep sleep, and when she awoke, her room was in near darkness except for a small shaft of streetlight coming through a gap in her window curtains. The bulb of the streetlamp must have been loose because the light flickered rhythmically, creating a strobe effect on the objects neatly arranged on Neffie's old desk under the window. Among these objects were a teddy bear nearly as old as Neffie, a 1970s lava lamp, a Wonder Woman statue that had once belonged to her mother, a cup of pens and pencils, the Napoleon chess set given to Neffie by her stepdad, and a glass jar of river agates collected by Neffie over the years.

To the left of Neffie's desk was a short table with an ancient color TV sitting on top and an old VHS player beneath it. Piled on the floor in front of the table were several stacks of well-used VHS tapes of old movies, more than a hundred of them, dating from the 1930s to the '50s, some in color but many from the days when movies were black and white.

Neffie loved old movies and shunned the new comic book releases relished by her friends. Seeing her treasures spread around her cozy bedroom made Neffie feel a little better. It was a perfect night to lock her door and get lost in two or three of her old movies, maybe a Hitchcock mystery followed by a Victorian romance.

Neffie heard voices coming from the kitchen. Her mother was doing most of the talking. Every once in a while, Neffie's stepdad spoke for a few seconds, his tone nasally and high-pitched, the twang of an Oklahoma man. Neffie had no doubt her parents were talking about her. She lingered in bed for a few minutes, getting a certain comfort from hearing them nearby even though their serious tone made her nervous.

Finally, she couldn't listen any longer and got up. Flipping the overhead light switch near her bed, Neffie walked to the body-length mirror. Looking at the reflection in the mirror, the first thing she saw was a girl who had slept in her tennis shoes. Slowly, she raised her eyes, taking in the long legs, wide hips, narrow waist and long torso. Finally, she fixed her eyes on the face in the mirror.

It was an unusual face, remarkable for its sharp lines and boniness. Her cheekbones were high and pronounced. Her chin was long and a bit pointed. Her forehead seemed to be built out of two flat surfaces that met with a noticeable ridgeline in the center. The nose was long and sharp, and her skin was the color of her old mahogany desk.

All these funny pieces might have fit together reasonably well except for two oddities that ruined everything for Neffie. First, the lips below the nose were too wide and too thick, and they had a pinkish tint that didn't match the rest of her face. Second, on each cheek were six very distinct freckles, each quite large, round, and of the same pinkish hue as her lips. Neffie sighed. She hated the face in the mirror.

Admittedly, it wasn't all bad. Four teased-out braids framed her face and were kind of cute. They were her mom's idea. The deep-brown eyes with startlingly yellow inner irises were pretty all on their own, without the help of any makeup.

Sighing, Neffie rubbed her eyes to get the sleep out, opened the bedroom door and walked noiselessly down the hall toward the kitchen. The hall was dimly lit, but the kitchen was bright, its yellow walls and white cabinets aglow in florescent light from the overhead fixture. Neffie was about to call hello to her parents when she saw they were not alone.

She froze as all conversation in the kitchen died. A strange man sat quietly in the rocking chair in the far corner, his kind eyes returning Neffie's gaze.

The man's face looked very much like hers—more angular, perhaps, and thoroughly lined from age. His forehead wasn't quite as ridged, but there was a definite line, and he had the same pinkish lips and the same color freckles, though he had four on each cheek, not six like Neffie. The biggest difference was in his eyes, which were sunk much more deeply in their sockets. They were also much yellower than Neffie's.

Those eyes transfixed Neffie. They were alert and probing, and as Neffie stared into them from the other side of the room, she felt as if he were peering into her soul. Too startled to think clearly, normally shy Neffie let the man's eyes study her freely for many seconds. Then, her self-consciousness returned, and she lowered her eyes and raised her emotional walls. The man seemed to understand because he turned his gaze from Neffie to her stepdad.

"Jack," he said, "would you kindly do me the honor of introducing me to your daughter?"

The man's accent was unusual, making *Jack* sound like *Jock*, and *daughter* like *dotter*. Jack Anderson nodded and gave a funny little bow, a gesture Neffie had never before seen him do.

Neffie's stepdad straightened and replied, "I will indeed. It is my honor." Turning to Neffie, he continued, "Neffie, may I introduce you to an old friend of your mother's and mine, a man who is much more to you, as you will soon hear. Neffie, this is Gannen Sargie Vong."

In response, the stranger eased out of his rocking chair and gave Neffie the same kind of bow that Jack had just performed. It began with a slight bend at the waist accompanied by a simultaneous dipping of the right shoulder as he crossed his right arm over the center of his chest. When he straightened, Neffie saw that he was noticeably taller than her significant height of six feet and an inch—plus a tiny bit more.

"It is my most storying honor to meet you, Neffatira Akou Sargie," he said in a deep voice, drawing out every syllable. "I have waited many years for this profoundly great moment. I am most honored, indeed."

The man gave another bow, this one deeper and with more of a flourish of the shoulder and arm than the first. Neffie had to grin, both at the strange gesture and at his odd way of speaking.

"What did you just call me?" she asked.

Nodding, the man seemed to think a bit before answering in his slow, formal manner.

"Yes, I understand that your blood-clan history here, the one *storytold* you by these fine two people, names you as Neffie McCormick Anderson, with McCormick being your mother's blood-clan name, Anderson being your stepfather's blood-clan name and Neffie being a form of familiar name given to you by your true blood-clan father. Is this not right?"

"Um, I don't know what you just said, but my name is definitely Neffie McCormick Anderson."

Smiling, the man shook his head. "In your blood-clan history here, in this place and in these times, with these people, that is indeed true. However, I am here at their request to storytell a different but even more real blood-clan history, from a different place, different times. I am here to storytell who you are besides being Neffie McCormick Anderson of this place and in these times."

Neffie looked stunned and turned to her mother.

"Mom, this is too weird. Like, who is this guy? And why is he talking so weirdly?"

Before Neffie's mother could speak, the man answered. "Neffatira, I am your Sargie blood-clan father's immediate next father."

When Neffie looked bewildered, her mother smiled before explaining, "Neffie, he's your grandfather. On your father's side."

"My what? Mom!"

The man spoke up before Katie could answer, saying, "Jack, Kathryn, would you please do me the kindness of leaving Neffatira and me for a little while. I feel the two of us need to be alone to talk of such things."

To Neffie's surprise, her parents both nodded and immediately turned to leave.

"Dad," she cried. "Mom!"

Neffie's mother gave her a reassuring look. "It's all right, Pumpkin," Katie murmured. "It'll be good for you to talk alone with your grandfather. We'll be nearby, waiting in the living room until you're finished. I promise."

Neffie was suddenly curious as she watched her stepdad close the kitchen door behind them. About the only thing she really knew about her biological dad was that he had supposedly gone on foot into the Sierra Nevada Mountains one winter's day for mysterious reasons. This was back when Neffie was less than a year old. Once in the mountains, he disappeared in a snowstorm without a trace, presumably dead as his body was never found.

Perhaps the man in front of her could explain about the man she thought about nearly every day but couldn't picture, the man who met Kathryn McCormick in Tanzania many years ago, fell in love with and married her, and then moved with his new wife from Africa to the United States. The man who had built a small house with his new bride in a little town in hilly California, where they conceived a child, a girl, before he unexpectedly died without a trace of him left behind. No photographs. No letters. Nothing. Not a single memento that might give his daughter what she had always wanted but never got—a connection that would help her make sense of her roots.

Neffie took a deep breath and faced this strange man.

# CHAPTER 4

# A NEAR JOURNEY

Neffie moved to her usual place at the family table, taking the seat closest to the wood stove. She hated the cold Iowa weather. Her fingers and toes were constantly numb from early fall until mid-spring, her body shivery and uncomfortable.

While Neffie took her seat, her grandfather went to her father's chair at the head of the table and solemnly sat. There was an awkward silence. The man seemed to be waiting for Neffie to speak as she searched her mind for something meaningful to say. Finally, a thought came to her. It was really quite trivial, but it was all she could conjure.

"Tell me your name again," she said. "I missed it the first time." In truth, her curiosity screamed at her. The problem was, mixed with her curiosity was a heavy fear that something terrible came with him. She couldn't name it, but she felt it. She did not fear the man himself, she noted.

After giving Neffie a small smile, the man answered slowly. "My name, as you mean the word, is Gannen Sargie Vong, and I have come here to storytell to you some of your own blood-clan history. Would you like to hear the storytelling of it?"

"Um, no, that's all right. Forgive me for saying this, but you don't sound like you're from Iowa."

Chuckling, her grandfather replied, "You are rootly correct and correct in times placement, as well."

"See," said Neffie, "that's what I mean. I totally don't know what you just said." When he failed to explain himself, Neffie sighed and tried again, asking, "On the subject of names, what did you say my, um, my blood-clan name is?"

Her grandfather thought for a moment. "Neffatira, I could answer that question and all your questions that followed, one at a time as they popped into your head. However, let me suggest you might instead allow me to recount some of your blood-clan history in storyline order, at least the small, storied part you need to hear right now. I think you will understand everything better if I follow this more logical, lineal storytelling course rather than answering your questions as you pose them."

Neffie giggled. "Once again, I have no idea what you just said, but go ahead and talk if you're going to tell me about my dad and about other things I should know."

"It's what you have always wished, yes? To know more about your father and your blood family and your special nature. You've wondered profoundly about these things, yes?"

"I've wondered what's wrong with me and why my dad disappeared—that's definitely true," Neffie said.

Her grandfather put his elbows on the tabletop and leaned forward. "Dear lass, there is nothing wrong with you; you are storyworthily special. The wrong is with the times."

"What do you mean, *wrong with the times*? You're not talking climate change and terrorism, are you?"

The man smiled. "I apologize, Neffatira, for I see how you have misunderstood me. You heard me to say *times*, but the word I used was *Tymes*, pronounced just as I have said it. Your *times* is not the same thing as my *Tymes*. My *Tymes* is hard to explain. Perhaps think of my *Tymes* as a place."

"It sounds the same to me no matter which way you say it."

"Oh no," he corrected. "Listen to the difference." He spoke slowly, starting with a pronunciation much like hers. "*Times* is your word. Now listen to mine." Pausing briefly, he exhaled his version of the word and then repeated it.

"Okay, I get it," laughed Neffie. Grinning, she said, "*Tymes*."

"Exactly so. Thus, the wrong I am speaking of is with the *Tymes*, my word, not your *times*, as you use—a different word. You will need to understand something of the terrible truth of the *Tymes* to understand your history and your future, which are tied together."

Neffie sighed and shook her head. "If you didn't look so much like me, I'd be tempted to think you're, like, some kind of weirdo. However, considering that everyone at school thinks I'm a total freak, I guess it's not a surprise to have a grandfather like you. Sorry to be rude, but I've had a really bad day and I just can't be polite right now."

Her grandfather chuckled. "You're not a freak and there's nothing wrong with you. As I say, the wrong is with the Tymes. And truly, I do not mean times like the *New York Times*, or Times Square or parsley, sage, rosemary and thyme." He winked at Neffie before adding, "See, I have spent enough time here to be chill about some things."

This made Neffie laugh.

"I hate to break the news," she remarked, "but this here is small-town Iowa, and no one is chill in Windmere. But, given my day, I'm happy to take your word I'm not a freak and you're not weird except you have this pretty weird way of saying *times*."

He chuckled again. "Then it seems we're making progress."

"Maybe, but whatever you say, there really is something wrong with me, and if you'd been up on the Spine this morning, you'd be totally agreeing with me."

"I'm here to convince you this is not true."

Neffie shook her head. "Don't mess with me. I know you're here because of Mom and Dad. My mom says you know something about my . . . um, condition. So talk."

Instead of talking, her grandfather leaned forward and peered into Neffie's eyes in a way that should have made her feel uncomfortable, though strangely it didn't. Once again, it was as if he were peering into her soul.

Taking a breath, she muttered, "Well?"

"I know more than you think," he finally said. "This morning, you went into a state that felt as if you were being transported, lifted and pulled away. Yes?"

This description surprised Neffie. It was not how she usually thought of her fits.

"Yeah, maybe," she agreed, "but I think it's epilepsy. My doctors say it's not epilepsy, but I've been researching on the internet and it seems like it to me. I haven't figured out why I only get my seizures in high places, but maybe I have, like, some rare kind of epilepsy."

"You don't have epilepsy. They're not seizures."

"You a doctor?"

"No, but I do know about you," her grandfather said. "You want to understand this thing you felt today, yes? You may call them convulsions or seizures or fits, but that isn't really what you feel when it happens, is it?"

"Epilepsy," Neffie insisted.

He shook his head. "Think carefully," he suggested. "You start shaking, but it's not the shaking you feel most strongly, is it? What you feel most strongly is the sensation you are floating, yes? Floating into the sky to travel somewhere."

Once again, his words had a ring of truth. When he raised a questioning eyebrow, Neffie had no choice but to agree.

"Yeah, maybe it's something like that."

"Think about the incident today. When it happened, you felt yourself being lifted and transported, yes? You felt as if you were moving to someplace else, did you not?"

Neffie didn't like where this was going. She didn't need some new craziness complicating her life. "I'm not sure what I felt, but I didn't like it."

"Take your mind back. Is what I'm saying not true?"

Part of Neffie desperately wanted to disagree, to hold out for her simpler explanation. She needed time to think, to figure things out. Lowering her gaze, she stared at her long hands while she collected her thoughts.

Finally, she mumbled, "I don't know what I was feeling. Maybe floating. Yes, possibly." Then her fear made her back down. "But how could that be?"

"Neffie, look at me," her grandfather said, his voice serious and urgent. "There's something important I must say."

Neffie raised her chin. Maybe it was the warmth of his yellow irises, but Neffie felt drawn to him despite the intensity of his gaze.

"Neffatira, would you like to learn exactly what you were feeling today and why? Really learn?"

Neffie looked away. The thought was too scary. "Let's stop this, please," she muttered. "You're talking like . . . I just want to know what's wrong with me and how to fix it. Is that too much?"

"Neffatira, you must look at this without fear. You say you want answers, you want to know. Well, I can help."

The woodpecker suddenly awakened in Neffie's chest. "Then fix my problem," she cried.

"Neffatira, you need to believe me when I say I can help you. You need to trust me."

"Then say something that makes sense," she countered.

For a long moment, her grandfather stared at the tabletop lost in thought. Then he sighed and leveled his gaze again at Neffie.

"All right," he murmured. "Let's try a different way. The difficulty is I don't know the right words to explain what happens to you in a way that will make sense to you. It's too far out of your normal experiences living here, in Iowa, in these Tymes. However, if you truly want to understand, there is something I can do to help. Do you want this help?"

Neffie wasn't sure she did, but his eyes gripped her powerfully, weakening her will.

"I guess," she conceded, nodding slightly.

"For me to help, you will need to take a journey. It's the only way. Nothing else will bring full understanding."

Taking a deep breath, she asked, "What do you mean, journey?"

"It is the only way. I'm going to suggest we go right now onto the roof of your house and learn about the Tymes together."

There must have been something hypnotic about the man's eyes because Neffie didn't object at first. Then the full meaning of his suggestion suddenly hit her.

"Oh my gosh," she cried, "I get it. You're saying go on the roof and have one of those attacks of mine right now. On purpose. You're crazy!"

"I assure you I am quite sane," he answered calmly, his eyes twinkling. "And believe me, Neffatira, you and I are of the same blood-clan, and being of the same blood-clan, I know exactly what happens to you because it happens to me. In your heart, you know this is true. You sense our blood-clan connection."

Suddenly tired of resisting, Neffie leaned back in her chair and sat quietly for a moment, allowing her mind to go blank and her emotions to calm. Gradually, the woodpecker in her chest quieted, and she was able to think clearly.

She asked, "Doing this will answer my questions?"

"Yes."

"And it's safe?"

"Yes."

"Then all right."

"Excellent. You have made the right choice. There's a hatch in your attic that opens onto the roof, yes? If you lead me, I will guide you on your journey, and you will then understand much more than you do now."

Neffie sucked in her breath. This had all been planned. It was the only way he could know about the roof hatch. She didn't like the idea of everyone plotting against her, and she didn't like the idea of going onto the roof. Not one bit.

Nevertheless, while this was the craziest thing she could ever have imagined—wilder than the wildest plot of any of her old-time movies—doing this somehow made sense.

Standing, she gestured for her grandfather to follow her. He stood and let her take him down the hall, past her parents' bedroom, past the door to her own bedroom and finally to a doorway at the back of the house. Opening the door and reaching up, Neffie pulled down the folded stairway from the ceiling. A string dangled from the attic. Giving it a pull, Neffie lit a line of bare bulbs, which dimly illuminated the unheated attic space above them.

Never before in her life had Neffie gone into the attic. For obvious reasons, she avoided most stairs, and even though the attic was windowless, just the thought of being in the highest part of her house made her uncomfortable.

"This is going to give me answers?" she asked again.

"Oh, yes," her grandfather replied.

Taking a deep breath, Neffie stepped on the first rung. Her hands instantly began trembling, but she pushed on, taking the steps one at a time. When she reached the top, she paused to peer around. The space was a typical open, unfinished attic, with low, sloping ceilings and bare rafters. Fighting her fears, Neffie stepped onto a long piece of loose planking laid across the floor joists as a makeshift walkway. Between the joists, Neffie saw pink rolled-out insulation. Other pieces of planking held all sizes of boxes, no doubt storing family treasures and family junk. Neffie had no idea so much stuff was in her family's attic and wondered what she might find.

Before she could give it much thought, her grandfather tapped her shoulder and pointed at a small steel hatchway on the other side of the attic.

"That's the way out?" he asked.

"Yes," whispered Neffie as her heart raced.

Her grandfather must have sensed her rising fear. "Be brave," he said. "You are in no danger, and many of your questions will be answered. I promise."

He slipped a bolt and opened the door. There was an immediate rush of cool night air, and a sky full of stars appeared in the opening. Neffie turned her eyes away. Fear gripped her, but before she could change her mind, her grandfather ducked his head and hoisted himself through the hatchway onto the gentle pitch of the roof. Crouching in the doorway, he reached down and held out a hand for Neffie.

"Come, Neffatira," he urged. "Step out and find your answers."

The woodpecker inside her chest went nuts. Neffie suddenly felt dizzy, and her stomach heaved. Her knees grew weak, but she struggled against the urge to run and somehow managed to move to the hatch. Closing her eyes, she took hold of her grandfather's hand.

His fingers were surprisingly cold, and his grip was strong. When she was unable to take a first step, he tugged on her hand, and she began to move against her fears, climbing toward the blackness and convulsions that undoubtedly awaited her on the other side.

"Once on the roof, you will need to open your eyes," her grandfather whispered as she climbed through. "It will be better if you do not hesitate."

Neffie nodded. Stepping onto the roof, she took a deep breath and forced her eyes to open and look up. It took only a moment to gauge how high she was. Strangely the blackness did not grab her immediately the way it should have. She had scant seconds to appreciate a sight she had never seen before: the full beauty of a starlit night's canopy.

Then she shuddered, and her eyeballs rolled up in their sockets. The stars brightened, crackled and began oozing from the black surface of the sky like drips of glowing water rolling down black glass. As the blackness engulfed Neffie, her grandfather wrapped his arms around her shoulders and held her tightly.

Moving his mouth to her ear, he whispered, "Find the reddest star and follow it. The reddest star will show you the way."

He spoke in a voice that reminded Neffie of her mother's—sure and strong and soothing. Neffie almost did as told, but in the next instant, a raw panic took hold of her. Shuddering and moaning, she shook herself out of his arms.

"No way!" she cried.

Her grandfather tried to pull her back.

"Neffatira, this is the only way," he said. "Trust me."

"No way!" she screamed. As the world spun dizzyingly around her, she gasped and stumbled away from her grandfather. The air seemed to ripple and bend.

"Neffatira," her grandfather cried, "grab my hand."

Neffie refused to touch him. A giant, invisible wave coursed through the air, making numerous ripples. Her grandfather's body bent and stretched, and suddenly he disappeared. Neffie thought she saw his hand close into a fist just before it rippled out of sight.

Her mind grew as fogged as her eyesight. Managing a few erratic steps, Neffie found the hatchway and tumbled through the opening, desiring only to reach the windowless attic below. She landed with a thud on the planking beneath the hatch, and pain shot through her right knee.

With her world spinning out of control, Neffie tried to stand but couldn't. Stretching her arm, she searched with a wobbly hand for something to grab, but there was nothing. Neffie did her best to climb onto her hands and knees, and she was about to make it when she passed out.

# CHAPTER 5

# RENEWING A FRIENDSHIP

S unlight flickering against her closed eyelids eventually woke
Neffie, who found herself safely in her own little bed in her own
little bedroom in Windmere. She wasn't entirely sure how she had
gotten there, but she assumed it was her parents' doing. She had no
memories after blacking out in the attic.

Climbing slowly out of bed, she walked across her room and
looked at the girl in the mirror. Instead of seeing the old Neffie, she
saw a startling resemblance to her grandfather. Despite the abrupt and
uncomfortable ending to his visit, she felt unusually calm and more
at peace than usual. After splashing water on her face, she practically
breezed down the hall and into the kitchen where her mother was
making pancakes. Neffie plopped in her chair at the table.

"I'm starved," she announced. "Four pancakes this morning, please."

Her mother turned to look at her. "Neffie, if I may ask, what
happened to Sarge last night?"

"You mean my grandfather?"

"Yes. Everyone calls him Sarge."

"Why are you asking?"

"Your dad and I don't know where he is. After we heard sounds in the attic, we found you alone and unconscious. Sarge was nowhere to be seen."

Hearing the worry in her mother's voice, Neffie's good mood deflated. For some reason, she didn't feel like sharing the night's happenings with her mother, but she needed to say something.

"Um, about the attic . . ." Neffie's voice trailed off. She really didn't know what to say. Fortunately, her mother helped her out.

"You don't have to say anything if you don't want. What happened between him and you is none of my business if you want it that way."

This surprised Neffie. Like many mothers, hers usually wanted as many details as possible about what was going on in her life.

"Thanks. It all happened so fast. I need to think about it."

"Well," her mother said. "I'm glad the two of you had a chance to talk." Then she paused before continuing. "Neffie, even though it's not my place to ask, I am worried about Sarge. Sure, he has his own way of doing things, but it's not like him to disappear. Is there anything you can say?"

Neffie answered as best she could. "I honestly don't know what happened to Sarge. We were together and then I blacked out, and when I came to, he was gone. That's all I know."

Katie sighed and gave Neffie a small smile as if to reassure her that everything was all right—or perhaps it was to reassure herself. "Well, that's fine," she said. "Your dad and I were just wondering, that's all."

"Mom, I have to ask—where exactly does Grandfather Sarge come from, and why have I never met him before?"

"I can't really give an answer," replied her mother, looking uncomfortable.

"What do you mean you can't give an answer? You obviously know him pretty well. I just want to know a little more than nothing."

"Unfortunately, I have to answer the same way as before," Katie said, shaking her head. "Pumpkin, you just have to believe me when I say I took an oath and I'm duty-bound not to say."

"Mom," she cried, "I'm your daughter. What about your duty to me? Come on, talk to me!" Neffie gave her mother an imploring look. Katie sighed and shook her head again, which really annoyed Neffie.

"I'm afraid that's just how it is," murmured her mother. "Pumpkin, I know this is hard to understand, but to say more could be dangerous. Trust me, I'm not forgetting you're my daughter."

Neffie grimaced. "Well, then get my grandfather back if he's the only one who will talk."

"That's the thing. I don't know how to contact him."

"You guys just did it yesterday. Have Dad do it again, same way."

"It's hard to explain, but that way only works once. Kind of an emergency call."

"Well, this really sucks."

"Please don't use that word. I tell you what, let's leave this conversation for now and we can talk later. Why don't you have some breakfast?"

"Fine."

"Then here, let me get you your pancakes," her mother practically sang, doing her best to lighten the mood.

Frustrated, Neffie decided to push down all the bad thoughts and focus on breakfast. After eating her mother's four fluffy pancakes in silence, she excused herself to go wash up for school. She left her house without saying goodbye to her mother, girding for the huge problem of facing the kids at school. As she started down the road toward town, she wondered if another terrible day loomed. *Probably*, she thought gloomily.

Unfortunately, she was right. Back in school, her classmates acted no better than they had the day before. There were still the sneaky looks, behind-the-back comments, giggles and smirks. In fact, with very few exceptions, Neffie's schoolmates all acted terribly. A surprise exception was Sarah.

On her way to lunch from biology class, Neffie suddenly found Sarah walking beside her, having stolen up from behind.

"Hey, Neff," Sarah whispered to her.

Cautiously Neffie answered back, "Hey yourself."

After a few steps Sarah whispered, "It's not as bad as it seems, you know."

Neffie remained defensive. "What do you mean?" she asked.

"Nothing," replied Sarah. Then she gave a little laugh. "Everything. I'm talking about school here. Life. The jerks everywhere around us. Just between the two of us, there's one thing I keep telling myself, no matter what happens."

"What's that?" asked Neffie, still cautious.

"I tell myself, thank goodness for Jessica and her adventures. You know? They take us out of the ordinary."

"Me, I'm not so sure about that. Right now, I could use a big dose of ordinary."

"I see that," agreed Sarah, chuckling. "Maybe there's ordinary good, but for me ordinary is mostly bad."

After thinking for a second or two, Neffie agreed. "Right," she said. "You mean Windmere ordinary."

"Yes, the totally boring kind," laughed Sarah.

They reached the cafeteria. Winking at Neffie, Sarah cocked her chin in the direction of Jessica and her gang, who were at their usual table at the far end of the cafeteria by the middle window. Sarah gave Neffie a playful tap on the arm before leaving to join Jessica and the group. "Don't worry," she said. "It'll get better."

Amazingly, the other surprise of the day came from Jessica. Twice during the morning, Neffie caught Jessica staring. Her appraising looks seemed more friendly than unfriendly. In fact, the second time Neffie caught Jessica looking at her, Jessica almost smiled before moving to join some of the girls from her gang.

When school ended, Neffie waited in her last class while the halls slowly emptied. Finally, when the coast felt clear, she left the safety of the classroom and started down the central hallway toward her locker in the side hall.

Before she had taken five steps, however, she heard footsteps echoing behind her. She was immediately too nervous to look back. Maybe the steps belonged to Sarah, but maybe they belonged to Hannah. Or to someone even worse.

Neffie tried to walk nonchalantly, but soon it became obvious the footsteps were closing on her, the time between them shortening and the sounds growing louder. This made Neffie even more nervous. She sped up, but to no avail.

There was only one thing Neffie could do. Unable to stand the mystery any longer, she whirled around. To her surprise, she found Jessica, and before she could react, Jessica put a finger to her lips and spoke.

"Come with me," she muttered, smiling as if it were perfectly ordinary for her to seek out Neffie. "There's something I want to show you."

Confused, Neffie managed only a meek, "All right."

Jessica led Neffie back down the main hallway and then down a side hallway leading to the parking lot. When they were about halfway down this smaller hallway, Jessica halted abruptly at the foot of a long, narrow stairway to her right, one that students never used because it led to the school's mechanical room.

"Do you remember the time we climbed these stairs?" Jessica asked.

"No," Neffie answered honestly.

"I didn't think you would," Jessica observed. "Honestly, Neff, I can see why you might want to forget, and I don't blame you."

Neffie had no idea what to make of this. "Um, I really don't know what to say," she answered, "cuz I totally don't remember anything."

Jessica stared into Neffie's eyes with the famously probing, ice-blue eyes of hers. "Oh no?" she remarked.

"What's this all about?" Neffie asked.

"Do you remember when we were best friends?"

"Are you kidding?" Neffie almost snorted at the idea. "When you and I were best friends? Um, I don't think so."

Jessica's fierce eyes bore into hers. "That's what I like about you, girl."

"What?"

"You don't say much, but when you do talk, you say exactly what's on your mind, even if it bugs someone, which it usually does. I suppose it's why no one wants to be your friend. Cuz you're too . . . forthright."

"Uh, is that a compliment?"

"It *is* a compliment," Jessica replied with a wink, sounding as if she meant it. "It's really pretty cool the way you say what you think."

Neffie truly didn't know how to take this unexpected praise from Jessica. On the other hand, she felt she had to make one point. "Just for the record, I do have friends," she said.

"That's the other thing I like about you, Neff. I like the way you stare at kids like you're looking right through 'em. Just like you're doing with me right now," she laughed. "Do you remember back in fourth grade when we used to stare at each other to see who could hold it the longest?"

Neffie searched her mind for a memory but found nothing.

"I honestly don't remember," she said.

"Yeah, for some reason you never talk about memories. It's like you've forgotten us," Jessica observed with a wrinkle of her brow. "But I'll tell you what. You always won our staring contests."

"If you say so."

The notion of Neffie once being Jessica's best friend sounded totally crazy, but Jessica talked as if she was sure. In truth, there were lots of things Neffie couldn't remember from the earlier years of her childhood. One doctor thought it was due to post-traumatic stress from her fits or seizures. Neffie always figured the memories were so bad they needed forgetting.

"I'm serious; you and I were best friends," Jessica pressed. "We hung together back in fourth grade. I mean, a lot. And one day we were standing right here, talking about something, and I noticed that the door up there had been left open, and even though you said you didn't want to go, we sneaked up these stairs to check out the room. And guess what?"

"What?"

Waving a hand toward the stairs, Jessica said, "That's why we're here. I want to show you."

Neffie did not want to climb the stairs, not even for Jessica, but the weirdness of the situation threw her off balance. "I don't think so," was all she could muster.

"You have to," Jessica urged. "It's important."

"No way," cried Neffie.

Jessica scrutinized her closely, wearing a determined expression. Neffie immediately realized she wasn't going to win a battle of wills with Jessica, a realization that scared her.

Giving Neffie a reassuring smile, Jessica said, "Don't worry. I know you hate heights. Same as back in fourth grade and every year since then. But I'm here to help."

"Really?"

"Believe me," replied Jessica. "I'm doing this mainly for you, though a little for me. So close your eyes. Let me lead you. It's all right. I promise."

Neffie got the feeling her life was about to take an unexpected dramatic turn and she had no choice but to go with it. Her stomach churned, and the woodpecker in her chest fluttered its wings, but these things could not and did not stop her.

"All right," she agreed, surprising herself a bit, "but at least tell me why we're doing this."

Jessica thought for a moment. "Something happened that we both need to remember."

"What?"

"I'll tell you when we get up. You can't say no cuz I've got it all planned. See, I even swiped the key from old Jerry while he was catching his nap after lunch."

When Jessica held up the maintenance guy's key with a flourish, Neffie had to laugh. Jessica certainly had style. Neffie had to give her that.

Abruptly, Jessica put a hand on her shoulder and whispered, "I mean it, close your eyes."

Neffie couldn't say no, and she couldn't delay the inevitable any longer. Taking a deep breath, she closed her eyes. Jessica took her arm and wrapped it in hers. Moving slowly and calling out each step as they climbed, Jessica methodically guided Neffie up the stairs. By the third step, Neffie's body was shaking, and the woodpecker busily thumped in her chest.

At the top of the stairs, Jessica whispered, "Hang here a sec while I get the door open."

Jessica let go of Neffie's arm and stepped away. Her whole body trembling, Neffie waited silently while Jessica fiddled with the lock. Then Neffie heard a click and the creak of the door opening.

Taking Neffie's arm again, Jessica led her through the doorway into the mechanical room. There was a smell of motor oil and old paint. Neffie heard the door close behind them. Then Jessica drew Neffie forward a few steps more.

"You can look now," she whispered as they came to a stop. "It's safe."

Opening her eyes, Neffie found herself in a small room with box-shaped pieces of machinery humming in front of her. To her left, propped against the far wall, was a tool bench, its surface covered with tools. To the left of the bench was a window with a blind drawn to cover it.

"Do you remember anything about this place?" asked Jessica.

"No," Neffie said, though a vague recollection began to surface. "But I have a feeling I've been here before."

Jessica again locked her eyes on Neffie's.

"Me, I have a vivid memory of the last time we were in this place," she said. "And I've thought about it, like, a thousand times. I'm not kidding—a thousand times."

"I don't like it here," Neffie protested. "We should leave."

"You don't remember, do you? You really don't?"

"Like, totally no."

Pointing, Jessica asked, "See that window over there?"

The woodpecker banged loudly against Neffie's sternum. "Yes, I see it," she acknowledged.

"The time before, that blind was closed just like today. We poked around this room looking for something cool, and when we went over to the window, do you remember what happened?" When Neffie remained silent, Jessica gave her a small smile before continuing. "My shoulder bumped against the blind, and you know what happened next?"

"I don't know," Neffie answered feebly.

"It's all right. I didn't bring you here to embarrass you. What happened is between us, our secret. The thing is, I got so totally scared I ran away. It's the only time in my life I ever ran from trouble. I panicked, which will never, ever happen again."

"I wouldn't worry about it."

Her eyes widening, Jessica said, "Well, I have worried about it. That's the point of us being here. Something bad was happening to you, and instead of helping you, my best friend, I ran. That sucks big time. After that, I was so embarrassed I couldn't be with you anymore, which also sucks. You deserved a better friend."

Neffie had no idea how to respond to this surprising confession. "I think . . ." she started to say, but her voice trailed off when she couldn't find the right words to finish her thought.

Quickly, Jessica spoke up. "So, here's the thing. After it happened again yesterday, I haven't stopped thinking about it. And guess what?"

"I have a feeling you're going to tell me."

"You bet. I've decided you, me—both of us together—we need to see it all, from beginning to end. I watched yesterday while everyone was being an ass to you. Then it came to me. I can make up for fourth grade by helping you figure it out."

Shocked, Neffie muttered, "You don't mean—"

Interrupting, Jessica confirmed, "We make it happen, and this time I'll be with you through it all. Then we'll figure out how to control it."

"Oh my gosh," answered Neffie, recoiling at the idea of someone watching. "I can't do that!"

"You can. And I really think we can fix it together."

"There's no way. You don't know how badly I lose control. Like, I have seen doctors and more doctors and they haven't been able to help me, so how could you possibly do it?"

"Listen, girl," Jessica persisted, her fierce eyes boring into Neffie's, "I'm convinced this is something we both need. I need it to make up for that time I ran. You need it because you can't be living half a life. So why not give it a try? I mean, ten to one, I'm smarter than any doctor you've ever seen."

Neffie smiled. Maybe Jessica wasn't smarter than her doctors, but she was certainly more confident. None of what she proposed made sense to Neffie, but Jessica was hard to say no to.

Something else tugged at Neffie. Her grandfather had proposed some version of the same thing. Well, Neffie felt a lot better putting her trust in Jessica than in some stranger, even if the stranger did have a face that looked like hers.

"All right, I guess," she surrendered. She did her best to give Jessica a brave smile.

"Good girl," cried Jessica, smiling back. "Let's do this!"

Before Neffie could change her mind, Jessica grabbed Neffie's arm and led her to the window. Once there, Jessica gave her another encouraging smile.

"You ready?" she asked.

"I guess."

Without another word, Jessica moved quickly, taking hold of the blind's cord and giving it a big tug. Instantly, the blind lifted, and sunlight poured through the open window.

"Let's go for it," Jessica urged.

Taking a deep breath, Neffie forced herself to look through the second-floor window, and instantly the thing hit her. Her eyes rolled back, and the convulsions seized her. In a matter of seconds, her body was trembling uncontrollably. She felt herself stretching, her body elongating. The sun dimmed until it was no longer the sun but a giant, bright-red star that began to move, oozing slowly across the sky like a big drop of oil rolling down a sheet of glass.

Remembering her grandfather's words from the night before, Neffie focused all her attention on that oozing red star. Immediately, her body lifted and floated toward it. Jessica cried out, and Neffie felt Jessica grabbing at her clothing. Jessica did her best to pull her back, but Neffie continued drifting toward the red star, taking Jessica with her.

"Holy crap!" cried Jessica as she lifted off the ground.

Above them, the sky dimmed and turned orange. The fiery red star changed color, transmuting to some deep shade of pink. Jessica's body suddenly began trembling and stretching too. Through fluttering eyelids, Neffie saw ripples running like staccato waves across the bare skin of her arms.

Out of nowhere, there was a great explosion followed by a giant flash of red-orange light, and Neffie felt a sensation like flying. Terrified, she closed her eyes as her body went hurtling through space. Stars exploded around her, and time accelerated until an hour took only a second. Neffie screamed and heard Jessica screaming beside her. Then Neffie's world turned upside down and her mind went spinning out of control.

# CHAPTER 6

# ON THE OTHER SIDE

"Yippee-ki-yay!" Jessica exclaimed. "That was intense!"

Neffie was on her back, eyes closed. A few tremors still ran through her, but otherwise she felt okay. She had remained conscious for nearly the whole thing, and unlike the recent event on the Spine, her mind was noticeably clear and alert now that the thing was over.

Opening her eyes, she looked at Jessica, who was sitting on the ground just a few feet away, her hair more windblown and messier than Neffie had ever before seen it. The girl's eyes were bright, her cheeks flushed a deep red, and there was a big grin on her face.

"You all right?" Jessica asked.

"I'm good."

Jessica stared around. "Like, where the heck are we?"

*That is a good question.* Neffie sat up and looked around. They were no longer in the little mechanical room in their school. Wherever they were, it looked like no place Neffie had seen or experienced. Memories of the conversation with her grandfather came back to her, but she wasn't about to repeat to Jessica the man's crazy talk about different

Tymes, whatever that meant.

"Dorothy, I don't think we're in Kansas anymore."

Jessica laughed. "I don't think we're in Iowa, either. What's the line from that old song? You know, the one about diamonds in the sky?"

Neffie shook her head. "Diamonds?"

"You know," laughed Jessica, "that old Beatles song."

Thinking for a second or two, Neffie suddenly remembered. And Jessica was right. The song described this place pretty perfectly. She was too shy to sing the line, so she spoke it. "*Tangerine trees and marmalade skies*; I think that's what you're thinking."

"That's it!" cried Jessica. Then she sang in a pretty soprano, "*Picture yourself on a boat on a river, with tangerine trees and marmalade skies.* That's totally this place, weird and psychedelic."

The sky above Neffie was lightly pumpkin colored, and despite the fact the sun was high in the sky, suggesting midafternoon, it didn't cast the kind of bright yellow light you'd expect from a high-sky Iowa sun. Instead, this one had the kind of dull reddish tint you got at sunset.

Neffie shifted her gaze to examine the scenery closer to the ground. They were in a small clearing carpeted by yellow-green grass tinged red by the strange sunlight. Around the clearing was a dense forest of trees that might have been normal Iowa pines except their trunks corkscrewed in bizarre contortions and their needles were five times the length of normal pines back home. All around them, Neffie heard the same melodic birdsong mixed with faint clicking sounds that were less pleasant. The air smelled like vanilla-scented candles.

"It's kind of pretty here," Neffie observed.

"It surely is," Jessica answered. "You ever been here before?"

"This is the first time," Neffie confessed. "When my thing happens, I always wake in the same place I started. At least, I always did before now."

Jessica raised an eyebrow. "So no orange skies before today?"

"No. Or maybe. I'm not sure," Neffie replied honestly, shaking her head. "The sky looks kinda familiar. Maybe from a dream. Heck, maybe I'm dreaming now."

"Right," Jessica chuckled. "You're dreaming and I'm really in Iowa. I like it."

"It sounds pretty good." Neffie grinned.

Jessica glanced around. "Since we're both in this crazy dream together, we might as well take a look around."

"Sounds good."

Jessica stood. "Um," she said, "just in case this isn't a dream, you do know how to get us back, don't you?"

"I guess. We just reverse everything, I suppose."

If Jessica heard the doubt in Neffie's voice, she didn't let on. "Then come on. I think there's a path on the other side of that funny-shaped tree. Let's have ourselves a little look-see."

"All right," agreed Neffie.

Leading the way, Jessica crossed the clearing and went around the tree. On the other side was indeed a path that led into the woods. Before Jessica could start down the path, a sudden movement in front of her caused both girls to freeze.

A small creature skittered across the path, mostly hidden by low-hanging branches. A second or two later, another short, fast something darted across the path before Neffie could see it clearly.

"Did you see that?" Jessica asked.

"I think so. I didn't get a good look. Some kind of animal, maybe."

"Well, I hope this place doesn't have lions and tigers and bears."

"Oh my."

"Um, you inviting me to sing again?" asked Jessica.

Just then, another something dashed across the path.

"That was definitely on two legs," observed Neffie. "Maybe some kids are fooling around in the woods."

"Kids . . . or something not human," Jessica said.

Neffie was about to make another observation when there was a sudden, extended burst of clicking nearby. To Neffie, the clicking sounded like a giant, agitated cricket. She guessed the sound was coming from one of the trees in front of her, and it didn't have a friendly feel.

Behind the girls, a second click-maker answered the first, and soon afterward a third to their left joined the chorus. Then another added its sounds, and before long, there were dozens of noisemakers all around them. As more and more joined the mix, the hubbub grew louder and more unpleasant.

"What the heck is going on?" cried Jessica above the din.

Suddenly, a strange-looking waist-high creature on two legs darted out of the trees. Its stunted torso topped seesawing legs that were long, thin and animal-like, reminding Neffie of one of those lean racing greyhounds, only this creature's head was not so dog-like. It was more of a rat's head, with a rat's nose and a rat's ears and rat's whiskers. Before Neffie could think much about this strange creature and its strange head, the thing abruptly veered, picking up speed and rushing headlong toward the two girls, clicking wildly. Neffie tensed as she debated whether she should run away or try fending it off. While she stood frozen, trying to decide what to do, the creature quickly closed the distance until it was no more than four or five feet away.

*Meet it,* Neffie suddenly decided.

Before she could react, the thing came to a halt in front of her, and there it stood on its two legs, its short body quivering but unmoving, its nose sniffing in Neffie's direction. Close up, the creature looked rather lightweight and fragile, which made it less scary. Suddenly curious, Neffie took a nervous step forward to get a better look at it. As she approached it warily, nerves tingling, the thing's clicking gradually subsided, replaced by a sound more like the high-pitched purring of an affectionate cat.

Now that the creature was near, its large, canine eyes appeared doleful and sweet, contrasting sharply with the ugly, rat-like appearance of the rest of its face. The sweet eyes softened Neffie, who relaxed her guard and cautiously reached out her hand, palm up in the universal gesture of friendliness.

"Here, little creature," she murmured gently. "What are you? You're kinda ugly but you're also kinda cute. Are you friendly?"

The creature sniffed the air and acted friendly. But then the purring stopped and the clicking resumed, starting slowly but rapidly increasing in rhythm and volume. Suddenly, the creature hissed, and its mouth stretched open, revealing fangs and a row of pointy upper teeth. With a leap, it suddenly latched its mouth on Neffie's leg, driving its fangs through her blue jeans and into the flesh of her thigh just above her knee.

"Ow," Neffie cried in pain, shocked and frightened.

"Get off her," Jessica yelled, kicking the creature's lowered shoulder hard with her right foot.

The thing yelped in pain and retreated with a whimper. This caused an explosion of clicks all around them. A host of creatures sprang from the trees, pouring into the clearing and rushing at the girls with fangs bared and sinister hisses coming from open mouths.

"What the heck," cried Jessica as the hissing creatures rapidly closed the gap between them. "What do we do?"

"Run!" Neffie cried.

One of the leading creatures dropped onto fours and lunged at Jessica, its head low, aiming its fangs at her right shin. Jessica leaped to avoid the thing's teeth. To both girls' surprise, Jessica exploded into the air, soaring three or four feet above the creature.

"What the heck," exclaimed Jessica as she flew over its head.

She landed gracefully on the ground a good five feet away. Before Neffie could wonder about Jessica's amazing leap, another creature rushed madly out of the pack, this one charging at her. Without thinking, Neffie duplicated Jessica's feat, rising high into the air as if she were doing a pole vault. She easily soared over the lunging creature, landing nimbly on the ground maybe a half dozen feet beyond it.

"Holy crap," she cried in amazement.

Neffie had no time to think about it. More creatures cascaded into the clearing, dozens upon dozens of them, hissing angrily and baring their fangs. Neffie shot a glance at Jessica just in time to see the girl hurdle powerfully over three or four creatures charging her in a pack, and then she disappeared into the trees.

"This way," she shouted, calling for Neffie to follow.

Neffie couldn't follow. Packs of snarling, hissing creatures moved between Jessica and her and turned to charge. Two great leaps brought Neffie to the edge of the woods, which teemed with more creatures dropping from the trees. Neffie scanned the woods desperately for a way to escape. She plunged through a hole in the foliage and followed a narrow path leading away from the clearing, leaving the terrible din behind her.

*Jess, where are you?* she thought as she ran into the woods.

# CHAPTER 7

# A CHANCE ENCOUNTER

Neffie couldn't believe how fast her feet were moving. She swooshed past trees, the ground in front of her nothing more than a blur. The hisses, snarls and clicks quickly faded, and all grew quiet. The quiet didn't make Neffie feel any safer, however. Frightened, she pushed on, running hard.

Neffie finally slowed to what would have been a half-sprint back in Iowa. Her heart beat loudly from the long run, but she felt too rattled to risk stopping altogether. So she jogged for many minutes more at this slower but still rapid pace. Finally, Neffie neared the middle of a clearing and stopped.

Glancing nervously back, she studied the path behind her. Nothing moved. All was quiet. Slowly, she let her muscles relax as she sucked in deep gulps of air to get her breathing back under control. For a minute or two, she rested, and then decided to move on, wanting to put as much distance between those unpleasant creatures and herself as she could. Before she took a step, however, she got a terrible shock.

A tall man stood motionless on the other side of the clearing, not more than a dozen feet from her. He seemed to be watching her, though Neffie couldn't see his face, which was hidden in the shadows of a deep hood pulled over his head. In his left hand, he slowly twirled a slender pole about three feet long. His right hand was on his hip. Neffie's muscles tensed, and her breath caught in her throat.

*Friend or foe?* she wondered.

When the man didn't make a move toward her, she relaxed a little, but only a little. *Who is this guy? Is he dangerous?* After debating for a second or two, Neffie decided she wasn't going to run. Not yet, anyway. Tired of running, she decided to confront this stranger. *Sound tough,* Neffie told herself.

Unfortunately, when she opened her mouth to speak, no words came out. She was still too rattled. Exhaling slowly, she closed her mouth. *Great,* she thought, *let's be a total coward.* Neffie tried again to speak, but once again words refused to come out. Her heart was beating loudly and her hands shook. *Give it up,* she chastised herself.

The man pulled back his hood, and although his face was partly obscured by the shadows of the tree limbs above him, she saw his lips curve into a friendly smile.

"Don't worry," he said in a raspy voice. "I'm on your side."

Neffie finally found her voice. "What side is that?" she called.

"The side of people like us," he answered with a small, friendly laugh as he stepped out of the shadows. "Seriously, you should take a good, close look at me and you'll see what I mean."

As suggested, Neffie studied the stranger. He was around her height, slender, and perhaps two or three years older. His complexion was somewhat similar to hers, and Neffie guessed he was Middle Eastern, though she had to admit this was just the notion of a small-town girl who had never traveled outside Iowa except for a few family trips into adjacent Wisconsin and Minnesota. The guy's unkempt hair was dark brown and slightly curly, and the forehead beneath his unruly bangs resembled hers.

What caught Neffie's eye most was the cluster of freckles on each of his cheeks. Except for Sarge, Neffie had never seen another person with large, bright-pink freckles like hers, though where Neffie had six freckles on each cheek, the guy in front of her had five of the long, uneven blotches on either side of his face. Like Neffie, his ample lips were a matching pink. Only, the pink freckles and matching pink lips looked okay on this guy.

Neffie wondered if attitude could make that much of a difference. He was posing for her examination as if he was proud of his looks and sure of who he was. *His sexy eyes might also explain the difference.* Neffie had never seen eyes so startlingly green, almost iridescent. They were the kind of stunning eyes you could get lost in.

"I have to say you don't look sixteen," he remarked, looking her up and down.

Once again, Neffie heard laughter in his voice. Considering she had never said she was sixteen for the obvious reason she was two years younger, she decided he must be making some kind of stupid joke at her expense. This annoyed her a little.

"Well, you don't look fourteen," she shot back impulsively.

"Who said anything about me being fourteen?"

"No one."

"Good, because I'm not fourteen," the boy muttered, his face reddening and his right eye twitching slightly.

"Then we're even. You don't look fourteen, and I'll try not to be offended if I don't look sixteen to you."

"My saying you don't look sixteen was just an observation," the boy pointed out, "so I don't know why you're getting so upset.

"I'm not upset," countered Neffie, though in truth she was a bit annoyed by the guy. "I just want you to be nice."

"I only said you don't look sixteen, which, by the way, was a totally reasonable thing for me to say under the circumstances, so let's react a little more calmly and rationally, please."

"I will if you will."

A little defensively, the boy mumbled, "Okay."

"Okay! Great. So, who's on first," she now remarked, relaxing into the game she was about to start.

"Um, you go first."

"No, no, who's on first is what I said."

"What?"

"No, what's on second," Neffie quickly replied, her tone dead serious.

The nervous tic of the boy's right eye increased noticeably.

"What do you mean, what's on second?"

"Exactly," Neffie replied in mock seriousness. "Now you're getting it."

Frowning, the boy asked, "Are you making fun of me? I think you are."

"No, no," replied Neffie, struggling to keep her face serious. "You could literally say I'm just covering all our bases. So let's do third, shall we?"

Giving a little snort, the boy shook his head in frustration. "Hah," he muttered. "You most definitely are teasing me."

"Come on," persisted Neffie, "at least tell me 'I don't know' so we can keep going."

"This is hopeless," the boy replied. "You're making no sense." His lips tightened, and the tic of his right eye became rapid. Neffie took this as a sign she might have taken things too far.

"Sorry," she murmured. "Really, I'm sorry. It's just an old comedy bit from the movies. You know, Abbott and Costello. I wasn't making fun of you, just making a joke from the movies."

Displaying a pained but friendly enough smile, the guy nodded. "Well," he said, "I'm glad you can joke in the face of danger. Aren't you even a little worried about those awful garffles following you?"

"Is that what they're called?"

"Of course. Who doesn't know about garffles? They're the scourge of these forests."

"Well, they're hideous things, that's for sure," Neffie laughed. "But how did you know about my run-in with the garffles?"

The boy moved closer to Neffie. When he was no more than a single pace from her, he gazed curiously into her eyes. "That's not important. What I want to know is, where on Earth did you come from?"

Neffie wasn't sure how to answer this question. "Um, that's a hard thing to explain."

"Why would you say that?" he retorted.

Neffie laughed nervously "Believe me, I haven't yet figured it all out."

Snorting, the guy shot back, "Well, if you cannot or will not give me a simple answer to a simple question, then at least tell me who's on first and what's on second."

Neffie suddenly understood what was going on. "Oh my gosh! You're teasing me, aren't you?"

"I am not."

"You are! And maybe I deserve it."

"Well, all teasing aside, in the case of me, I can easily answer the incontestably simple question you seem inscrutably incapable of answering," the man remarked, enjoying his choice of words.

*Smart aleck,* Neffie thought. Still, she was suddenly curious to hear what he had to say.

"Okay," she answered. "Tell me."

"Where on Earth I am from is Turkey," he said. "From Istanbul, to be precise. My name is Kerem Alp. Kerem is my Turkish first name. So there's my answer. I am Kerem from Turkey on the planet called Earth."

"You're from Earth? You're . . . Kerem from Earth?"

"Yes and yes. You are very quick, and you pronounced my Earthly name exactly right, though you might try rolling the *r* a bit more while stretching the syllables the way they do here. *Keer-rem.* Actually, you can call me Rem. That's what my non-Turkish friends call me."

"Kerem," repeated Neffie. "Or Rem. Got it."

Smiling, Rem continued, "And on the planet Earth, you're called what? And where on Earth did you come from? I'm betting you really can answer my simple question."

This time, Rem's teasing did not bother Neffie.

"I guess we're even," she laughed. "Me, I'm from Iowa, United States of America. The town I live in is called Windmere. It's a tiny place, really. My name is Neffie. Pronounced *Neff-fee*," she added. "Are you really from Turkey?"

With his brow furrowing, the guy answered, "As far as I can remember, yes." Then his face relaxed as he continued, "Seriously, I'm very happy to meet another Earthling, even if she is a Yank from Iowa." Rem held out his hand for a shake. When Neffie took his hand, his warm, strong fingers wrapped around hers, and the warmth felt good. Rem held her hand for an unusually long time.

"A profoundly storyworthy meeting," he said to her, bowing slightly.

Rem had altered his voice, Neffie noted, and now sounded like her grandfather, Sarge.

"I didn't expect to meet someone like you. Are there many here? You know, many like us."

"That is a most interesting question," Rem replied. "Walk with me, Neffie of Windmere." He motioned for her to follow. "We mustn't stay in any one place too long. It isn't safe for a number of reasons."

Rem started across the clearing. Neffie only hesitated for a second before following. He set a brisk pace, taking long, vigorous strides that she matched easily. When they had gone maybe a dozen paces or so, Neffie suddenly remembered something extraordinarily important. Stopping abruptly, she slapped her forehead, horror-struck.

"Oh my gosh," Neffie cried, "I've totally forgotten Jessica! It's all because you were, like, suddenly standing there in front of me and I got so freaked I totally forgot about her. Rem, we need to go back and find Jessica."

Frowning, Rem asked, "Who's Jessica?"

"If you must know, I'm Jessica."

Neffie turned as Jessica came striding up the path, her face flushed from running and both her shirt sleeves torn.

"Oh my gosh, are you all right?" called Neffie, feeling terribly guilty about forgetting her.

Jessica came up beside her. "Nice of you to ask," she replied without any sting of reprimand in her voice. "And who's this?"

Neffie was about to answer when she noticed Rem's shocked expression.

"You're completely human," Rem said to Jessica. "What a mightily and astonishingly storied moment. I am truly here in these Tymes, and yet I am looking at a completely human girl! You are human, aren't you?"

Rem's question was so odd Neffie almost laughed. For her part, Jessica reacted to his question with a fair amount of good humor.

"That's, like, the weirdest thing any boy has ever said to me," she said.

"I'm sorry," answered Rem, blushing slightly. "What I meant is—" Pausing before continuing, he eventually explained, "It's just that . . . well, it is quite amazing to see you here, in these Tymes. Seriously, it is storyingly amazing to see someone as Earthly and normal looking as you."

"Gee, thanks, glad to know I'm at least normal looking. So great," said Jessica, rolling her eyes while glancing at Neffie. "Neff, you hear how this guy lays on his compliments?"

Rem said nothing to defend himself. Instead, he took two steps toward Jessica and locked his eyes on hers in the same way he had done earlier with Neffie. Jessica kept her cool and simply stared back.

"I'm serious," Rem repeated. "Looking the way you do could be very bad. Very dangerous." Pausing to think, he suddenly cried, "I've got it!"

Pulling away, he quickly stripped off his hooded coat and handed it to Jessica. "Take it. I beseech you," Rem urged. "Wear this for me, and when you're around others, keep the hood up and your face as much as possible in the shadows and out of sight."

"Well, I have to say, you're really making me feel weird, mister . . . um, mister—"

"Rem," he told her. "I mean it; you need to trust me. It's not safe for you to be seen. Please, please put on this coat and use the hood."

Jessica gave Neffie a look that begged for help.

"Why not?" Neffie shrugged. "As you say, everything about this place is weird. I think Rem is all right and we should trust him. It certainly sounds important to him."

"Well, the coat won't bite me," Jessica said. Taking the coat from Rem, she slipped it over her head. The garment was made of a soft brown material that resembled well-worn suede, except it wasn't suede, and from what Neffie could tell, it smelled like dried hay. Blotchy stains marred the surface, and most of the original brown dye had faded to a lighter tan color. Once Jessica had the thing on, it proved much too big for her, its cuffs hanging past her wrists to her knuckles and the bottom hem falling well below her waist to mid-hip.

"A little big," Jessica said, stretching her arms to show the poor fit of the sleeves.

"Don't worry, it's a servant's coat," Rem answered. "You'll be just another maidservant wearing bad-fitting, used clothing. We can only hope no one will notice a poorly dressed maidservant."

This prompted a wink from Jessica to Neffie. "Hear that, Neff?" she remarked. "After some serious slams, this guy is now turning me into a servant." Pausing, she jabbed a finger at Rem. "I hope you don't think I'm your servant. You don't, do you?"

"No, no," Rem replied hastily, his face coloring, "what I meant was—"

"She's teasing you," Neffie interrupted with a laugh.

"Oh," he answered. "Not another teasing girl from Iowa?"

"I'm afraid she is. And in fact, Jessica makes my tongue sound pretty dull."

Rem laughed. "Well, it's good the two of you have your sharp tongues since I see you don't have your *zabbaton*. Is it lost?" he asked Neffie.

"I don't know what you're talking about," Neffie said. "What's a—"

"*Zabbaton*," Rem said, holding up the stick still in his left hand.

Neffie reached out and touched it, and Jessica did the same.

"It's just a wooden stick," she remarked.

"Not a wooden stick but a specially crafted tool," Rem answered. "Wasn't this explained to you?" He gave Neffie a curious look.

Neffie shrugged. "There wasn't much time for explanations."

"Well, you need to know how it works. Watch and see."

Taking a step backward, Rem flipped his wrist, making the stick twirl rapidly in his hand. Once he had it spinning, with another flip he launched it into the air. To Neffie's astonishment, it soared thirty feet above them, spinning as fast as a helicopter blade as it rose. Once it crested, down it plunged. With nonchalant ease, Rem thrust out a hand exactly when the thing reached eye level and nabbed it.

In the next instant, he flung it at Neffie. The stick zoomed at her with the speed of a fastball hurled by a strong-armed pitcher. Neffie threw her arm up to fend off the stick, which struck her forearm with a loud thwack. Luckily, the stick only nicked her arm before glancing off.

"Hey!" she cried. "That could've hurt. You can't go throwing sticks like that."

Picking up the zabbaton, Rem offered it to Neffie.

"Believe me, you could have caught it easily had you but tried. As I say, it is not a stick. This is an elegantly designed zabbaton, a wondrously effective instrument for self-protection." Pausing, he added, "Among other uses."

With a slight bow, he placed the zabbaton into Neffie's hands.

"Here," he said, "keep it. Learn to use it and it will do you well."

"But it's yours."

Laughing, Rem replied, "Hardly mine. Wrong gender and all that. I insist, you keep it."

He thrust the zabbaton at Neffie, who took hold of the thing and instantly noticed how light it was. Its surface was smooth, and its texture reminded her of a wooden baseball bat. Instead of tapering from a wider hitting end to a narrower handle, however, the zabbaton was uniform in diameter from end to end and perhaps three times the thickness of a drumstick. Neffie liked the way it balanced in her hand, and holding it did indeed make her feel safer.

"Thanks," she said.

"*Bir şey değil,*" Rem responded.

"What?"

"That's *you're welcome.* One of the few Turkish phrases I can remember. And for you, Jessica, here, take this."

Reaching into a pocket, Rem pulled out a round object slightly larger than a golf ball. Attached to it was a fine, braided rope about ten inches long with a ring at the far end.

"You slip the thumb of your throwing hand into this ring here," explained Rem, demonstrating with his hand. "And then you use the line to twirl it to get up speed. When you have it really going and it spins in the direction of your target, you let the ring slip off your thumb and it goes flying. It's called a *lobbie* and it is remarkably effective if used correctly."

Rem unhooked his thumb and tossed the lobbie at Jessica, who caught it easily, exactly as you'd expect from the captain of the Millard Fillmore girls' fast-pitch softball team.

"I want to try it," exclaimed Jessica, slipping her right thumb through the ring.

"Practice later," Rem suggested. "Right now, there's a thing or two I need to explain. First off, in the Tymes of this side—"

"Tymes," cried Neffie, interrupting him. "I've heard that word before."

"Yes, yes, you're on the other side of the Tymes. You must know this."

"Of course we do," said Jessica before Neffie could answer. "Go on, Rem. You were about to explain."

Rem nodded. "Right. I don't know exactly what you were taught, but if the zabbaton wasn't explained to you, let's start with some basics."

"Yes, let's," Jessica said.

Rem laughed nervously. "Right. First, I wouldn't go showing your athletic skills to just anyone. The reasons are complicated and I can't explain them in the little time we have, but trust me on this. Also, don't go believing things you hear here. Truth isn't the same as on Earth. Also, you need to be very careful when you—"

Before Rem could finish, an explosion overhead drowned out his words. Startled, Neffie glanced up to see a purplish hole opening in the sky below the sun. At the same time, the sun quivered and turned blue. Then another explosion rumbled.

Jessica cried, "What the heck is—"

Interrupting her, Rem shouted, "No time to explain. My stars, this is bad!" The pitch of his voice rose. "Very bad."

"What do you mean, very bad?"

"Bad like getting swallowed whole," answered Rem, his voice cracking.

Jessica asked, "What do we—"

"No more time!" Rem shouted. "We need a place to hide. But where? Wait! I think I know."

Without another word, Rem turned and sprinted away, making for a path on the other side of the clearing. Neffie hesitated a second before taking off after him, clutching her zabbaton to her chest with no idea why she should trust Rem.

"Come on," she cried to Jessica over her shoulder. Another explosion followed.

"I'm with you," Jessica called to Neffie.

Rem plunged into the woods, following the path at breakneck speed, leaping agilely over fallen limbs and ducking nimbly whenever a low-hanging tree limb got in his way. With her newfound jumping ability and remarkable speed, Neffie had no trouble keeping up, and she heard Jessica's footsteps close behind. Another explosion sounded. The three of them burst out of the trees into another clearing, this one much larger than the earlier one. In the middle of this clearing was a frighteningly wide and deep gorge. As they neared it, she glimpsed a churning river at the bottom.

Rem veered to run parallel to the gorge. After maybe twenty strides, he suddenly turned and headed straight for the edge at full speed. Neffie turned too, running blindly and putting all her trust in Rem. Behind Neffie, she heard Jessica's loud breathing and sharp footsteps as the girl kept pace. When Rem was no more than a step or two from the edge of the gorge, abruptly he leaped into the air, hurling his body out and over the shockingly wide chasm.

*Impossible,* Neffie thought.

It was all too sudden for her to think. In two steps, she was at the gorge's edge, and mimicking Rem, she threw herself upward and outward as he had done. Amazingly, she shot into the air and soared far out over the deep gorge. Time slowed as she soared to the mid-point of the chasm, and then it sped up as she descended in a long arc toward the other side.

Not sure she was going to make it, Neffie screamed. In front of her, she saw Rem land on the other side and tumble forward into a tight body-roll, then pop to his feet and resume running. Neffie closed her eyes and waited, desperately hoping for the best but fearing the worst. Her feet hit the ground on the other side with unexpected force, and instead of rolling as Rem had done, she lurched off-balance for several steps and then tripped over a rock, sprawling headfirst. Jessica crashed to the ground not far behind her.

The explosions continued, and the hole yawing in the sky was now wider than ever, and the sun had turned black.

Ignoring the pain of skinned palms and bruised knees, Neffie quickly climbed back on her feet and resumed running, with Jessica following. Rem was waiting for them maybe fifty feet ahead. As soon as they caught up, he took off down a long cut through the trees away from the gorge.

In the distance, Neffie saw a tall cliff at the end of the cut. Rem made for the cliff's hard, rocky face at full speed. This time Neffie dropped back in order not to be so totally surprised when Rem again did something utterly astounding and dangerous like leaping over a giant gorge. To Neffie's dismay, Rem kept churning toward the cliff, closing the distance rapidly.

*Please no,* she thought.

Just when it seemed Rem was going to crash into the cliff, he suddenly dove headfirst, stretching his arms in front of him like a diver, his body knifing through the air. Neffie watched in horror, expecting him to smack against the cliff wall, but instead his body disappeared through a narrow crack that opened out of nowhere.

"Oh my gosh!" Neffie screamed as she raced toward the looming cliff.

Two strides later, Neffie mimicked Rem, aiming for the same crack and trusting Rem to know what he was doing. As she flew through the air, she brought her zabbaton against her chest to keep it from catching the edges of the crack.

In the next breath, she was on the other side of the cliff, and again Neffie found herself crashing headfirst to the ground and skidding to a painful stop. And once more Jessica crashed to the ground behind her.

# CHAPTER 8

# LOST IN A CAVE

"**O**w," Jessica moaned. "That friggin' hurt." She gingerly touched a patch of bleeding skin through a long tear in the knee of her beige jeans.

"You all right?" Neffie asked.

"Peachy," replied Jessica, flexing her knee to see if it still worked.

Neffie's eyes gradually adjusted to the darkness. Climbing painfully to her feet, she took a slow look around. They were in small, dimly lit chamber. In front of her a long tunnel sloped gently into the ground. Neffie peered down the tunnel's length. As far as she could see, the tunnel was a narrow tube with smooth walls of grayish rock and a low ceiling. Nothing moved inside the tunnel; nothing breathed. All was quiet.

"Looks pretty dark and empty," she said to Jessica.

"Yep," Jessica agreed, "like a tomb."

The reality of this struck Neffie with full force. The place wasn't supposed to be empty.

"Where's Rem?" she asked.

Jessica shrugged. "Beats me."

"What do you mean, beats you? Doesn't that worry you? Oh my gosh, Jessica, he's not here. Rem is gone!"

Jessica shrugged again. "You're asking if I'm worried about Rem disappearing after everything else that's happened?" Gesturing with her hands, she continued, "After going through that beam-me-up-Scotty transport from our little school to this totally bizarre place with orange skies and a red sun and these ugly little critters with rat faces and beastly little fangs, only these critters walk on two legs, not four, and suddenly they're attacking us, like, probably to eat us?"

"Rem said they're called garffles."

"Garffles, snarffles, whatever," said Jessica. "So . . . to finish my point, next we run from these ugly garffles and end up meeting this dude who shows up out of nowhere and who is, like, totally weirded out I'm one hundred percent human—which means, by the way, he probably isn't—and then the sky starts exploding and this giant hole opens in the middle of the sky . . . and now you're asking if I'm worried about Rem?"

Having finished her rant, Jessica mugged a wide-eyed look of disbelief while turning her palms dramatically upward as if asking a cosmic *why*. This finishing touch was too much for Neffie, who giggled and then laughed. Soon, Jessica was laughing too.

"What do we do now?" Neffie finally asked when she could laugh no more.

"I'm thinking we should go home," replied Jessica. "I mean, while this place has its charms, right now I wouldn't mind being back in sleepy old Windmere where everything is boring and crazy stuff like garffles never happens. So, why don't you do your beaming thingy and take us home?"

Neffie had to admit she liked the idea, only there was something she needed to admit that Jessica wasn't going to like.

"Um, I have to tell you something important," she slowly confided.

"If it's bad, don't tell me."

"Okay," Neffie agreed with a shrug.

Jessica rolled her eyes. "Just kidding. Say what you need to say."

"I'm not sure how we get home. Rem's gone, and don't forget, my thing only happens when I'm up high," said Neffie. "Right now, we're in a cave, which is, like, the opposite of high."

"True 'nough. I guess we should look around and find a way out. If we can get outside, there were plenty of hills."

"Right," agreed Neffie, pointing to the tunnel. "This is the only way, so we might as well go this way."

"Solid thinking, girl," chuckled Jessica.

Neffie searched and found her zabbaton, which she had dropped during her hard landing in the cave. She gripped it firmly. Nodding, Jessica patted a bulge in her pocket where her lobbie was safely tucked. "I guess we're good to go," she said.

"You think garffles like caves?" asked Neffie.

Giving her a disapproving look, Jessica answered, "Please shut up about garffles."

Then she took Neffie's arm and tucked it under hers, and the two of them started forward, nervous but determined to find a way out. The long, downward-sloping tunnel was wide enough for the two girls to walk side by side so long as they squeezed together, and fortunately there was plenty of light to see, which surprised Neffie. The light had a soft blue hue and seemed to come from the cave roof above them. Neffie couldn't spot any source for the light, but she wasn't going to complain when light meant no darkness.

They walked wordlessly. The tunnel seemed to go on forever. Now and then, they had to unlink arms to avoid a solitary stalactite dangling from the ceiling, blocking their way. Mostly, the tunnel was featureless, with walls, ceiling and floor all of the same drab, gray rock.

To Neffie's dismay, the farther they went, the colder the air became. Before long, they could see their breath, and soon after that Neffie began shivering. As they traveled deeper and deeper into the cave, Neffie grew colder until her teeth were chattering and her fingers numb.

Finally, when she couldn't stand it any longer and was about to suggest they turn around and go back, Jessica spoke excitedly.

"There's light up ahead."

"Really?"

"Yes, I can barely see it, but it's there. Look!"

Neffie made out an orange-yellow light flickering faintly in the distance.

"A fire?" Neffie asked. The thought of a warm fire ahead was pleasing in some ways, but it was also scary.

"Come on," Jessica whispered. "Let's have a closer look."

Taking the lead, Jessica moved cautiously forward. Neffie followed. As they neared the light, the air grew warmer and the cave became brighter. Soon, Neffie heard voices. A man was talking. Then a woman spoke. Then a different man said something.

"Voices," Neffie whispered to Jessica.

"Yes, I hear them. From the other side of the tunnel."

Neffie squeezed Jessica's arm nervously. She couldn't make out what was being said, but she guessed there were at least three persons speaking. There was definitely a man's voice that seemed to have the right pitch to belong to Rem, though Neffie couldn't be sure.

"What should we do?" she whispered to Jessica.

They made their way slowly down the curving wall of the tunnel and the voices grew ominously near.

"I guess we should keep going and see who they are."

"You think?" asked Neffie, trying her best to be brave. "At least they sound human, not like those garffles."

"We don't know that for sure," Jessica reminded her. "In this freaked-out place, maybe garffles can talk."

"*Ssh*, let's be quiet and try to get a peek at them before they see us. If things look bad, we turn and try to sneak away, hopefully unseen. And if we have to, we run. Agreed?"

"Absolutely."

The two girls inched forward, walking as lightly as possible. Luckily for them, the glow originated well on the other side of the tunnel's long bend, and so they were able to get very close to the voices without being seen. Eventually, though, they came to a point where there was nothing left to do but step around the remaining curve of the cave wall and reveal themselves. Jessica gave Neffie a wink.

"Ready?"

"Ready." Neffie gripped her zabbaton with both hands.

"Then let's go," said Jessica, starting forward.

Suddenly remembering Rem's warning, Neffie grabbed Jessica's shoulder. When Jessica looked back, she pointed at the girl's head. "Hood," she reminded her.

Nodding, Jessica pulled up the hood and drew it forward to cover her face as much as possible. Then the two girls went around the bend, stepping into the dim light of a small fire flickering inside a neat ring of rocks piled ankle-high. Six or seven creatures were sitting on low stools around the fire, each with shoulders hunched, heads lowered. A few of them held clay mugs, and one was taking a sip from her or his mug.

Neffie and Jessica stayed close to the wall, watching and waiting. Eventually, one of the creatures must have noticed the girls because suddenly he stood and stared. All conversation immediately ceased. One by one, the others stood. All of them had dark faces, and they were tall, Neffie noticed, ranging from Neffie's height to a good half a head taller. Neffie caught her breath, not knowing what to expect. Then she recognized the tallest man.

"Sarge!" she cried, her spirits lifting at the sight of her grandfather.

Relieved to see a familiar face, Neffie rushed forward to greet him. Unfortunately, after only a few steps, the shadows obscuring the man's face dissolved, and she realized he was not her grandfather but a stranger with yellow eyes that now dug into hers with a fierceness that caused her to stop. Her first instinct should have been to turn from that fierce gaze, but for some inexplicable reason, she felt compelled to stare back. Their eyes locked, and a long, strange silence followed while the two of them stood staring.

"What in the name of Hentas did you call me?" the man finally asked.

"I don't know what you're talking about," answered Neffie.

"You called me Sarge."

"I did what?"

"You called me Sarge. I heard you."

"Um, I may have said something that sounded like Sarge," said Neffie, still nervous about revealing too much too quickly.

"Why would you say something that sounded like Sarge?" the man replied in the same slow manner of speech used by Sarge back in Neffie's kitchen.

As Neffie stared into the man's eyes, she suddenly decided he had an open, trustworthy face. Moreover, the man resembled Sarge, but without pink spots on his cheeks. Also, his complexion was darker, and his features were a bit more compressed between his forehead and chin. He was also slightly taller and more muscular than her grandfather, whom Neffie remembered as being slender and willowy. He had the same yellow eyes, however.

"Sarge is my grandfather," admitted Neffie, suddenly deciding to take the risk.

To her surprise, the man looked shocked and was speechless for a moment. When he finally spoke, he sounded so awestruck he stammered a bit.

"You're Neffatira Sargie? You are truly and incontrovertibly the granddaughter of Gannen Sargie and true blood-daughter of his blood-son?"

Neffie didn't know quite what to say. "Um, yes, I guess. You know my grandfather?"

"Of course!" the man cried. "We both live in the same compound, have lived there together for many years. He is truly a friend. And who is this with you, Lady Neffatira?"

Neffie chose her words carefully. "This is Jessica, who is traveling with me."

The man bowed before the two girls, using the same formal gesture Neffie's dad and grandfather had used when they made their introductions back in her family's kitchen. That meeting now felt ages ago. Finishing his bow, the man again spoke softly and slowly, just as her grandfather had.

"It is my storyworthy honor to meet you, Lady Neffatira of the Sargie blood-clan," he said, bowing again. "And to meet your maidservant, Jessica," he added with a nod in her direction. "My common name, my lady, is Jedd Planck, formerly a servant to the Clatchie blood-clan. I am now husband-consort to the woman here, who won me in a most storyworthy contest."

Pausing, the man tilted his head in the direction of a tall woman to his right before continuing. "My lady, it is thus my great honor to introduce you to my wife-consort, Lattiana of the Wurthers and Vong blood-clans." Jedd paused while the woman named Lattiana bowed respectfully.

"The others here are friends of mine and friends of Lattiana, and therefore they are friends of yours. You are most heartily welcome to join our fire, Lady Neffatira, as is your maidservant, and we most humbly and reverentially mark the storyworthiness of this moment in which you have graced us by joining our fire."

"Thank you," Neffie answered, doing her best to match the formality of the man's speech. "And may I ask you, sir, where here is? It feels to us we have been walking in these caves forever. We would most greatly appreciate your help, sir, with you pointing us in the right direction."

Planck raised his eyebrows and gave Lattiana a surprised and uncomfortable glance before composing himself and answering Neffie with the same kind of slow solemnity as before, though his tone had changed in some way Neffie was unable to read.

"Imagine, Lattie," Planck muttered, "that a lady of such storied worth as to be marked with six spots has just called me sir." He shifted his wide eyes to gaze at Neffie. "Lady Neffatira, are you testing me? I humbly ask this because of course you must know that you are in the secret and hallowed passageway of our storied alliance, the alliance of the blood-clans from which have sprung countless noble Tymes benders and the greatest light guardians of the ages. Given that you must know this even as you ask for direction, I humbly beg you to forgive me for not understanding your purpose and for answering only inadequately."

Crossing an arm over his chest, Jedd folded his body in such a deep bow his hat tumbled from his head and his mass of hair fell forward. Ignoring the hat on the ground, he finished his bow with the same exaggerated formality with which he had started it, rising slowly and stiffly and uncrossing his arm from his chest with so much pomp it was almost comical. Neffie found this whole performance exceedingly silly, and she struggled to stifle a tiny giggle bubbling up inside her.

Instead she tightened her lips and waited silently, unsure about what she should say or do in response. For his part, the man stood bareheaded and unmoving in front of Neffie, his hair a mess, his eyes popping unnaturally. Above his forehead, the man had a bowl-shaped bald spot that added to his silliness.

*What the heck,* Neffie thought. *Go for it.*

The perfectly round, brightly shining bald spot above the man's forehead looked so totally ridiculous she couldn't take her eyes off it. Still, she did her best to match the formality of his speech.

"Indeed, of course. And I will tell you that I am most deeply contemplating what you just said," she continued, "yet verily and truly where we are is perhaps obvious to you, but it is a strange and new place to us and thus my purpose is to have you give us some advice on the direction we want to go."

Finished, Neffie waited and hoped for the response she wanted. Planck looked dismayed. In fact, he looked so forlorn Neffie giggled.

"Please forgive me, Lady Neffatira," the man mumbled miserably. "It seems truly I have displeased you."

"No, no—" Neffie started.

"Indeed, lady, I am deeply dismayed to have displeased you so profoundly."

Jessica now interjected, trying to help. "If I may say so, Lady Neffatira is not displeased. She just wants to know where in these hallowed passages we are. We have gotten a bit lost and could use your help finding our way out."

"Ah, now I see," Planck replied, doing his best to maintain his dignity. "I understand and it is my honor to assist by informing her lady's maidservant that her lady is near the end of the Lower Galleyton Passageway, nearly beneath the mountainside edge of Galleyton High Main. I am profoundly pleased to be at her lady's service in any way her lady might ask."

Planck dipped into another deep, formal bow, his long hair spilling everywhere as he bent so low his head nearly touched the ground.

"Well, my lady greatly appreciates your kind help," Jessica said. "And on behalf of my lady as her maidservant, we thank you, sir."

"It will be my great honor, maidservant, to assist by guiding Lady Neffatira and you to the city."

"What do you think, my lady?" asked Jessica, giving Neffie a private little wink. "Shall we go with this good man to the city of, um, Galleyton High Main? Shall we leave now?"

Taking a deep breath and growing as serious as she could manage, Neffie replied, "In a minute we can go. First, I need to ask you one question, Mr. Planck. By any chance, did you see some boy go by who was about my height but he had lighter skin and, like, really green eyes?"

"Green eyes?" the man cried, his face paling visibly. "You mean to say there's a Tymes stealer in the passageway? Why didn't you say so right away, my lady?" Shooting a glance at the others he cried, "Is this possible?"

Lattiana shot a nervous glance down the tunnel. The others around the fire murmured anxiously.

"No, no," Neffie reassured the bunch without understanding why she chose to hide the truth. "I was only asking just in case. I didn't say there was actually anyone with green eyes here."

Planck seemed to relax a little, and when he next spoke, his words were again slow and well mannered.

"My apologies for reacting so strongly, my lady," he murmured. "But your lady knows well that there are many enemies everywhere about. It is certainly true that not all green-eyes are evil, but most of them are undeniably liars and thieves and so we must be ever vigilant and wary. Truly, we must be wary. But I am again confounded by your question, my lady. It seems I have no ability to discern your purpose and thereby to serve you properly. Undoubtedly this is my failing and for it I am most profoundly sorry."

Planck was studying her closely, Neffie noticed. And it seemed to her his eyes were now a bit distrustful. She glanced at Lattiana, and the woman also had a suspicious look.

"Let's not talk any more of it," Neffie said. "Why don't you just take us up to the city and help me find my grandfather? If you will do that, you will be of profoundly great service to us, Mr. Planck."

This change of subjects seemed to work. With a great flourish, the man gave his formal bow again. When he finally lifted his head, there was a pleased look on his face.

"Thank you, Lady Neffatira. You honor me with this task, and I shall not fail you. This way, my lady. My Lattiana will lead and I will take my proper place at the rear."

Lattiana stepped forward. She was around the same height as Planck, with a long face and three pink spots on either cheek. Like Planck, her eyes were bright yellow, and there was a stylized tattoo of a sun in matching yellow on her cheek. She wore loose brown trousers, a comfortable-looking green tunic or dress nearly down to her knees, and a wide-brimmed hat, which was also green. With the exception of Planck, whose brimless hat he now fetched from the ground, all the others were wearing wide-brimmed hats. Giving Neffie a small smile, Lattiana indicated a narrow side tunnel branching off the main one.

"This way will take us to the city," Lattiana said. "Once we have guided you into the city, my lady, and we have found you a safe place to wait, Planck and I will locate your grandfather and bring him to you. Now please, my lady, it is my profound honor to guide you."

The woman gestured for Neffie and Jessica to follow. Starting down the side passageway, which was only wide enough for one person to pass at a time, she set out at a healthy jog but nowhere near as fast as Rem's earlier rush through forests and hills. The girls fell in line behind her, first Neffie and then Jessica. Planck followed a short distance behind. The others remained at the fire.

"I don't think Rem is trustworthy," Jessica whispered to Neffie as they jogged down the narrow tunnel. "He gives me the creeps."

Neffie didn't answer. Rem had struck her as friendly—even cute—so it now troubled her to think he might be something else. *What? An enemy? A doer of evil, as Planck suggested?* That hardly seemed possible. *A Tymes stealer?* Planck had all but called him that. Whatever a Tymes stealer was, it didn't sound good.

# CHAPTER 9

# A TERRIBLE EVENT

The tunnel sloped steeply upward, but Neffie jogged effortlessly with a strength she had never before experienced. Lattiana seemed to maintain the rapid pace effortlessly as well. At last, the tunnel leveled off and soon ended in a small, round cavern that gave the impression of being intentionally carved into the rock. At the far end was a wide, tall door. Moving to the door, Lattiana drew a large, brass-like key from her jacket pocket and slipped it into a keyhole in the center of the door.

Instead of opening on side hinges as Neffie would have expected, the door swung down from hinges hidden in the ground. There was creaking followed by a loud thud as the door crashed to the ground on the other side of the threshold. The thud echoed down the tunnel behind Neffie, leaving her strangely unsettled.

There was no time to think, however. With Lattiana hurrying forward, they stepped one by one through the open doorway into the back end of a long, narrow alleyway. Stone-faced, windowless buildings lined both sides, giving it a close, dark feeling. At the distant end of the alley, Neffie saw the brightness of a sunlit day.

"There lies the city of Galleyton High Main, my lady," Planck announced with a smile.

"Come quickly, my lady," urged Lattiana, leading Neffie and Jessica down the alleyway while Planck lingered behind to hoist the door back into place.

At the far end, Lattiana paused, giving Neffie a chance to take in the scenery. A wide street extended in both directions, seeming to go on forever. Heavy traffic flowed both ways, but it was not the kind Neffie knew back on Earth. For one thing, there were no cars, buses, trucks, motorcycles, or noises of engines. Rather, everyone traveled by bicycle or on foot.

The street was wide and grassy, and extending down its middle were four evenly spaced rows of willowy trees growing out of planters that looked to be made of clay. On both sides of the wide street, long rows of tall, closely packed buildings ranged in height from seven to ten stories. There were no sidewalks. Instead, the fronts of buildings came right up to the grassy thoroughfare, and their ends were packed so closely together that each building practically touched its neighbor. The effect was to create a nearly endless wall of building facades on either side of the street, punctuated by an occasional alleyway.

Everything about the scene in front of Neffie looked odd. Strangest of all were the giant birdhouses. These bizarre structures dotted the boulevard every half mile or so. They weren't actually birdhouses, Neffie observed, though they certainly had the look of birdhouses from a distance. On closer examination, they appeared to be three and four-story buildings sitting on long, slender columns of stone rising perhaps two stories high. The buildings perched on top of these columns were nearly the full width of the boulevard, coming within a dozen feet or so of the buildings along the sides.

As soon as Planck caught up, Lattiana muttered, "Come, my lady, we mustn't linger." Hastily, she led them out of the alleyway, but the minute they moved onto the street, a small group of people lingering on the edge of the boulevard sauntered away, heading against the traffic down the boulevard. Neffie thought this was somewhat odd, and apparently Lattiana did too.

"I don't like how those folks reacted," she observed.

"Like they knew you?" Neffie said.

"Quite so," agreed Lattiana. "I do believe we need to move quickly, my lady, and find you a place that's safe."

"Whatever you say."

Nodding, Lattiana gestured to her left. "Then please follow this way, my lady."

Lattiana moved with the traffic down the near side of the street. With the others following, she hugged close to the fronts of the buildings, no doubt to draw as little attention to them as possible. The first building they passed was seven stories tall and very long. When they reached the end of the next one, abruptly Lattiana turned down a small alleyway.

This alleyway was even narrower than the previous one, and again the walls were windowless. To Neffie's relief, no one was in this alleyway, though its darkness was unsettling. There was light in the distance, and this made Neffie feel a little better.

With Lattiana leading them, they jogged quickly, their footsteps echoing in the deep canyon created by the buildings. Before long, they reached the halfway point, and Neffie saw the sunshine brightening at the far end. She grew almost optimistic until she heard voices behind her. Glancing over her shoulder, she glimpsed four or five tall figures now hurrying after them.

"There are people behind us," she whispered ahead to Lattiana.

"Yes, my lady," the woman replied. "And likely they are not friends."

Lattiana sped up. The familiar woodpecker stirred in Neffie's chest. Again, she glanced back. The strangers were quickly catching up.

"Oh dear," muttered Lattiana when another bunch of tall figures suddenly appeared in front of them at the far end of the alley.

"Not friends?" Neffie guessed.

"It's as if they were waiting for us. I fear we will need to fight, my lady. I wonder how in Hentas they knew."

Neffie felt a pang of guilt. *Could this be Rem's doing? Rem with the green eyes? The Tymes stealer?*

Lattiana reached under the lapel of her jacket and took out a short stick perhaps ten inches long. Grasping one end, she flicked the stick downward. There was a pleasant sound like wind chimes jingling, and wondrously the stick grew, its length quickly tripling.

Other chimes tinkled behind Neffie. When she twisted her head to look, the tall strangers in the back group were grasping long sticks. The group in front of them did the same.

*They're zabbatons,* Neffie reminded herself as she tightened her grip on the zabbaton Rem had given her, holding it in the center the way all the others were doing.

Lattiana glanced at the zabbaton in Neffie's hands.

"No, my lady," she said. "Today's is not your fight."

The group in front of them all appeared to be women, though Neffie couldn't be entirely sure of genders since they were wearing wide-brimmed hats that covered their faces in shadows. None was more than half a head shorter than Neffie, and they seemed uniformly lithe and agile.

All of a sudden, one woman separated herself from the others, taking two steps ahead and performing an elaborate ritual with her zabbaton, twirling it in front of her, then over her head, then behind her back and finally in front of her again. The woman looked young to Neffie, perhaps no older than Rem, but she was very tall—even taller than Planck and Lattiana. She had broad shoulders and wide hands with long fingers. She wore her hair split into numerous braids hanging to her shoulders in alternating bands of bright green and teal blue. Her bright eyes blazed at them, and they were green, Neffie noted with alarm. *Like Rem's.*

Calmly removing her brimmed hat and handing it to Planck, Lattiana took two long strides forward and performed a similar ritual with her zabbaton. Her movements were graceful, sure.

"Are you acting as champion then?" the other woman called, her voice loud and defiant but the words drawn out and deliberate. "For I am here to challenge."

"Yes, I stand as champion," Lattiana answered, her own words equally measured and slow, "and I demand to hear your name spoken."

"I am Gwenlie of the mightily storied Charmaine blood-clan."

"And I am Lattiana of the profoundly storyworthy Wurthers blood-clan, answering your challenge."

"How shall we fight?" the other woman demanded.

"In the profoundly storyworthy style of the Sargies," answered Lattiana, glancing back to give Neffie a little wink and smile.

"I acquiesce in your choice of styles," the woman calling herself Gwenlie announced, taking a great leap forward and landing only a few feet from Lattiana. "In the style of the Sargies it shall be."

Each woman now shifted her grip to hold her zabbaton with only one hand in the middle while placing the other hand behind her back. Rather than twirling their zabbatons, the two of them oscillated the ends up and down with quick, energetic motions of their hands, their wrists acting as pivots, their zabbatons held roughly parallel to the ground as the ends seesawed up and down. While Neffie watched with a mix of fascination and concern, the two women's bodies swayed as they circled each other, their zabbatons moving rhythmically up and down while each studied her opponent with unblinking eyes.

Gwenlie suddenly flicked one end of her zabbaton at Lattiana's head. The movement was no more than a flash, but Lattiana managed to parry the intended blow with the end of her zabbaton. Gwenlie took a step back and gave the low, formal bow that was now becoming so familiar to Neffie.

"Well met," she said to Lattiana.

"Thank you," replied Lattiana, bowing gracefully in return.

Both women again took up their fighting stances. Abruptly, Lattiana leaped forward, closing half the space between them. Skipping the elaborate, circling dance of their previous round, she jabbed the leading end of her zabbaton at Gwenlie's head. The movement was so fast, so unexpected, that Gwenlie barely managed to react in time. And yet, by luck or skill—or through some combination of the two—she was able to shift her zabbaton just quickly enough to brush aside the attack.

There was a loud click as the dueling instruments struck each other, and Lattiana twirled her wrist to slide her zabbaton off Gwenlie's in the direction of the other woman's head. To avoid being hit, Gwenlie had to roll her head sideways, and Lattiana's zabbaton swished by so close it rustled Gwenlie's hair.

As before, the attacker didn't press her advantage. Rather, Lattiana took a step away and gave Gwenlie a low, formal bow.

"A good parry," she complimented.

"Thank you," was the other woman's cool reply.

Taking up fighting stances again, the two women now resumed their graceful dance. Lattiana's torso swayed backward and forward as she controlled her zabbaton in front of her. Reacting to this change in Lattiana's movements, Gwenlie matched her opponent's swaying with controlled, compact movements of her own.

On one of Lattiana's backward sways, Gwenlie suddenly plunged forward and flicked the end of her zabbaton at Lattiana's head so quickly Neffie barely saw it. Lattiana tried to parry, but this time she was not quite quick enough, and the blow struck her temple with such force it knocked the woman to the ground. Neffie gave a cry and started to move to Lattiana to help her, but instead of continuing her attack as Neffie feared the woman would do, Gwenlie took a step backward and waited, her eyes shining, her face flushed.

Taking a deep breath, Lattiana struggled to her feet, and with a rueful look in Neffie's direction, she gingerly touched the nasty-looking red welt forming on her temple.

"Today, the Charmaines are victors in the challenge," she called to her opponent.

"You fought well, Lattiana," Gwenlie answered. "It is the first challenge in which I have ever defeated you. Perhaps it marks a new turning, a new ascendancy. I claim my rights as victor. Whom do you choose as my prize?"

Lattiana turned and glanced from Neffie to Jessica to Planck, looking uncertain. Neffie had no idea what was going on. The whole affair had been so strange yet also so formal and elegant she hadn't thought to worry much. Now, fear flashed through her. Lattiana's eyes fixed on Jessica. Without knowing why, Neffie vigorously shook her head to signal a firm no. Sighing, Lattiana turned to Planck.

"Planck, step forward," she said gently.

With a gasp, the man took one grudging step forward and then another. Neffie noticed his hands were trembling, and the color of his face turned from brown to red. With his lips tightening, he took several more unenthusiastic steps forward until he was about midway between Lattiana and Gwenlie.

Gwenlie looked puzzled.

"It is profoundly strange that you do not choose the maidservant," she remarked, pointing the end of her zabbaton at Jessica. "Planck has been your husband-consort for nearly four years. Why would you choose him?"

"I have made my choice," Lattiana answered. "I choose Planck."

"Well, Lattiana, suppose I don't want old Planck? What use do I have for a man of such limited talents as your old Planck?"

"You may challenge again, Gwenlie, but do remember this was the first challenge in which you have ever prevailed over me. You may not do so well in the next one."

Gwenlie laughed and twirled her zabbaton over her head.

"You're old, Lattiana," she scoffed, "nearly as old as your man, Planck. Your days of prowess are passing and you know it. It's a good bluff, but I believe I prefer the maidservant."

Lattiana countered. "Then you choose to challenge again, Gwenlie? Are you so willing to risk Jedd? Are you so willing to risk one of such incontestable talent for a mere maidservant?"

Gwenlie hesitated, and Neffie shot a quick glance at Jessica, who stood behind Planck, her face hidden inside her hood. Instinctively, Neffie took a protective step toward Jessica while tightening her grip on her own zabbaton.

"Very well," Gwenlie finally said, yawning to suggest a boredom that was obviously feigned. "It is unquestionably your right to choose Planck if you wish, and to be honest, I am not in the mood for a second challenge."

"Not in the mood or afraid?"

Gwenlie laughed. "I have just eaten lunch, and it was a deliciously large one. I need a nap more than I need another fight," she answered. "Let us finish. I am growing bored."

"Then the choice is final," Lattiana agreed. "So be it."

"Yes, so be it."

In the next instant, the group behind Gwenlie sprang forward. Hands reached out and grabbed poor Planck, raising the man into the air and then throwing him to the pavement. Hitting the ground hard, Planck rolled onto his stomach and covered his head with his hands as Gwenlie's companions beat him with their zabbatons, raining fierce blows. Neffie watched in horror while Planck cried out in pain, sobbing and moaning.

Neffie expected Lattiana to do something, but when she gave the woman a horrified look, Lattiana remained still and silent, her lips drawn tightly as she watched the beating of her man.

"Do something!" Neffie cried. "They're killing him!"

"There's nothing to do. It is their right," the woman answered grimly, tears welling in her eyes as she stood watching.

Dumbfounded, Neffie glanced at Jessica, whose face was invisible inside the shadows of her hood. And yet Neffie had no doubt that Jessica was thinking as she was, that they should be coming to Planck's defense.

When it seemed that Planck could take no more beating without permanent injury, Gwenlie suddenly called out, "Enough!"

Immediately, the terrible thumping stopped. Gwenlie's comrades flicked their zabbatons upward, and with a tinkling sound, the zabbatons retracted. Slipping the small sticks under the lapels of their jackets, they stooped and picked up the moaning Planck.

"The day is ours," Gwenlie cried gleefully, twirling her zabbaton over her head with a flourish before retracting it and stowing it away.

In response, Lattiana gave a low bow and said nothing, which dumbfounded Neffie even more. How could Lattiana take this gloating from the woman who had just directed the beating of her man? It was utterly mind-blowing to Neffie.

"I say again, the day is most undeniably ours!" repeated Gwenlie, her gloating arrogant and ungracious.

Lattiana gave another low bow as Gwenlie and her group turned and retraced their steps up the alley, moving fast now, carrying Planck with them. Very soon, they disappeared around the corner, their footsteps fading away.

"Oh my gosh," Neffie now cried. "They took Mr. Planck away. They beat him nearly to death and then they took him away. Oh my gosh," she again cried.

"Yes," Lattiana answered in a cold, quiet voice. "And now, my lady, you and I need to talk about the man with the green eyes whom you earlier asserted you did not see in the passageway. Like Planck, I don't understand the private counsel you are choosing to keep, and of course, I would not think of questioning your right to keep it. And yet I believe I now have earned the right to know the reason why I have sacrificed my man for your maidservant, of all people."

## CHAPTER 10

# A LONG CLIMB

Neffie knew she should be apologizing, but for some weird reason, she remained silent about the boy, Rem. Giving Neffie an accusatory look, Lattiana muttered, "Am I not owed this courtesy for what I've done?"

When Neffie remained silent, the woman sighed and gave up.

"In that case," she said, glancing up and down the alley, "let us now get you someplace safe. So please follow me, my lady. Our talk can wait."

Setting a quick pace, Lattiana led Neffie and Jessica to the end of the alley, which opened onto another boulevard, this one somewhat narrower than the first. Turning and heading away from the direction taken by Gwenlie and her gang, Lattiana merged into the line of traffic. Neffie felt a bit nervous about being back in the open where anyone could see them, but she followed Lattiana without complaint, with Jessica matching strides just behind her.

There were more people on this new boulevard than on the previous one. As a result, the traffic moved more slowly, with most of the people shuffling along, some alone, others in small groups. Neffie didn't hear much conversation, only quiet mutters.

Nearly everyone wore a hooded coat or sweater, and in all cases, the hoods were up.

Even the tallest folks' heads were at least a foot or more below Neffie's. Ambling on short legs and swinging short arms, none appeared to pay much attention to Neffie and her entourage. Every once in a while, they passed someone around Lattiana's height or taller, and these taller folks always wore a brimmed hat and moved at a pace faster than the others.

When Neffie slowed to study one of them, Lattiana called to her, "Better we keep moving, my lady."

"As you wish. Please continue."

Lattiana led them for four blocks or so and then abruptly turned left down yet another alley, this one somewhat wider but also ominously canyon-like. Following her into the gloomy darkness, Neffie felt the woodpecker again stirring in her chest but forced herself to keep moving, sticking close to Lattiana and hoping for the best.

*Please no more attacks,* she thought.

They passed safely through the dark alley and emerged into another boulevard. Nearby stood one of the birdhouse buildings on four columns. To Neffie's surprise, Lattiana walked purposefully to the nearest column. Without a word, she gripped the sides of the column just above her head with both hands, stretched her arms, arched her back, and with a quick little hop, she caught the column with her feet about a foot off the ground and began climbing, shinnying like a lumberjack up a tall tree.

Pausing, Lattiana called down, "This way, my lady."

Sucking in a deep breath, Jessica whispered to Neffie, "She's got to be kidding."

"I don't think she is," Neffie said.

Gazing up, Jessica said, "That thing has to be, like, thirty feet tall."

"At least," Neffie unhappily agreed.

Neffie surveyed the column from top to bottom. *No way,* she thought.

Above her Lattiana stared down from her perch. When the woman gestured for Neffie to follow, Neffie searched for any excuse to say no, but she couldn't come up with one. Jessica and she were strangers in a strange land, and for better or worse, Lattiana was their guide.

Gloomily, she thought, *I'm dead.*

Jessica didn't help when she asked, "You really going to climb that?"

"Is there a choice?"

Frowning, Jessica said, "Maybe this is the time for us to go beaming away. Just warn me so I can grab you first."

For some reason, Neffie didn't like this idea. The thought of going home should have had some appeal, but it didn't.

She answered, "Now's not the time."

"Why not?"

"It just isn't."

Sighing, Jessica quickly accepted the verdict. "Right," she said. "You go first, and believe me, I'm gonna follow close behind in case you change your mind and start shaking." Glancing up, Jessica shouted to Lattiana, "Don't you people believe in stairs?"

Laughing loudly, Lattiana called down, "The compound of the light guardians of the Vongs would hardly project the storied image it has so storyingly earned if we had stairs anyone could climb. Now come. It is a poor choice to linger."

Nodding, Neffie moved to the base of the column where she made the mistake of looking up. Lattiana had moved higher now, maybe twelve feet off the ground. It seemed dizzyingly high to Neffie, and the woman wasn't even halfway to the top. She shuddered.

*Do or die time,* she thought.

Hesitating was only going to make things harder. She slipped her zabbaton inside the belt of her jeans to free her hands. Giving the stick a little tug to make sure it was secure, she sighed.

"Come," Lattiana called again, "we mustn't linger."

"Yes, yes, I'm coming," cried Neffie. Hardly believing she was saying it, Neffie whispered back to Jessica, "It will be all right. Really."

Imitating Lattiana as best she could, Neffie gripped the column on either side with her hands. She was about to heave herself up when Jessica spoke again.

"You just make sure you keep your eyes closed while you're climbing. Seriously, I don't want you beaming away and leaving me all alone in this whacked-out place."

"Believe me, my eyes are going to be firmly closed," Neffie promised, meaning every word. Swallowing hard, she looked up one last time. The column towered above her, and now that Jessica had been so kind as to remind her again of the dangers, the old, familiar dizziness felt frighteningly close to taking hold of her before her feet even left the ground.

*I'm dead,* she thought. Taking a deep breath, she closed her eyes, ignored the woodpecker in her chest, and started climbing with remarkable and unexpected ease. *Oh my gosh,* she thought as she scampered up with her eyes tightly shut.

All of a sudden, one of her hands encountered a narrow metal tube. Risking opening her eyes, Neffie discovered the tube was the lower end of a narrow ladder whose color so perfectly matched the material of the column it was invisible from below. Relieved, Neffie grabbed the first rung and worked her way up the column until her feet were safely on solid metal. After that, Neffie climbed easily—still with eyes closed—until finally she heard Lattiana's voice, which sounded no more than a half dozen feet above her.

"Watch your head coming through," the woman called down.

Neffie had no idea what that meant. Her instincts told her she needed to look. Cautiously, she raised her chin and opened her eyes a tiny bit. Above her, Lattiana peered through a small, round opening that had miraculously appeared in the base of the building just above the top of column. From the bottom of this opening, the ladder angled through a narrow tunnel. Neffie was unable to see what was at the end of the tunnel.

Neffie resumed her climb, moving rung by rung and making fast progress. As she climbed, a small temptation tugged at her to steal one tiny, quick glance down to see how Jessica was doing. However, after the bitter lesson on the Spine, Neffie was smart enough not to look.

At the top of the ladder, she finally opened her eyes to discover she was at one end of a large, empty room with a well-polished wooden floor and wooden walls paneled in the same color, which was as dark as molasses. Acutely aware that one glance through the open tunnel could trigger her thing, Neffie kept her chin tilted unnaturally upward as she peered around the room.

The space was dimly lit. Most of the light came from the open tunnel below. In the middle of the wall on the far side was a double door illuminated on either side by fancy wall sconces that looked to be made of gold or brass; the small, sputtering flames cast only a pale light.

Lattiana had already moved across the room and was waiting by the door, her form fluttering in the firelight. Neffie lingered at the top of the ladder, waiting for Jessica, whose breathing was labored.

"You all right?" she asked.

Jessica smiled back. "I was going to ask you the same thing."

"It was kinda weird but all right," Neffie said.

Nodding, Jessica observed drily, "Makes you wonder how these people get their groceries home."

Neffie laughed.

"I hadn't thought of that. Let's hope they know a trick we don't."

"You know, Neff," whispered Jessica, changing subjects abruptly, "we could, like, transport out of here right now if you wanted to try. It's wide open below us. One look down would probably get your thing going."

"I still want to wait. There's a thing or two I need to discuss with Lattiana."

"You mean Rem? What's up with that?"

"Um, no," Neffie answered slowly. "I was thinking of other stuff."

"Really?" probed Jessica. "Like what?"

Neffie laughed. "So suddenly you have a hundred questions? You're not becoming another me, are you?"

"Maybe," she chuckled. "And it's more a thousand questions I have . . . but none so important it would keep me here."

Lattiana called. "Please hurry, my lady."

"We're coming," Neffie said. When she got to the other side of the room, she asked, "Where are we?"

"My lady, this is the main compound of the famously storied blood-clan of the Vongs, long the allies of the Sargies. It is not one of the compounds under the charge of your storyworthy grandfather, but it is gloriously and worthily led by his half sister, Maggus Jonesy, of whom much has been storytold. Have you not met her, my lady?"

"No, but I'd like to," replied Neffie.

"It will be my storyworthy honor to introduce you, my lady. But first, I must beg leave to complain. It is incontestably your right, of course, to withhold your counsel from me. However, I believe that my sacrifice of my man should entitle me to some small explanation, at least as much as you deign to give to ease my . . . my . . ." Tears formed in the woman's yellow eyes.

Neffie swallowed hard, feeling terrible. "I don't know what to say. How about you help me by answering one or two of my questions and then I'll try to help you. Okay?"

"As you wish, my lady," answered Lattiana, bowing slightly.

Not sure how to proceed, Neffie asked the first, obvious question in her head.

"If you didn't want to give away Mr. Planck, then I'm wondering why you didn't pick me instead."

Lattiana's eyes widened and her brow creased.

"My lady, when you shook your head most emphatically, telling me not to offer your maidservant, surely you had to know Planck was of the next lowest position and therefore the only choice."

Neffie's eyebrows shot up before she could stop them, and she saw Lattiana taking note of her reaction. Hurriedly changing subjects, she asked another question, the one most likely to distract Lattiana—and perhaps even please her.

"How can I help you get Mr. Planck back?"

Lattiana paused, carefully weighing her words.

"You might tell me something about the man with the green eyes," she said. "I implore you, my lady, please share some of your hidden purpose. I am assuredly on your side, and while I know it is not my place to ask, still, I have sacrificed my Planck, and if you would but deign to share some piece of your purpose, this would bring comfort to me, my lady."

Her voice cracking with the final words, Lattiana looked imploringly into Neffie's eyes. Neffie still didn't know what to say. If there were some connection between Rem and Planck, she couldn't see it. Neffie glanced at Jessica, who gave her a nod obviously meant as encouragement for her to tell Lattiana about Rem.

"There's nothing to tell," Neffie finally said, feeling bad about it but not bad enough to change her mind.

Lattiana's lips tightened, and although a tear loosened and rolled down her cheek, she didn't complain.

"So be it," she said instead. "It is my storyworthy honor, my lady, to do your bidding, which is now to take you to Maggus Jonesy Vong. Please, this way," she added with a bow, turning to lead them.

The second Lattiana's back was turned, Jessica shot Neffie a critical look. Neffie lowered her eyes and hurried past Jessica, following Lattiana while ignoring her friend.

She felt horrible about her choice. It should have felt all wrong, except her gut told her it was the right choice. But why?

# CHAPTER 11

# MAGGUS JONESY

Leading them through the double door, Lattiana proceeded down a short hallway and up the polished, wooden treads of a long staircase. The sides of the stairway had tall walls paneled in wood of a lighter, almost honeyed color. Along both walls, every ten feet or so, flickering wall sconces filled the air with a sweet, floral smell.

At the top of the stairs was another double door. Lattiana grasped the handles and swung the two doors inward, stepped across the threshold and signaled for Neffie and Jessica to follow. Inside, Neffie found herself in a large room that was bright and cheerful and sweet-smelling. Loving the scent, Neffie searched for its source, and against the wall to her left, she spotted a huge bouquet of flowers arranged in a giant vase on top of a large, wooden table. The flowers reminded Neffie of daisies, only they were much larger, and the petals on each bloom showed three colors that reminded Neffie of lime, mango and honeydew.

Above Neffie's head, hanging from long poles that crisscrossed the entire breadth of the room, was a gauzy, pink canopy with tiny red stars sewn into the fabric in giant whorls. The lightness of this canopy gave the room an airiness. The walls bore the pleasing sea-green hue of Mediterranean waters. Underfoot, the floor reminded Neffie of marble, if there were any marble on this planet in these Tymes.

The room was windowless except for a huge opening the size of a barn door on the right wall. Covering this opening and filtering the sunlight was a curtain so filmy its pinkish color could hardly be seen. Looking at the opening made Neffie uncomfortable, and so she quickly shifted her gaze to what really mattered—a three-step dais in the center of the room.

Atop this dais was a simple wooden chair, and in this unremarkable chair sat a remarkable woman. She wore a form-fitting, cottony dress in a shimmery gray. On her hands were black gloves, on her feet black, ankle-length boots, and on her head perched a very wide-brimmed purple hat. In the woman's right hand, she held a long, purple zabbaton with gray tips at either end. Her hair was curly and mostly black, with tight braids of gray and green arrayed in alternating rows down the sides of her head. The woman's eyes were almond shaped and glowed with a pure, yellow fire. Her face was perhaps a little darker than Sarge's, and more wrinkled, giving Neffie a sense of great age.

Although this woman was certainly unusual looking, she was normal compared to the creature lying at her feet. Cobalt blue with a head and body that reminded Neffie of a large cat, this creature had bright-pink eyes and a pink-tipped tail. At first, Neffie thought it might be wearing a collar, but then she realized she was looking at a narrow strand of tiny golden feathers growing around its neck. The thing emitted low sounds like the coo of a mourning dove.

*Way cool,* Neffie thought.

She would have liked more time to study the creature, but the woman spoke, drawing her attention up from the creature, which rested its head on her feet.

"Come closer," the woman directed, her eyes fixing on Neffie. "And please tell your maidservant to remain where she now stands until I summon her."

Neffie glanced back at Jessica, who grunted, "Got it. Me stay."

With the woodpecker again stirring, Neffie took a couple of steps toward the woman.

"I know who you are, my lady. I know you are Neffatira Sargie Akou."

Neffie mimicked the low, formal bow she had seen performed so many times, and the woman seemed pleased. "If you already know my name, you are indeed of the Sargie blood-clan. For we Sargies learn quickly what we need to know."

"Then I take it you know who I am."

"I do," Neffie answered politely. "You are Maggus Jonesy Vong. You are . . . um, my great-aunt, I believe."

Neffie was about to say how honored she was to meet Maggus Jonesy when the cat-like creature surprised her by standing suddenly and stretching languorously before padding in her direction. The thing was at least the size of a mountain lion, and Neffie couldn't help but notice the very large, pointy front teeth protruding out of its mouth. The creature moved beside her and rubbed the side of its face against her leg. Neffie's muscles tensed. Then it licked Neffie's ankle with a long, bright-red tongue. Neffie had no idea how to react, and the woman's next words didn't help the situation.

"Your arrival here is most unexpected, Neffatira Sargie Akou. In fact, I confess to being equally perplexed both as to the why of your untimely arrival and the how of it." When Neffie said nothing the woman continued, "I have many questions for you, lass, but I suspect you have even more for me. Ask one."

The creature licking Neffie's ankle made it hard for her to think. "I don't really have any," she answered. "I mean, I've had a million questions since arriving here, but right now I can't think of any."

"Ah yes," the woman answered, her eyes now shifting from Neffie to Jessica. "There is also the matter of your so-called maidservant here, your Jessica, as you name her." The woman shifted her gaze past Jessica to Lattiana, who had remained silent. "Lattiana," she called to her, "will you please leave us now? Take the door in the corner over there," she directed, pointing to a small doorway to her right. "Follow the hallway on the other side of the door, use your nose and you will find a kitchen soon enough. You may take food while we finish here."

Lattiana bowed deeply and then departed as commanded. Maggus Jonesy waited until she was gone, the door clicking shut behind her, and then she turned her attention back to Jessica.

"I'd like to see your face," she said in a friendly enough way. "Would you please remove your hood?"

Jessica hesitated a second before reaching up and slipping the hood from her head.

Immediately, Maggus Jonesy gasped and then exclaimed, "This is profoundly the most storying moment of my life! A life, by the way, that has seen many storying moments. I must say, your appearance here is quite remarkable."

"That's just how Rem reacted," Jessica answered with a small chuckle, "totally surprised."

Neffie caught her breath. Had Jessica just spoken Rem's name without thinking? Or had she intentionally chosen to speak the name Neffie was keeping secret? Neffie shot a sharp glance at her friend, but neither Jessica's facial expression nor her eyes betrayed anything of her intentions.

"We'll get to the matter of this Rem in a minute," Maggus Jonesy said, turning her eyes from Jessica back to Neffie. "But first I have a few questions for your maidservant, your Jessica here, questions I wish her to answer alone, without any help from you, lady. Do you understand?"

Neffie nodded.

"The most pressing question, Jessica, is of course how you came to be on this side of the Tymes. In other words, how did you get here from your home? Before we discuss anything else, I'd like to hear from you about this."

"I came with Neffie. We were in school and I, like, grabbed hold of her when she started to shake and float and we ended up here."

"That is profoundly interesting," Maggus Jonesy said. "So, Lady Neffatira carried you here, did she? How bendingly interesting." Maggus Jonesy leaned back in her chair and thought for a moment before resuming. "Is there anyone besides your lady and me here—and besides the Rem we will soon discuss—who knows a human girl has arrived to grace us?" she finally asked.

Without hesitating, Jessica replied, "That's the whole list. And it might be one too long."

Maggus Jonesy eyed Jessica closely. "What do you mean?"

"There's one on your list—namely Rem—who maybe saw the color of my hair," she lied, "but I'm not sure what else he saw or knows."

It was the first time Neffie had ever heard a straight-up lie from Jessica. In school, Jessica was pretty well known for her blunt honesty. Not that she couldn't evade when she needed, but lying was something she simply didn't do. Not ever.

Maggus Jonesy locked her eyes on Jessica's and peered into them for a long time. Jessica stood her ground, returning the woman's powerful gaze without wavering.

"Interesting," Maggus Jonesy commented at last. "Did Lady Neffatira here teach you how to control and use your eyes in the storied manner of a true light guardian?"

"Um, I don't understand what you just said, but no, probably not."

Maggus Jonesy's fierce eyes continued to probe.

"It's time to speak more about this Rem. Who precisely is he?" Maggus Jonesy finally asked.

"A guy we met in the woods after the garffles attacked us," Jessica said.

"You were attacked by garffles? How did you escape them?"

"We hoofed it. After we got away, we ran into this guy who called himself Rem."

"What happened next?"

"He gave me this lobbie," answered Jessica, pulling the ball with braided rope out of her pocket. "And he gave Neff—oops, I mean Lady Neffatira—a zabbaton."

"He possessed a zabbaton, did he?" murmured Maggus Jonesy, her eyes shifting to Neffie.

"Yes," Jessica answered.

"He was tall, this Rem?"

"Kind of."

"How did he not see you were human?"

To Neffie's relief, Jessica again lied. "I had my hood up and he saw only the hair sticking out, which did kinda surprise him," she explained. "He was more surprised to meet Lady Neffatira than me, I think."

Maggus Jonesy sat back in her chair, deep in thought. Neffie had the impression Jessica's answers to the woman's questions, although kept short, simple and to the point, had revealed much. Maggus Jonesy shifted her eyes to Neffie.

"Ask your questions now."

Neffie thought for a bit. The creature beside her had stopped licking her ankle, which helped her concentration.

"I have a few," she admitted. "First, you might tell me exactly where we are. What does it mean to be on the other side of the Tymes?"

"Ah," Maggus Jonesy replied, "the essence of everything. An excellent question deserving of a full answer. So you might understand, I'll try to give a simple answer to your complex question."

"That would be good," said Neffie.

Nodding, the woman explained, "In your world, you believe there is only one universe—your universe. In fact, there are at least four universes we know of." The woman gave a fluttering wave of her hand. "Think of each universe as a giant wave traveling through what appears to be nothingness, though it isn't. Our universe is spreading in every direction, a great wave of stars and planets and other objects moving through the cosmos. Your universe is another wave that started after or before ours, we're not sure which. The two universes have some of the same rules, but other rules are different."

"And the Tymes?" asked Neffie.

"There's an overlap between your universe and ours, marked by a series of cosmic ripples that can be—and this is an imprecise way of putting it—ridden by some."

"That's what you call Tymes?"

"Correct. You are now on our side of those ripples, on our side of the Tymes."

"And somehow I'm able to cross these ripples?"

"Cross is not the right word, but generally speaking, you are correct," said Maggus Jonesy with a smile. "We call it bending the Tymes, a wondrously fanciful term for something frankly no one here completely understands."

"Um, what do you call this planet we're on? You know, your world here."

"Its modern name is Fastness. Long ago, we called it Esh, but with the discovery of multiple universes, we began leaving our superstitious past behind. The modern era demanded a new name to go with new understandings."

"What are light guardians?"

"Light guardians are the champions, the keepers of proper order here on this side of the Tymes."

"Now tell me about blood-clans."

"You do get to the heart of things, Lady Neffatira," Maggus Jonesy chuckled. "On Earth, as I understand it, you have small families formed around parents. Here on Fastness, in these Tymes, we count many more relationships as part of a larger family we call the blood-clan."

"You mean extended families?" interrupted Jessica.

Maggus Jonesy shook her head. "Here, each blood-clan is more than just relationships; it has its own unique role to play. There are blood-clans of builders, blood-clans of mechanics, blood-clans of doctors and blood-clans of farmers."

"You're saying blood-clans are giant families with everyone doing the same kind of work?" asked Jessica.

"Indeed."

"Wow. Strange."

Before Maggus Jonesy could reply, Neffie had another question.

"So, are light guardians the police? Or maybe they're more like soldiers."

"No, the light guardians are neither," Maggus Jonesy said. "Light guardians prevent crimes and wars from ever happening. You see, Lady Neffatira, unlike on your world, war never happens here. Crimes do not exist."

"Well, that's cool, I guess," Neffie said.

"Indeed," Maggus Jonesy agreed. "Now, you may ask one more question, and then we will stop this game for now."

That sounded good to Neffie. She was suddenly tired. "I really can't think of anything more to ask."

Maggus Jonesy nodded. "We've spoken quite enough for now. You should rest while I think on the weighty matters we've discussed. And I'm certain you could use a meal."

Immediately, Neffie's stomach rumbled. *How many hours since Mom made me pancakes?* Really, she had no idea. She looked at Jessica. "Hungry?"

"Totally."

"Oh, may I ask one last question before we go?"

"Ask it."

"What is a Tymes stealer?"

Maggus Jonesy stood and descended from her dais, her pace slow and measured, her posture erect. She stopped directly in front of Neffie, and stared into the girl's brown-yellow eyes with her bright-yellow ones.

"You need only understand this, my lady," she muttered. "Tymes stealers are your enemies. They threaten this entire world. You will recognize them by their green eyes. They speak in lies and must never be trusted. Never. Do you understand me?"

"I understand," answered Neffie, breaking eye contact.

"I profoundly hope you do," she remarked. "Now go. Take the same door as Lattiana, follow your noses and find your way to food and a meal. Afterward, rest, and later we'll talk again."

Maggus Jonesy turned and went back to her chair where she sat, placing her chin on the palm of one hand and closing her eyes. Neffie started toward the door. Immediately, the creature at her feet stood to follow beside her.

"Go away," she said. "I don't want you following." Ignoring Neffie, the beast stood its ground, looking up at her with bright-pink eyes. "Go on," Neffie repeated. "You can't follow me. I mean it."

Neffie started for the door, and the creature moved with her. When Neffie halted again, it stopped beside her. Confounded, Neffie looked to Maggus Jonesy for help.

Maggus Jonesy called from her seat in a gentle, coaxing voice, "Nobila, come here. Come to Jonesy." The cat looked her way but didn't move. "I said, come here, Nobila," Maggus Jonesy called again, more insistent.

The cat didn't budge.

"Go on, kitty," Neffie coaxed.

"Don't insult her by calling her kitty," Maggus Jonesy said sharply. "She will not like it."

"Oh, cat," said Neffie, quickly correcting herself.

"Not cat. Nobila is a felinx-wan."

"A what?"

The woman glared at the animal.

"A felinx-wan. And this particular one is apparently a fickle creature who has grown much too curious about you, as if there were any reason to be so curious." Standing, Maggus Jonesy called again. "Come here, Nobila. Your place is here."

Again, Nobila refused to budge.

"Fine!" the woman cried, suddenly angry. "If she's your new hobby, then by all means go, stay with her. Just don't expect me to be kind to you when you decide to come back, which you most certainly will."

Neffie shrugged and gave Maggus Jonesy her most apologetic look.

Waving away the felinx-wan with an impatient twist of her hand, Maggus Jonesy cried, "Go then! I've had quite enough of both of you."

# CHAPTER 12

# A STRANGE ENCOUNTER

Neffie hurried to the door. To her chagrin, the second she opened it, Nobila sprang through and bolted down the hallway on the other side, disappearing around a far corner.

"So much for my new friend," muttered Neffie as she stepped through the doorway, with Jessica following.

Neffie closed the door, and the two of them started wordlessly down the hallway. Neffie felt terrible about everything. Her conversation with Maggus Jonesy had been a total disaster. And that darn cat had only made it worse. On top of everything else, Neffie was pretty sure Jessica was not judging her kindly.

*She's right. I am stupid,* thought Neffie.

Fortunately, her gloomy thoughts were interrupted by the sound of laughter ahead of them, and with the laughter came the welcome smell of food. With the likelihood of a meal in front of them, she quickened her pace. However, before Neffie took five steps, a tall figure emerged from a side door and quickly moved to block Neffie's path.

Startled and fearing the worst, she slipped a hand behind her back to find her zabbaton.

Before she could speak, the figure lifted her face, and Neffie saw it was a young woman with girlish, plump cheeks, pouty lips and pale eyes. She wore a bronze-colored ring in her nose, and on each cheek she had two round, pink spots. Halting in front of Neffie, she extended her hands in front of her chest with palms up and fingers spread to show she was unarmed. The woman seemed nervous.

"Please, my lady," she said, "I have a message for you. An urgent one."

Like others of these Tymes, the woman spoke with a slow, measured cadence. Jessica placed a hand lightly on Neffie's elbow to silence her and then addressed the woman.

"Who are you to stand in my lady's way?" she demanded.

The woman stuttered. "Ah . . . of course your lady should know these things. Maidservant, please inform your lady I am Mallaine of the Wurthers blood-clan. Lattiana is my cousin, though I am not here at the bidding of Lattiana. I speak for another."

"And who is that?" asked Jessica.

"I speak secretly for Kerem, to whom I am sworn in friendship as if by blood."

"Kerem? You mean Rem?" Neffie interjected.

"Yes, my lady," the woman nodded.

Neffie relaxed the grip on her zabbaton and brought her hand back in front of her.

"Thank goodness," she murmured.

"And what makes you think we want to hear from Rem?" Jessica asked, stepping forward to glare at the woman.

"I am told he is friend to you," stuttered Mallaine, sounding confused. "Is this not so?"

"Friend?" Jessica snorted, gripping Neffie's elbow very hard to signal her to remain quiet. "Why would we trust a Tymes stealer?"

"He is not a Tymes stealer," Mallaine huffed. "Most emphatically not!"

"You're the only one who says he isn't," Jessica shot back.

"I speak the truth."

"Why should we believe you?" Jessica demanded.

"You must!"

"I mean it. Why should we trust you?" demanded Jessica. "Or this Kerem."

Rather than argue the point, Mallaine sighed and shifted her gaze to Neffie.

"My lady," she murmured, "to settle this, I offer to open myself to your light."

Before Neffie could speak, Mallaine stepped forward. Opening her eyes wide, she drew her face close to Neffie's so each woman could peer into the other's eyes. Mallaine's eyes were mostly light brown, with the centers of her irises shading toward yellow and dotted with flecks of amber.

Unblinking, Mallaine continued to stare deeply into Neffie's eyes, seemingly waiting for something to happen. At first Neffie felt only weird and embarrassed to have the woman's face only inches from hers, but then something very strange did happen. Neffie sensed a deep and compelling certitude the woman would and could speak only the truth with their eyes now locked together.

"Ask me anything, my lady," Mallaine whispered to her, "and I will answer while thus exposed."

Neffie took a second to decide on the question she should ask.

"You said Rem is your friend. Is this true?"

"Yes."

"Okay, then what is Rem's message to me?"

"You are not safe here. They plan to use you for evil purposes. Already, they will be forming dangerous plans in secret."

Neffie knew for certain the woman was speaking the truth.

"Go on."

"You need to escape, and you must do so quickly. Kerem says tonight. I will be waiting for you on the ground below the compound.

You must come at the third hour. Do not let anyone see you. I will lead you to Kerem."

"Anything more?" Neffie asked.

"There is one thing more, though I do not understand it. Kerem says I don't know is on third."

Neffie quickly broke eye contact to choke down a laugh. Mallaine immediately relaxed and gave Neffie a smaller version of the formal bow now so familiar to her.

"It is my storyworthy honor to serve you, my lady."

"Okay, um, thank you."

"Ask anything of me, my lady, and I will do what I can to serve."

Nodding, Neffie smiled. "Well, you can serve me by telling us how to know when it's third hour."

"Ah, yes," Mallaine murmured as she reached into her pocket and took out a strange-looking watch, which she now handed to Neffie. "See here, lady," she said, indicating the watch face with her hand. "Rem told me I would need to explain. Our day has thirty-eight hours, and on our clock's face, there are nineteen numbers, one for every even hour. Right now, we are just past twenty-fourth hour, see." Pausing, Mallaine pointed to a number on the clock's face. "Thirty-eighth hour is at the end of our day, which falls roughly in the middle of the night's darkness. We call it the deeply hour. Third hour comes three hours afterward."

"Your day has thirty-eight hours," Jessica wondered aloud, lifting an eyebrow.

"Quite so. Rem chose third hour precisely because it is deep in the night when all will be asleep. Keep and use this hour piece. Do not sleep when they take you to your sleeping chamber. Stay awake. Be vigilant. Make excuses if you must. I'll be waiting for you."

Neffie took the odd-looking watch and shoved it in her jeans pocket. Mallaine was about to leave when Neffie suddenly had an important question. She put a hand on Mallaine's shoulder to stop her.

"Why are we in danger here?" she asked.

"My lady, all I can tell you is what Rem believes, that many wish to use you. I myself cannot tell you why this is so or how they wish to use you because I do not really know."

"What do you mean use?" Jessica interjected. "What exactly did Rem tell you?"

"I mustn't say more. But please, be careful. You are at great risk here!"

With that, Mallaine turned abruptly and slipped through the side door, leaving the two girls standing alone.

"Great," Jessica remarked to Neffie. "Weirdville just got even weirder. We should definitely get out of here. I vote for beaming home the first chance we get. I mean it. Go back to safe old Windmere where the only danger is dying of boredom, which sounds pretty good right now."

"I'd really like to talk with Rem before we go."

"I totally don't understand that. Why the heck would we stay?"

"Mainly it's just curiosity," answered Neffie. "I mean, he's from Earth like us, and I'd like to hear what's going on here."

"In case you've forgotten," Jessica reminded, "Rem may be from Earth, but he probably isn't human, and everyone says he's a Tymes stealer."

"Maybe, but the thing is, I need to know what it means that I look more like Rem than I look like any kid back in Windmere."

"You might not like the answers you get," Jessica said.

"I still need to talk to Rem. I have to find out."

"Okay, Neff, if you're sure you want to find this Rem and talk to him, then heck, let's go find this Rem and talk to him."

"Thanks," she said, smiling appreciatively. It made a difference to have Jessica on her side.

Jessica laughed. "Before we go on our Rem quest," she said, "let's get back to the more serious question of where to find food. You're still hungry, aren't you?"

"Starved," Neffie heartily agreed.

"Then let's go eat," cried Jessica. "Before I seriously starve to death," she added with mock seriousness.

# CHAPTER 13

# FOOD AND TALK

The two girls shuffled down the hallway and through a door at the end. On the other side, they found a long room lined with shelves full of ceramic jars and wooden boxes. At the end of this room was a doorway with a small window. From the other side of the door came cheery noises.

Neffie walked to the door and peered through the window. In the middle of the next room was a long table at which sat Lattiana and several others. Mallaine was now at the far end talking to a woman with very broad shoulders and grinning. Neffie couldn't see the others' faces, but there was a lot of eating going on.

"Food," she remarked to Jessica.

"My lady, lead the way and your maidservant will happily follow," urged Jessica.

When Neffie stepped through the doorway, all conversation died. Lattiana stood and looked at Neffie with narrowing eyes, her lips pursed and eyebrows raised.

"So, my lady, I see you have finished with Maggus Jonesy. Did it go well?"

Playing it safe, Neffie simply answered, "For now, yes."

"You told her everything she needed to hear, I assume."

Neffie heard bitterness in the woman's voice. Of course, she had a right to be bitter, Neffie reminded herself. After all, she had lost her man, and maybe it was Neffie's fault.

"May we join you and eat?" Neffie asked. "It has been a long while since our last meal and we are really, really hungry."

Quickly, Lattiana found her manners. Giving the formal bow of the Tymes, she said, "Of course. Please, my lady, let's have your maidservant and you take these chairs near me. Your light at this table is welcome indeed."

After taking her seat, Neffie said to Lattiana, "Does the thing you just did have a name?"

"Does what have a name, my lady?"

From her seat, Neffie performed a smaller version of Lattiana's formal bow with arm across her chest. "You know, this thing."

"Ah, I see. My lady doesn't know," replied Lattiana. "It is called the Gesture of Honorium, my lady. It is said to be nearly as old as the sign of reverence and the Ritual of the Hand, though I doubt this is true."

"The Ritual of the Hand? What is that?"

"It is no longer permitted and therefore I cannot show you, though I am allowed to explain. It was an act of great respect made with the hand, and it was given only to someone who possessed the power of true light. It was a sign of great respect from the ancient times."

"The power of light? What's that?"

"Not *light*, my lady. *True light*. It is a myth, a storytelling from our deepest past," said Lattiana. "But let's not speak of it now," she continued, suddenly adopting a lighter, friendlier tone of voice. "Please, my lady, do please eat."

One of the others stood and began cutting thick slices from a congealed, brownish goo that looked disgusting to Neffie. Lattiana pointed at a stack of plates near them, and Neffie took this to mean they should each take one. Before Neffie could move, Jessica grabbed two and handed one to her. Giving a friendly smile, Mallaine passed to them two long forks, each with seven prongs.

Taking turns, Neffie and Jessica took a piece of the gooey mass from the platter. Neffie didn't know what to make of it. If she were forced to guess, she would have said it was a thick pudding made from squash or something equally mushy and thoroughly dusted with some kind of gray powder. The dish had a spice smell somewhat like curry. Cautiously, Jessica used her fork to take a small taste, and then she grinned at Neffie.

"It's delicious."

"Really?" Neffie answered, slicing off a small amount with her fork.

Lifting the goo to her mouth, she carefully tasted it. Jessica was right. Not exactly delicious but adequately good, with a spiciness that was both tangy and sweet at the same time, flavoring some kind of vegetable mix with an earthy mustiness that melted gently in her mouth.

*Not bad,* Neffie thought.

Famished, the two girls ate their slices of goo quickly and then took a second helping each and then a third. Mallaine watched them bemused. Lattiana said a few words here and there to others at the table, but she didn't again speak to Neffie. Or to Jessica. When they finished eating, Lattiana finally addressed them, pointing to a man seated at the other end of the table—the only man in the room.

"My lady, may I introduce you to Vondra, a vassal of the Vongs. He will escort your maidservant and you to your sleeping chamber. He will then stay within hearing distance. If you need anything, my lady, call outside your door for Vondra. He will serve you as you wish, as I have tried so poorly to do to the best of my ability."

Neffie again heard the bitterness in Lattiana's voice. Quickly, she decided to give Lattiana the bow she now knew to be called *honorium*.

"Thank you for being of such fine service," she said, bowing while doing her best to use the formal manner of speaking. Then Neffie turned to Vondra. "Please, sir, lead the way for us."

Giving a curt nod, Vondra had a quirky little smile, Neffie noticed, no more than a tiny twitch of the corners of his mouth. Quickly, Neffie realized what it meant. Just as Planck had done earlier, Vondra was reacting with amusement to the fact she had called him *sir*. Obviously, it wasn't right to address men like Planck and Vondra as sir. Neffie quickly made a mental note never to do it again.

"This way, my lady," Vondra now mumbled, giving her an honorium before turning to leave.

Vondra exited through a different door and proceeded down a hallway, then up a set of stairs, then down another hallway and around a corner, then up a shorter flight of stairs before leading them down a final hallway that ended at a door. Neffie walked silently behind the man, concentrating as best she could on memorizing the route, making mental notes of tables, wall sconces, windows and other telltales that might help her find her way back at third hour. In the right pocket of her jeans, she felt the weight of the watch given by Mallaine.

"Your sleeping chamber, my lady," Vondra announced as he opened a heavy door at the end of the hallway.

While he waited respectfully outside, Neffie and Jessica walked into a room that was quite spectacular, with a wide window on the opposite wall through which streamed the light of Fastness' bright, red-tinted sun. Knowing how high they were, Neffie was careful to avoid looking out the window.

The room was at least the size of three of Neffie's bedrooms back home, with blond, wood-paneled walls and a polished wooden floor the color of maple syrup. Strewn on the floor were maybe a half dozen small round rugs in bright colors. For furnishings, the room had three comfortable-looking stuffed chairs and two enormous beds as wide as they were long and obviously designed to fit tall sleepers. Jessica walked to the nearest bed and perched on its edge.

"Comfy," she pronounced, taking a measure of the mattress's firmness by bouncing up and down. "So this is our sleeping chamber, huh?"

"Yes, of course," Vondra confirmed from the doorway.

"Or prison," Jessica whispered to Neffie.

Jessica hopped off the bed and moved to the window. After a quick glance outside, she found a bundle of dangling cords and closed the two gauzy curtains. Vondra remained standing in the doorway, looking awkward and uncomfortable. Neffie decided she'd better say something.

"Thank you for bringing us here, Mr. Vondra," she called.

Vondra gave her a curious look. "They say you're new to these Tymes, my lady. They storytell you have lived your whole life on the other side and you are half human."

Neffie stepped toward the man and peered into his eyes, probing them. There was nothing lurking there to disturb her.

"Who are they?" she asked. "The ones saying all these things about me?"

"My lady?"

"Mr. Vondra, I wish you to open yourself to my light."

The man looked startled. Then he swayed uncomfortably, his mouth falling open.

"My lady!" he cried.

"Lattiana said you are here to serve me as I wish," Neffie pressed. "So I want you to open yourself to my light. That's how you can best serve me."

Eyes widening, Vondra shook his head vigorously.

"What you ask is forbidden, my lady. If you were from these Tymes, you would know it is an impossible thing you ask."

This surprised Neffie. After all, Mallaine had voluntarily opened herself to questioning.

"You're right, Mr. Vondra," she continued, "I am not from these Tymes, which is why I have lots of questions that need answers. I'm asking you to serve me in this way. In fact, I'm requiring it." Pausing, Neffie searched her mind for things she'd heard since coming here, looking for the right words. "As a lady from a most profoundly storied blood-clan, I am asking it of you; I am asking it as a lady of the true light."

Vondra cried out and his face flushed. He then hastily performed a deep honorium in front of her. Neffie noticed how visibly unsteady was the hand he placed across his chest.

"My lady, it is my profoundly deep honor to be of service in whatever way you desire," Vondra muttered.

"Excellent," Neffie replied. "You have my profound gratitude, Mr. Vondra."

Taking a deep breath, she pushed her face close to his, peering deeply into his eyes now only inches from hers. The man caught his breath, and then he opened his eyes wide as he stared into Neffie's. Immediately, Neffie felt herself pulled into the man's thoughts and emotions. Right away, she sensed fear, though it was not clear what he feared. She sensed something else, too—awe.

"Who here can I trust, Mr. Vondra?" Neffie asked.

"I truly don't know, my lady."

"May I trust you?"

Neffie immediately sensed confusion and conflicting emotions.

"I don't know the answer to that question, my lady. You may trust me to do whatever you ask of me, but I owe service to others, as well."

Neffie thought about this for a moment.

"What if I asked you to put your service to me first at all times, ahead of your duty to others?"

"If you ask it, my lady, you will have my service first, above all others."

"Then I ask it, and I also ask you always to be completely honest with me, Mr. Vondra."

Taking a deep breath, Vondra slowly answered, "It will be my honor, my lady, to do whatever you ask of me."

Satisfied, Neffie broke eye contact, and Vondra staggered backward. When next he looked at Neffie, he appeared bleary-eyed, as if he had just spent an all-night sleepover with friends. Neffie felt a little drained, too.

"Are you all right, Mr. Vondra?" she asked.

"Yes, my lady," the man answered.

"Why does everyone call me that, Mr. Vondra?" Neffie asked. "Call me *my lady*?"

"My lady, you bear the mark of six spots. You are not yet of an age to be called Maggus. Girls of your status and age are honored instead with the title of *lady*. You really do not know our customs, do you? Mallaine told me you didn't, but I must admit I failed to understand her words precisely enough."

"Mallaine told you?"

"Yes, my lady. Mallaine and I speak in confidence. I hope to be her husband-consort someday, if she can win me."

"Can I trust Mallaine?"

"I believe so, my lady."

"You aren't sure?"

Vondra thought for a moment. "That is a difficult question, my lady. What I can say is that Mallaine has her own ideas, and they're not the ideas of most light guardians. She most certainly wants what is best for you, and what is best for all of us. However, I cannot say for certain she is right in her thinking, although she may indeed be so. That is the best and most honest answer I can give."

Jessica interrupted. "Do you know someone named Rem?"

"No, maidservant," Vondra answered.

"How about Kerem?"

"Maidservant, I have not heard that name. It is not from our Tymes."

"I have a quite important question for you, Mr. Vondra," she continued. "Should we, like, ever trust any guy with green eyes?"

"Maidservant, you ask a profoundly difficult question," Vondra said, speaking slowly and choosing every word carefully, "and it is not one I would normally hear from one of such lowly rank in the presence of her lady." Vondra shifted his gaze to Neffie. "What would you have me do, my lady?"

"You should answer her as best you can," Neffie commanded.

"It is profoundly complicated, my lady. The best I can say is you should trust very few of those with green eyes, though I do believe some of them are trustworthy and well intentioned. The difficulty would be in the sorting of the trustworthy from the untrustworthy, a task that would confound me, I must admit."

Neffie couldn't decide whether Vondra was being straight with her. Despite his claim to the contrary, he certainly hadn't said all there was to say on the subject. That much was obvious to her. She was about to press him with another question when suddenly a shadow loomed behind him.

It was a small, low shadow that grew quickly larger. The leading edge formed into the shape of a head with ears that came to sharp points. A mouth opened, displaying two long, sharp incisors.

Neffie gasped.

# CHAPTER 14

# AN UNCOMFORTABLE REUNION

The shadow morphed into the form of Nobila, who crouched immediately behind Vondra, her pink eyes shining brightly. Then the creature scampered away. Neffie heard footsteps in the hallway followed by voices. She was pretty sure she recognized one. A wrinkled old face appeared in the doorway.

"I am profoundly pleased to have found you at last, my young lass," the owner of this well-worn face said in his slow, measured manner of speech.

"Sarge!" Neffie cried, running to the door and giving her grandfather a hug. Grinning, Sarge hugged her back.

"Greetings, my itinerant lady," he murmured.

"I am so happy to see you," cried Neffie. "You cannot believe what has been happening to me!"

Over her grandfather's shoulder, Neffie saw Maggus Jonesy standing quietly in the hallway, curiously watching the reunion. Although the woman's lips were turned upward in a small smile, it was a forced smile, and the overall impression she conveyed was not a happy one. Instantly, Neffie's defenses went up, and she pulled away from Sarge.

Letting her go, the old man joked, "So here you are, the girl from Iowa who would not bend with me across the Tymes."

"Guilty as charged," she agreed with a smile.

"It was most profoundly a dangerous and untimely thing for you to do. Imagine, to go bending unguided and untrained across the Tymes. By all that is right and proper, and in more ways than one, you should not be here."

Before Neffie could ask what he meant, Jessica interrupted. "It was my fault. I kinda encouraged her to do her bending-'cross-Tymes thing."

"So, you are the human who came in the bending with Neffie, are you not?"

"Guilty as charged," admitted Jessica, giving Neffie a quick wink.

"Did Maggus Jonesy explain to you that you are the first human ever to bend into these Tymes? That this was perhaps the most storying day in the history of the light guardians?" Before Jessica could answer, the man laughed loudly, looking quite delighted as he continued, "Well, it is profoundly true. And because of it, I have come here more quickly than I have moved in a long, long while, just to see you for myself."

Jessica rolled her eyes and tried to make a joke of it.

"Well, here I am," she laughed, "the most storied human of the Tymes."

"You are indeed," cried Sarge. "This is indeed a dizzyingly storyworthy moment, believe me, to be standing in these Tymes in front of a completely human girl. It is most extraordinary."

"Thanks, I guess," replied Jessica, rolling her eyes again, this time in Neffie's direction. "And just for the record," she added, "every moment here has been, like, totally extraordinary for Neff and me, too."

"I am sure it has," Sarge agreed. "However, I am also here because I have been hearing whispers about a man with green eyes who is involved somehow."

His words startled Neffie. Before she could react, Sarge looked at Vondra, and with a pleasant enough smile, he directed, "Will you please leave us, Vondra? I need to speak in private with my granddaughter and her maidservant."

Giving a low bow, Vondra moved behind Maggus Jonesy in the hallway. With a small bow of her own, the tall woman closed the door. Sarge then turned to look at Neffie. His voice low, he muttered to her, "I hear you are being strangely silent about the green-eyed man."

"It's because there isn't anything to say," answered Neffie, who, for some reason, was still intent on keeping Rem a secret, even if it meant going against her grandfather.

Sarge looked deeply into Neffie's eyes.

"Neffatira, this is a profoundly important matter. For quite some while, there have been rumors circulating of a man who has come from your planet, from Earth, and who is here to cause trouble. They say he has extraordinarily green eyes and five blighted spots on each of his false cheeks. I tell you this because if the rumors are true, this man is most certainly a danger to you, to your blood-clan here, and to all kindred light guardians. And so I am asking most seriously and urgently for you to tell me honestly and clearly, have you seen such a man?"

Sarge's eyes bore into hers. Neffie felt them probing deeply, searching for the truth. She returned her grandfather's gaze, hoping her eyes wouldn't betray her.

"No."

"Interesting. Jonesy told me you have mastered your light even without training. Your eyes give the impression you are speaking the truth, and yet I am left entirely unsure of what I am seeing, which is profoundly interesting."

"Um, I don't understand what you mean by my *light*," said Neffie. "I've heard others say it."

"No, of course you don't," her grandfather answered. "It is something you would normally learn as part of your training. A *training*, by the way, that was supposed to start before you came here, not after."

"Yeah, Maggus Jonesy said something about my coming early."

"Indeed. You were supposed to cross the Tymes at age sixteen or seventeen, not fourteen. I am profoundly uncertain what to make of this situation you have created. That you have brought a *human* only complicates things even more."

"I'm sorry," was all Neffie could manage to say in reply. "I mean, my bending here was totally an accident."

"Well, for now we shall leave this conundrum for later conversation. I must think on it and you most certainly must be tired and need to rest. Jessica and you should sleep. Vondra will guard your door and we will talk again tomorrow. Yes?"

"Sleep sounds good," agreed Neffie, happy to get a break from Sarge's probing questions and even more probing eyes.

"Excellent," Sarge confirmed.

Giving a low bow, he opened the door and left. The second he was gone, closing the door behind him, Jessica gave Neffie a sharp look.

"I see you won't come clean to literally anyone about Rem. What gives?"

Neffie sighed. "I don't know. I can't explain it."

"And what was that stuff you said to Vondra about being of the true light?"

"I can't explain that, either. It just popped into my head."

"You don't even know what it means," Jessica suggested to her.

"I know," Neffie agreed. "Still, it turned out to be the right thing to say, I guess."

"Well, I hope you're right about old Rem of the green eyes."

"Me too," answered Neffie. *Me too*, she repeated to herself.

"I suppose we should get some sleep," Jessica remarked. "How long 'til third hour?"

Neffie pulled the timepiece out of her jean pocket. It took a little effort to calculate the time remaining.

"A little more than seven hours."

Jessica gave a long sigh before asking, "You think an hour here is like an hour back home?"

"Don't know," she said. "I don't suppose your phone is working, is it?"

After checking her phone, Jessica gave the expected answer.

"Not working. What a surprise, huh?"

"I suppose we can watch the clock and guess about hours."

Jessica yawned. "Be my guest. Me, I'm going to sleep."

Neffie felt her eyelids growing heavy just thinking about all the work of staying awake. *Maybe just a quick nap,* she thought.

Jessica suddenly sprang up. "Neffie, no! We can't both sleep. We might not wake up."

"You're right," admitted Neffie. "How about we take turns sleeping? Half the time for each."

Jessica gave her a grin. "Great idea. I sleep first."

"Deal," agreed Neffie.

# CHAPTER 15

# AN UNEXPECTED TURN

For Neffie, the halfway mark until third hour was painfully slow in coming, and the time spent alone proved tedious. To top things off, Jessica snored. Finally, the time to wake Jessica arrived, and she put a hand on her shoulder. Jessica's eyes instantly popped open, and she gave Neffie a friendly grin.

"Man, I had a great sleep."

"It was only three hours, give or take," Neffie said.

Climbing off the bed, Jessica answered, "Neff, I don't think it was three Earthly hours. In fact, all day long I've been getting this funny feeling everything moves slower than normal on this crazy planet."

"You think?"

"Definitely," replied Jessica. "I mean, look how people talk. Like, they *take forr—evv—err* to say one sentence. Heck, it takes someone here more than a minute just to say the word *hhhhhhonor*."

"With your profoundly observant observations, I totally agree," Neffie said, speaking slowly and drawing out every syllable of every word.

Jessica laughed. "Just for the record, it makes me worry about the time between meals."

"Well, there's nothing we can do about it," Neffie pointed out.

"True 'nough. Now it's your turn. You go to sleep and I'll just sit here, like, forever."

Jessica drew out the final word so much Neffie had to laugh.

"I'm not arguing," she replied. Yawning, she offered Mallaine's timepiece to Jessica. "Take this and wake me with enough time to get my thinking straight."

"Okay," replied Jessica, "though I don't know how quickly you wake up."

"I'm guessing it'll take three times longer in these Tymes," laughed Neffie. Giving another big yawn, she pulled her zabbaton out of her belt and laid it on the bed. Untying and removing her boots, she stretched out and closed her eyes. Instantly, she fell soundly asleep. She awoke to the sensations of Jessica gently shaking her shoulder and calling her name.

"Neff. It's time."

Yawning and climbing out of bed, Neffie looked at Jessica.

"How much time before we have to go?"

"Pretty much none. I let you sleep."

Giving another yawn, Neffie answered, "Okay."

"I've been wondering, what about that guy, Vondra? What if he's standing guard outside our door when we go?"

Neffie gave this question some thought before answering, "I guess we should just walk up and tell him not to follow us or tell anyone we've left. He promised to serve me, so let's just hold him to his promise."

"What if he asks where we're going? Or why?"

"I don't know. I guess we say it's none of his business."

Jessica stretched, then pulled up her hood. Neffie slipped on her boots and tied them. Tucking her zabbaton into her belt, she was about to start for the door when Jessica put a hand on her shoulder to stop her.

"Let me handle Vondra," she said with a wink. "I have an idea. You just wait."

Jessica went to the door, opened it and slipped outside. Listening curiously through the door, Neffie heard Vondra greet Jessica in the hallway. Then Jessica spoke in a voice too low for Neffie to make out the words. After a few minutes, Jessica's head reappeared in the doorway.

"Come on," she said. "Don't talk. Just follow."

In the hallway, Vondra stood in front of a small stool he had obviously set up for his night's watch. When Neffie looked at him, the man fidgeted and stared at his feet.

"My lady," he murmured with lowered eyes.

Jessica walked quietly past the man. As instructed, Neffie said nothing as she followed her friend. Vondra waited for them to pass, and then he sat on his stool, his gaze still aimed at the floor. When the two girls reached the end of the hallway and turned a corner, Jessica started giggling.

"Oh my gosh, what did you say to Vondra?" Neffie demanded. "The man looked totally weirded out."

"I told him you were having these really bad cramps and needed to do some walking to feel better. I told him you didn't want any man around 'cause you were, like, embarrassed."

"Oh my gosh, you didn't say that," Neffie exclaimed.

"I was only being the good maidservant," Jessica replied with a grin.

"Gee, thanks," muttered Neffie, though she had to give credit to Jessica. "Only, next time, why don't you be the one with cramps?"

"Heck no, I hate cramps," replied Jessica. "In fact, back in Iowa I refuse to get 'em."

The two girls reached the end of the first hallway. Halting, Jessica gave a long look both ways down the intersecting hall.

"Do you have any idea which way we go?" she finally asked. "I'm totally not sure."

"This way," answered Neffie, noting a small table with a blue vase she had marked earlier as one of her telltales. "We go down this hallway, then go left to the stairs at the end."

Neffie had always possessed a good sense of direction, and it served her well this night. Except for one wrong turn requiring a short retracing of their steps, Neffie led them surely through the building. All was quiet, and they encountered no one after leaving Vondra. At last, they reached the lower room where they had first arrived in the compound.

"Wait here while I climb down and open the door," Jessica whispered to Neffie when they reached the top of the ladder.

"Right," answered Neffie, more than happy to stay where it was safe.

Jessica climbed down the ladder and managed to open the portal at the end of the tunnel. A gust of cool air blew through the opening, tickling Neffie's bare skin and raising goose bumps on her forearms.

"Come on," Jessica called up the tunnel.

Taking a deep breath, Neffie closed her eyes and climbed down the ladder. Her hands trembled slightly, and the woodpecker inside began to flutter.

When she joined her friend, Jessica said, "I'll go first. It's dark, but I still think you should keep your eyes closed while you're climbing. No beaming away without me, okay?"

"I'll be careful," Neffie agreed.

"Once I get a little ahead, I'll let you know and you follow. I'll tell you when you're near the bottom."

"Okay."

Moving agilely, Jessica started down the ladder. After a few seconds, she called up, "Come on."

Taking a deep breath and keeping her eyes closed, Neffie worked her way carefully down the ladder until her feet reached the bottom rung. After that, there was only column below her, and so she wrapped her legs tightly around the stone and slid down hand over hand, rung by rung, until there were no more rungs to grip. Before letting go, she sucked in a deep breath and then shifted her hands to the stone and shinnied down, feeling her way along the column.

For what seemed a long time, Neffie worked her way blindly, waiting and hoping to hear Jessica's voice telling her she was reaching the bottom.

"Another couple of feet and you're there. Take it slow," Jessica called.

Neffie did as instructed, and before long, her feet touched the ground. Opening her eyes, she glanced around. The night was dark, with only a tiny sliver of a bluish moon in the sky, visible just above a nearby wall that disappeared in the darkness down a narrow roadway. With a start, Neffie suddenly realized it wasn't a single moon she was seeing. Rather, there were two slivers of moons aligned side by side, each glowing with a similar, pale bluish light.

That Fastness had two moons seemed pretty cool to Neffie—definitely a scene out of one of those epic sci-fi movies. She was about to say something to Jessica when the girl spoke first.

"Where's Mallaine?" she whispered, abruptly bringing Neffie back to the here and now of their situation. "I thought she said she'd be waiting for us."

"I don't see her," Neffie answered.

"Not good if she's not here," replied Jessica.

"Mallaine," Neffie called in a hushed voice, trying to remain calm while looking around for a sign of the woman. "Mallaine, you there?"

"*Ssh*," whispered a female voice from a particularly deep shadow along the tall wall.

"Mallaine?" Neffie called into the darkness.

"No," answered the woman as she emerged from the shadow and nimbly skipped over a low hedge that paralleled the wall. With long strides, she closed the distance between them.

"Gwenlie!" cried Jessica, reaching for her lobbie.

Neffie gasped and reached back to pull her zabbaton from her belt.

"*Ssh*," Gwenlie warned. "I'm a friend. You must be quiet."

"Friend, my ass," cried Jessica, twirling her lobbie in her right hand.

"I mean it," replied Gwenlie, opening her hands to show she was unarmed. "I'm here to talk, not fight."

"Where's Mallaine?" demanded Neffie, making no effort to keep quiet or to put away her zabbaton.

"She couldn't come, so I'm here in her place. Believe me, I'm your friend."

"Friend? I saw the way you beat poor Mr. Planck," cried Neffie. "Did you do the same to Mallaine?"

"Please lower your voice," Gwenlie urged.

"Not until you tell us what happened to Mallaine!" cried Neffie, her voice growing even louder.

Footsteps sounded in the distance. Jerking her head in the direction of the sounds, Gwenlie muttered some fierce, unfamiliar words under her breath.

"You're cussing, aren't you?" surmised Neffie, suddenly worried.

"Indeed, my lady," confirmed Gwenlie. "Now you must either trust me or face alone what's coming to get you."

Before Neffie could answer, a bunch of figures came striding out of the shadows, maybe a hundred feet away. Leading the group were two tall women in brimmed hats, both holding zabbatons. Behind the two women were a dozen or more shorter men and women, all of them wearing hoods and carrying stubby, club-like sticks. They were closing quickly.

"This way," Gwenlie urged. "We go down the alley. Follow me."

Turning, she headed away from the oncoming crowd. Unfortunately, before she had taken two steps, a second armed group appeared, coming out of a building maybe fifty feet away. Leading this group was a single tall figure followed by seven or eight shorter folks. The leader bore a zabbaton, and all the rest carried clubs. Gwenlie froze.

"Crossed and cursed," she muttered.

"Oh crap," Neffie agreed as the ominous figures quickly closed the distance between them.

"They mustn't take us," Gwenlie muttered.

"What do we do?" whispered Jessica.

"We go over the wall. Hurry."

Gwenlie hurled herself into the air, and her body went soaring over the hedge toward the top of the wall. The peak of her trajectory took her a little short of the wall but close enough for Gwenlie to grab the edge with both hands. With only a little struggle, she hauled herself up, and from her perch atop the wall, she gestured for the two girls to follow.

"Quick," she called, "this way!"

By now, the two groups were almost upon them. The soles of their heavy boots clattered loudly on the pavement, and Neffie heard angry mutters. She had no doubt it was better to try the wall than to face the two crowds of enemies. Slipping her zabbaton in her belt, she sucked in a deep breath and sped toward the wall. When she was a couple of paces from the hedge, she summoned all her strength and leaped, throwing herself outward and upward while hoping with all her heart she'd do as well as Gwenlie. As she flew off the ground, Neffie stretched her arms in front of her, ready to grab the wall as Gwenlie had done.

To Neffie's surprise, she soared much higher—in fact, she nearly flew over the wall. Her shins banged against the top edge, and her body pitched forward out of control. Desperately, Neffie grabbed for the wall and somehow managed to keep from tumbling headfirst over the other side.

With her breath coming in excited heaves, Neffie looked back and waved for Jessica to follow. Taking aim, Jessica leaped and landed gracefully on her feet just beside Neffie, her flight easily covering the twenty feet or so as if the height and distance were nothing.

"Now what?" Neffie cried to Gwenlie.

Without a word, Gwenlie launched herself across the empty space, aiming for a large window that was more or less straight across from them. Her hands caught the molding along the top of a window frame while her feet landed softly on the sill. One of her knees must have banged against the bottom windowpane because Neffie heard glass breaking.

Gwenlie didn't hesitate. Crouching, she balled her hand into a fist, and with two quick blows, she punched out the remaining shards of glass. Crawling through the window to make room for them, Gwenlie waved a hand for the girls to follow.

"Come," she cried across the alleyway, "be quick."

Neffie hesitated. There wasn't much of a sill to land on, but by now, the two hostile crowds had gathered below them.

"Oh, why not?" muttered Jessica. Before Neffie could react, the girl leaped from the wall and landed lightly on the sill. Bending, she slipped through the opening.

*Fine,* Neffie thought.

Giving her zabbaton a quick check to make sure it was securely tucked in her belt, she jumped. To her surprise, she covered the distance easily, landing on the sill as gracefully as Jessica had done. Quickly, she stooped and followed her friend inside.

Neffie found herself in a small room with pale lighting. Gwenlie stood just to the side of the window with Jessica beside her. Neffie was about to ask what was next when the woman unexpectedly grabbed Jessica's hood and yanked it down, revealing Jessica's blond head of hair and fair-skinned face.

"*Hah,*" Gwenlie cried. "I see you are frighteningly much more than you pretend to be, maidservant."

Jessica took a nervous step back, her hands instinctively going up for protection. At the same time, Neffie reached behind her back for her zabbaton, fully intending to defend her friend.

"Easy, my lady, no need for worry," Gwenlie said. "I said I am your friend and it is most definitely true. I just needed to see for myself the why and how of a maidservant so prodigiously and unusually talented."

"Next time, ask," muttered Jessica, pulling up her hood.

Gwenlie gave Jessica a slight bow, not exactly an honorium but nonetheless a small gesture of apology.

"Perhaps you are right, but I had my reasons," replied Gwenlie, "and they're important reasons. Unfortunately, we do not have time to discuss them. We need to keep moving until we are safely away from your enemies. Then we can talk."

Without another word, Gwenlie turned to head for a door on the opposite wall of the room. Jessica moved to follow, but Neffie suddenly wasn't ready to put any more trust in Gwenlie. Holding her ground, she called, "Not until you tell us about Mallaine."

Sighing, Gwenlie halted, turned. "I told you, Mallaine could not come."

"Why not?"

"She simply could not."

"That's not much of an answer," Jessica chimed in. "You need to do better for my lady."

Sighing, Gwenlie replied, "She was being watched; that is the heart of the matter. The rest is complicated."

Outside the window, from the alley below, there sounded a threatening clatter of boots. Gwenlie moved to the window and glanced out, taking care to avoid being seen.

"They're coming," she whispered in a low and urgent voice. "We need to find a way to the roof."

Neffie refused to budge.

"Not until I get some answers. Who was watching Mallaine?" she demanded. "And why?"

Gwenlie sighed. "Mallaine was being watched doubtless because Maggus Jonesy ordered it, just as she had you watched."

"Why is she so interested in us?"

"Because, my lady, here on Fastness, you and your maidservant are incontrovertibly the two most dangerous creatures alive."

Instantly, Neffie had what felt like a hundred questions for Gwenlie, but there wasn't time to ask any of them. The footsteps outside the window were quite loud now, and more ominously, a door creaked open below them.

"We must go!" Gwenlie urged. "Please, my lady, trust me."

"I don't trust you," Neffie answered, "but I agree we should get the heck out of here."

Giving a perfunctory honorium, Gwenlie moved quickly, leading them through the door and down a hallway that ended at a staircase. Without hesitating, she hurried up the stairs. With the two girls following, they covered four flights in no time, each of them speeding along, taking the stairs three or four at a time.

At the top of the staircase was a door, but its handle refused to turn. Gwenlie threw her shoulder against the wood, and with a crack, a lock broke and the door flew open. Gwenlie again took the lead, and they hurried onto the roof. Its odd surface was soft and spongy like a rain-soaked lawn. Pausing, Gwenlie quickly looked left and right. No one was in sight.

"This way," she directed, running to her left. As they ran, Neffie was acutely aware of how high they were. *Thank goodness it's dark,* she thought as she hurried to keep up with Gwenlie.

At the edge of the roof, Gwenlie launched herself into the air, and her body easily spanned the narrow alleyway between buildings.

"Oh heck," muttered Neffie as she followed, closing her eyes just before she leaped.

Neffie made it across the alleyway to the next building, with Jessica following right behind her. On the other side, they quickly crossed the wide expanse of a second roof, and then Gwenlie jumped again, soaring over another narrow alley to a third roof with Neffie and Jessica close behind.

They were running hard, perhaps not quite as fast as Rem had run during that first flight from whatever it was that frightened him so much. Still, their pace would have been a full sprint back on Earth. Despite the danger, Neffie liked the feeling of flying along like this. They were going so fast the still air turned to a whistling wind streaming across Neffie's face and through her hair. It was all so exciting and enlivening, unlike anything she had ever experienced.

After maybe eight or nine roofs, Gwenlie finally slowed and came to a halt in front of a door. With a powerful smack of one shoulder, she broke it open and led them inside a dark building. They encountered no one as they hurried down a long staircase. Upon reaching the ground floor, they found themselves in an empty hallway and hurried down its length, coming at last to one of the building's front doors, which Gwenlie again broke open with her shoulder.

Once outside, Gwenlie looked up and down the street. It appeared empty. Letting out a long sigh, she turned to Neffie.

"My lady," she said, "I believe we're—"

Before Gwenlie could finish her sentence, Neffie put into action a plan she had formed while they were running from roof to roof. Amazingly, her hand moved with such blinding speed Gwenlie had absolutely no time to react. Grabbing Gwenlie's lapels and plucking her zabbaton from the inside pocket, Neffie tossed it to Jessica, who caught it easily.

"What are you doing?" cried a shocked Gwenlie.

"What does it look like I'm doing?" Neffie answered coolly. "I'm taking your zabbaton."

"You can't do that," said Gwenlie, her hands tightening into fists. "It doesn't belong to you; you haven't won the right to take it. Give it back."

"Not until I get some answers."

"My lady, if you weren't who you are, I would take it from you. Please, you must give my zabbaton back. You have no idea what you're doing, but it is very unacceptable behavior. Believe me."

"If you try taking it from me, you're not my friend."

Neffie glowered at Gwenlie, who shook visibly with emotion.

"Please, my lady, if you are determined to get answers, that's fine, but you should return my zabbaton, and we should keep moving until we have reached a safe place. Then I will answer all your questions, I swear."

"No, we stay here until I have answers."

"I suggest you give my lady her answers," Jessica added. "She can be very stubborn."

"All right, my lady, what would you like to know?"

# CHAPTER 16

# SOME NEW LESSONS

"The thing is," said Neffie, "the only way I'm going to believe what you say is if you open yourself to my light."

Her eyes widening, Gwenlie shook her head. "My lady, you don't know what you are asking. It is profoundly worse than taking my zabbaton to make this demand."

"After what you did to Mr. Planck, taking your zabbaton is the only way I can feel safe with you," countered Neffie. "Do you not agree, my maidservant?"

"Oh, I definitely agree, my lady," Jessica said.

Gwenlie shook her head.

"You don't understand, my lady. Planck was utterly the rightful prize after a properly made challenge with an honorable ending. To take a champion's zabbaton without first challenging is a very improper way of behaving. And opening one's light to another is truly dishonorable."

"Mallaine did it for me," Neffie countered. "It helped me to trust her. I don't trust you, Gwenlie, but if you do what Mallaine did, it would help."

Gwenlie annoyed Neffie by shaking her head again. Neffie really disliked this woman.

"My lady," said Gwenlie, "Mallaine could do it because she is a believer in the ancient ways, like Rem."

Neffie's heart beat a little faster when Gwenlie mentioned Rem.

"You know Rem?" she asked.

"I do. And he knows who's on first, my lady. I don't know what this means, but Rem told me to say it as a gesture of friendship."

Neffie softened a bit. "That's fine, but I still want you to open yourself to my light. It's the only way for me to be sure."

Neffie expected to get turned down again, but Gwenlie caved.

"If it is the only way, I acquiesce. I do this with a great deal of reluctance, though perhaps Rem is right. Perhaps we must all return to the ancient ways. Who knows?"

"Good," Neffie replied. "Let's get started." She glanced around. "It's too dark for me to see your eyes. Anyone got any ideas?"

"My lady," Gwenlie said, "why don't you have your maidservant use my zabbaton. I now give her my permission to use it."

"What do you mean, use your zabbaton?" Neffie asked.

After giving a surprised look, Gwenlie recovered and explained, "My lady, your maidservant may use it as a lamp."

"That thing's a wooden stick," Jessica said.

"It is quite easy to modify, maidservant," Gwenlie said. "Simply hold the end with both hands and squeeze it firmly. Then extend one of your thumbs and move it slowly in small circles widdershins against the wood while still gripping very tightly with all your other fingers."

"*Widdershins*? What's that?" asked Jessica.

"It's an ancient word once used on Earth, too. It means going against the direction of the clock hand," Gwenlie explained. "Now please do as I explained."

"Um, can you repeat? I missed what you said."

"Actually, what is on second," responded Gwenlie, giving Neffie a quick wink. "Is that not correct, my lady?"

Neffie chuckled. It seemed her teasing with Rem was making the rounds among Rem's acquaintances. "Quite correct," she agreed. "Now, please help my maidservant."

Nodding, Gwenlie went over the steps a second time. When she was done, Jessica took the end of the zabbaton in both hands and squeezed it. Next, she extended her thumb and began making slow, counter-clockwise circles against the wood. For a few seconds, nothing happened. Then the upper half of the zabbaton began to glow faintly with a white-blue light. Jessica was so surprised she stopped moving her thumb.

"Keep going," Gwenlie urged. "You mustn't stop."

Nodding, Jessica resumed making counter-clockwise circles on the wood, and the glow of the zabbaton grew gradually brighter with each rotation of her thumb until it was as bright as a lightbulb. Amazed, Jessica kept going, and soon it was glowing like a car's headlight.

"That's quite enough, maidservant," said Gwenlie.

Jessica ignored Gwenlie and kept at it until the light was so bright it hurt everyone's eyes.

"Oh my gosh! How bright does this thing get?" Jessica exclaimed.

"My lady," Gwenlie begged, "please tell your maidservant to stop. She risks us being seen."

"You're right," Neffie agreed. "Jessica, stop." Jessica stopped making little circles with her thumb. "How do we turn it down?" Neffie asked.

"Your maidservant should turn her thumb in the opposite direction, what we call *clockings*—or *ershins* in the ancient tongue."

Nodding, Jessica reversed the direction of her thumb, and the light rapidly diminished. Jessica reversed again, adding a little more light. "Is this about right?" she asked. "Or how about this?" she added, dimming the light again.

Neffie laughed. "I see you have a new toy. Yes, that's about right, I think."

"Okay," said Jessica, "I'm ready to be serious. Let's get started."

Jessica was right—it was time to be serious. Neffie squared herself in front of Gwenlie. Jessica moved beside her and raised the glowing zabbaton to position it over Neffie's head, just high enough to let the light fall between the two women. With the expression of a school kid waiting glumly for her flu shot, Gwenlie moved her face a few inches from Neffie's, and then she peered into Neffie's eyes.

Now that Neffie was seeing Gwenlie's eyes for the first time in decent light, she discovered they were a vivid green. Not as vividly green as Rem's but quite green. Taking a deep breath, Neffie stared into those green eyes, delving deeply into the dark, round pupils.

For a moment or two nothing happened. Then, suddenly, the connection was made. It was different from the one with Mallaine—a bit vaguer, weaker. Neffie moved her face closer to peer more intently into Gwenlie's eyes.

Now that she was deep inside Gwenlie's being, Neffie sensed a true desire for honesty, though there was a lot of shame and discomfiture, too. Neffie felt bad about this.

"Are you all right?" she whispered to the woman.

"Yes, my lady."

"Okay, so let's start. You know Rem, right?

"I do."

"He trusts you?"

"I believe so, my lady."

"Can I trust you?"

After a noticeable pause, Gwenlie answered. "That depends on what you would have me do, my lady."

"That's fair enough, I guess," she replied. "Before we talk more about that, here's another question. What exactly happened to Mallaine?"

"My lady, I'm afraid I cannot give a complete answer. Rem asked me to hide below Maggus Jonesy's compound tonight, waiting and watching from the shadows to make certain the two of you met up with Mallaine, but when the hour of your meeting drew near and Mallaine failed to appear, I was obliged to take her place because this was what Rem told me to do."

"Then have you come to take us to Rem?"

"Yes, my lady, if you wish it."

Gwenlie's answer was exactly what Neffie wanted to hear. "Maybe I do and maybe I don't," she answered. "I guess it depends on your answer to my next question."

"What is your question, my lady?"

"Should we trust Rem?"

"I'm sorry to say the answer is most certainly no, my lady, although you may be safer with him than you might be without him."

Neffie suddenly had a load of questions, but it was hard work having to share Gwenlie's shame and embarrassment while knowing she was the cause. *Enough,* Neffie decided as she stepped back and broke the connection between them. Immediately, Gwenlie's whole body sagged, and she staggered and practically fell. In fact, the woman was so weak she had to bend and put her hands on her knees, like a runner at the finish of a demanding race. Neffie, too, felt a little like she had just run a long distance. But she was glad to have gotten some important information from Gwenlie, and she sensed she could trust Gwenlie.

*Things are getting better,* Neffie thought.

○◉○

Neffie decided it was time to offer an apology. Taking Gwenlie's zabbaton from Jessica and dimming the light, she handed it to the woman.

"I'm sorry I took it," she said.

Gripping her zabbaton, Gwenlie gave a nod of thanks. "It is entirely all right, my lady. You have not yet learned our customs. I feel it is I who should apologize most profoundly for my overreaction. I believe you are very wise and it would be my honor to serve you."

Gwenlie then performed a deep honorium. Neffie sensed her offer of service was sincere. When Gwenlie straightened, Neffie gave a thankful nod.

"To have your service, Gwenlie, makes me profoundly honored," she answered. "And it would be totally great if you would now lead us to Rem." Neffie performed an honorium of her own. It must have been the right choice because Gwenlie's face lit in appreciation. Quickly, she returned the reverential bow, her head nearly touching the ground.

"This way, my lady. Please follow me."

When Gwenlie started down the street at an easy jog, Jessica grabbed Neffie's arm and briefly held her back, allowing the woman to get out of hearing range.

Giving Neffie a quizzical look, she whispered, "So, tell me about that thing with your eyes. Are you telepathic or something?"

Shaking her head, Neffie answered, "It's hard to explain, but I can tell a lot from looking into someone's eyes."

"You really trust this Gwenlie, even after what she did to Planck?"

"I don't know. There's some kind of, like, weird conflict going on in her, but I'm sure she's telling the truth about taking us to Rem."

"Rem again!" Jessica exclaimed. "I still don't get your deal with Rem. Didn't Gwenlie just say we can't trust him?"

"I can't explain it, but I *know* she's wrong. You just have to believe me."

"I've gone along this far, haven't I?" Jessica pointed out. "At least no one—"

"Please hurry," Gwenlie called back to them, interrupting Jessica. "Now that we're decided on the destination, we should get off these streets as quickly as we can."

With a nod, Neffie hurried to catch up, and Jessica followed without complaint. Once they were all together, Gwenlie resumed her course down the street, jogging at a comfortable pace.

After about the eighth or ninth block, one of the buildings on stilts came into view, looming over the street ahead of them. Immediately, Gwenlie came to a halt.

"We don't want anything to do with that place," she said to Neffie.

Neffie stared at the building, which was a little different from the other birdhouses, this one's four stone columns even slenderer and angled so that they came together at the center of the building's base to support the structure in a way that seemed impossible to Neffie.

"Then why did you take us here?" asked Jessica.

"It was unavoidably on our way, maidservant," Gwenlie explained. "From this place, however, we must veer away and follow a different street."

Of course, Neffie immediately had a bunch of questions about the building, but she decided it was best to save them. "Lead us," she directed.

Nodding and turning to her left, Gwenlie was about to start down an alley when three figures emerged out of the shadows of a building. The lead figure was tall and looked exceedingly elegant in her flowing cloak and extremely wide-brimmed hat.

"Jonesy," Gwenlie hissed.

"Yes," the woman answered. "Surprised are we, Gwenlie?"

Behind her were two short men in hooded jackets, each carrying a small club. Though their faces were hidden in the shadows of their hoods, Neffie sensed they were grinning.

"You get around, Maggus Jonesy," remarked Gwenlie, her voice icy.

"So do you, ma'am," the woman rejoined. "I am here because ganglies like you are so distastefully sneaky. And now, I must insist on having my protégé and her maidservant back."

Standing her ground, Gwenlie answered, "I am deeply sorry, Maggus Jonesy, but they're with me now, under my protection."

Maggus Jonesy turned her eyes to Neffie. "Is this true?"

"Yes," said Neffie.

Maggus Jonesy gave her an angry look.

"Why in the name of Hentas would you want to travel with this gangly here?"

"She is my friend," replied Neffie. The word seemed to fit, and whatever a gangly was, she didn't like hearing it used on Gwenlie by Maggus Jonesy. She herself had suffered too many racial slurs over the years. Raising her eyebrows, Maggus Jonesy took two steps closer and focused her probing eyes on Neffie's.

"And it is with your free will you make this choice and not because you are somehow being forced?" she queried. "You may speak freely for

I will protect you if need be."

Neffie had to admit she felt a little weird about choosing Gwenlie over one of the leaders of her own blood-clan, but her gut told her to trust Gwenlie and to stay with her. *Hope you know what you're doing,* Neffie thought.

"I am with her by choice," she slowly answered, "and I guess Jessica and I are going to stay with her."

"A poor choice, my lady," Maggus Jonesy remarked as she turned to flash her fierce eyes at Gwenlie. "So be it, Gwenlie. I am obliged to challenge. Choose the style of fighting and let's get this done."

"As you wish," Gwenlie replied, giving a low bow. "The challenge shall be met."

"Excellent," said Maggus Jonesy, returning Gwenlie's low bow.

"Not another fight!" Neffie cried. "Are you people crazy?"

"It is not a fight," Maggus Jonesy corrected. "Rather, it is a storyworthy challenge."

"Indeed it is," agreed Gwenlie with a small, polite bow toward Neffie.

Neffie couldn't believe it. *Do these people do nothing but fight their stupid fights?* "You people are crazy," she cried.

"It is profoundly inaccurate to say such a thing, my lady," observed Maggus Jonesy, giving Neffie a rather patronizing smile, "and yet I take no offense for you have not been in these Tymes long enough to understand the great and important purpose of the challenge." Facing Gwenlie, she called out, "The challenge is made and answered. Let us begin."

Taking off her hat and handing it to Jessica, Gwenlie took two long strides and, as she had done when facing Lattiana, performed an elaborate ritual with her zabbaton, twirling it in front of her, then over her head, then behind her back.

Tossing her hat to one of the hooded men and then reaching into her cloak and extracting her own zabbaton, Maggus Jonesy flicked her wrist, and with a sound of small bells, the thing extended to its full length. Taking a position in front of Gwenlie, the older woman now performed a similar exercise with her zabbaton. For a woman of her age, she was remarkably graceful, her movements fluid and powerful.

"Are you acting as champion?" Maggus Jonesy called, her words drawn out and carefully enunciated. "For I am here to challenge."

"Yes, I am," Gwenlie answered in an equally measured, formal manner of speech, "and I demand your name."

"I am Jonesy of the storyworthy Vong blood-clan, making the challenge."

"And I am Gwenlie of the profoundly storied Charmaine blood-clan, answering your challenge."

"How shall we fight?" Maggus Jonesy demanded.

"In the profoundly storyworthy style of the Island Traditions," Gwenlie replied.

"I acquiesce to your choice," Maggus Jonesy called.

The women gripped their zabbatons by one end as the two short men handed each of the women his club. Standing very straight and still, each woman began beating her club against the side of her zabbaton slowly and steadily in a simple rhythm, wood against wood in stereo.

All of a sudden, Maggus Jonesy hurled herself forward with so much speed it astonished Neffie. Gwenlie sidestepped and met Maggus Jonesy's club and zabbaton with hers, the movements of the four weapons a blur until they smashed together. Twisting to the side, Gwenlie tried to bring her zabbaton down on Maggus Jonesy's head with a fast, overhead motion, but Maggus Jonesy was quicker. She tipped her zabbaton sideways and brought the butt up very quickly, cracking it against Gwenlie's chin. Groaning in pain, Gwenlie tumbled backwards and fell, her back hitting the pavement with a loud thud as she collapsed onto the ground.

Neffie couldn't believe it. Just like that, the challenge was over, within seconds after it had begun. With a cry, she rushed to Gwenlie's side.

"Victory belongs to the Vongs," Maggus Jonesy crowed. "The old warrior is still the fastest of all." When Gwenlie moaned and failed to answer, Maggus Jonesy crowed some more, mocking her opponent.

"That's right, Gwenlie, old Jonesy is too fast for you, far too fast and far too strong."

Gwenlie's only response was to moan again.

Jessica quietly joined Neffie, kneeling on the other side of Gwenlie, who lay very still, her eyes closed, her breathing coming in alarmingly quick and shallow puffs.

"Fast and strong is old Jonesy of the Vongs," cried the victorious woman. "Faster and stronger than Gwenlie of the Charmaines."

"Gwenlie is badly hurt," Neffie cried, unable to believe how boorishly the other woman was behaving.

"Decidedly that is most true," Maggus Jonesy chuckled.

"Gwenlie," Neffie whispered into the young woman's ear, "are you all right?"

Gwenlie moaned again, and her head rolled back on its neck. An ugly purple welt was forming on her chin, Neffie noticed.

"It looks bad," Jessica whispered.

"Gwenlie, are you all right?" Neffie said.

Gwenlie opened her eyes. "It is only my pride that is mortally hurt, my lady," she labored to say, "and I fear I have been of profoundly poor service to you."

When Gwenlie struggled to get up, Neffie put a hand on her shoulder to restrain her.

"You haven't failed me," Neffie reassured her. "Don't move until you feel better."

"Get up, Gwenlie," Maggus Jonesy called, laughing. "Stop stalling. You have a choice to make."

Gwenlie looked at Neffie, and tears welled in her eyes. Instantly, Neffie had a bad feeling. Images of Mr. Planck's cruel beating came rushing back.

*No, no,* she thought, resisting the urge to glance at Jessica.

Gwenlie forced herself into a sitting position.

"It is not right to do this," she called to Maggus Jonesy. "They are strangers here and deserve better from us."

"No, ma'am," Maggus Jonesy countered. "On that point, you are utterly and entirely wrong. It is profoundly and storyingly my right to demand my prize. Now name her or challenge again!"

Gwenlie shot Neffie a pained look, causing Neffie's stomach to tighten.

"Although I heartily wish I could say differently," she whispered to Neffie, "it would be useless to challenge her again. I am sorry, my lady, but there's no choice."

"No freakin' way!" Neffie blurted, her whole body shaking at the thought of what was about to happen.

Neffie felt angry—not scared. Gripping her zabbaton, she glared at Maggus Jonesy. Impulsively, she climbed to her feet and glanced at Jessica. Not surprisingly, her friend was grim-faced. She, too, had to know what was coming.

"I challenge," Neffie cried, unable to control her anger.

Maggus Jonesy laughed.

"It is a very good thing, my lady," she answered with a broad grin, "that you are of too young an age to make a challenge."

"I challenge," Neffie cried defiantly, taking a step toward Jonesy while reaching behind her back to grip her zabbaton.

Neffie felt a hand on her shoulder. It belonged to Gwenlie. Somehow, the injured woman had managed to get to her feet.

"My lady, you cannot. You are not of age and you are of the same blood-clans as Maggus Jonesy."

Neffie wasn't hearing any of it. She was fed up with all the nonsense of these Tymes, fed up with the brutality of these people. And she was not going to let them do to Jessica what they had done to Planck.

She cried, "I don't care about what can and cannot be done. Maggus Jonesy," she called to the woman, "unless you are a total coward, I challenge. Fight me!"

She took a step forward.

With all her rage focused on Maggus Jonesy, Neffie didn't see Gwenlie's zabbaton as it came whizzing at her. The zabbaton cracked against the side of her head, knocking her to the ground. Her fingers loosened, and quickly Gwenlie pulled her zabbaton from her hands and tossed it away. Dizzy from the blow, Neffie rolled onto her back and looked up.

"I'm sorry, my lady," said Gwenlie, staring down at her, "but I am obligated to protect your honor. At your age, you may not challenge, and I must decide her prize. This is the way of it."

Neffie was too dizzy to protest.

Gwenlie called to Maggus Jonesy, "Of course, I make the only choice I can. Take the maidservant."

"No way!" cried Jessica, reaching into her pocket to yank out her lobbie. "You're not taking me without a fight."

Her face reddening, Jessica twirled her lobbie, but it was no good. The two short men were too quick for her. Before she could react, they slammed into her, knocking her to the ground. Jessica tried to escape, but one of the men jumped into the air and came down feet first, on her chest. Horror-struck, Neffie heard Jessica gasp as the terrible blow knocked the air from her lungs.

The other man then kicked Jessica several times in her side. Neffie tried getting up to help, but Gwenlie had both hands on her shoulders, holding her down. After four or five vicious kicks to her side, Jessica lay quiet, moaning.

"Bring her," Maggus Jonesy called to the two men.

With ease, they picked up Jessica's limp body and hoisted her over their heads.

"Lady Neffatira, you may come with us if you wish," Maggus Jonesy called to Neffie. "Come and be with your maidservant, rejoin your blood-clan and stand with your grandfather and me. It is a poor choice to journey with this evil gangly."

Neffie's gut told her she had only one choice to make. It was not an easy one.

"I stay with Gwenlie," she called back. "But someday soon, I am going to challenge you, Maggus Jonesy. You won't keep Jessica, I promise you that."

"My dear lady," Maggus Jonesy answered gently, "do think on this. I vehemently urge you to come with us. I offer you the proper place to get the correct training with the right people, to learn the ways of these Tymes with those of your own blood-clan. Don't be foolish. We are your kin, and whatever Gwenlie here may claim, this little witch is on the side of your enemies."

Neffie remained stubbornly silent, and Maggus Jonesy gave a frustrated wave of her hand.

"So be it," she cried, and then immediately she turned and, without another word, led the two men carrying Jessica into the shadows, where they quickly disappeared.

"Oh my gosh," Neffie cried. "They've taken Jessica! I can't believe it."

Gwenlie took a few steps, stooped and retrieved Neffie's zabbaton.

"Please, my lady," she urged, "take your zabbaton. We have much to do."

Reluctantly, Neffie gripped the end of her zabbaton. Gwenlie let go, and the full weight of the thing fell to Neffie.

"You will need it, my lady," Gwenlie said.

Neffie said nothing in reply. What was there to say? Jessica was gone, taken from her. Just like that, she was suddenly all alone in these strange Tymes.

# CHAPTER 17

# TRAVELING WITH GWENLIE

Neither Neffie nor Gwenlie spoke as they jogged through the desolate streets of Galleyton High Main. All Neffie could think about was the loss of her friend.

*Jessica is gone! She's gone!* she kept thinking

Gwenlie never paused to check on Neffie as she hurried down the streets of the city. Eventually, she led Neffie into a different part of Galleyton High Main where the streets were narrower, the buildings smaller and more dilapidated, and absent were the columned compounds of the light guardians.

*The light guardians,* Neffie thought bitterly. The name sounded so lofty and heroic, yet all Neffie had seen from the light guardians so far was brutish, violent behavior. *Just look at what they did to poor Mr. Planck. And what they just did to Jessica. I hate them,* Neffie thought.

Nearing a squat, beat-up-looking building, Gwenlie slowed to a fast walk. After a dozen or so small steps she stopped. Lifting her chin to glance around, she took a slow, quiet breath.

"What?" Neffie whispered.

"Shh," Gwenlie hushed before breaking into a sprint. "Follow," she called as she darted down an alley.

Mystified, Neffie followed, moving so fast the air flowing across her face rustled her hair like the wind from a storm. In a way, it felt good to be running. The exertion emptied her mind, and her heart was now thumping, flushing away feelings of self-pity.

Reaching the end of the alley, Gwenlie turned onto a wider street where she ran for many more minutes. Beyond the alley was a small, empty square where Gwenlie finally stopped.

"What's going on?" Neffie asked. "Why did you run like that?"

"To throw them off your light, my lady. It won't be for long, however. We've got to do something about you."

"About me?"

Nodding, Gwenlie answered, "I'm talking about tracking. I don't know how, but they're tracking you. I had a very strong sense of it back there."

"What do you mean, tracking?"

"I've been embarrassingly stupid. It's the only way to explain how Maggus Jonesy found us after we fled from the compound," replied Gwenlie. "Tracking, it's hard to explain. Think of it as a connection that follows you wherever you go."

"Kind of like a homing device?" Neffie asked.

"*Homing device?*" asked Gwenlie, furrowing her brow. "I don't know what that is."

Neffie didn't know why she had said homing device. Probably a memory from one of the many spy movies she liked to watch, the kind with secret agents using a load of super-techno-gadgets. Thinking about the big pile of old VHS movies back in her bedroom in Windmere made her homesick.

"You don't have James Bond here, do you?" she asked.

"My lady?" said Gwenlie.

*Don't be an idiot,* Neffie thought. "Skip it," Neffie said. "You'd never understand."

"At least tell me about homing devices."

"Um, a homing device is an electronic thing that bounces a signal off a satellite, I think. You hide it on someone or something and it sends you the location. It's kind of hard to explain since you don't have much technology here."

When Gwenlie suddenly chortled, it was Neffie's turn to look confused.

"Why are you laughing?" she demanded.

Gwenlie answered, "You must think us very primitive to believe we don't have sufficient knowledge of technology to make your homing device."

"That's not what I meant," Neffie quickly replied. "It's just that . . . you know, from what I've seen technology-wise, you just don't seem too advanced."

Gwenlie rolled her eyes. "Well, we don't have homing devices, but we are most assuredly not as primitive as you apparently think."

"I didn't mean to be rude."

"My lady, no offense taken," she chuckled. "You are new to these Tymes, and so you perhaps have not yet learned that electronic devices and other manipulations of nature are only used for high purpose. They would never be put to so crude a use as a homing device. However, we have quite advanced technology working for us when and how we need it."

"If you say so," a dubious Neffie replied. "I mean, you folks don't even use lightbulbs."

Gwenlie chuckled again.

"My lady, the fact that we don't like lightbulbs doesn't mean we couldn't make them."

This made Neffie curious. "Are you saying you just don't like cars and smartphones? Or computers? Cuz I haven't seen these, either."

"You think there are no computers here, my lady?" Gwenlie laughed. "Truly, you must think us primitive indeed."

"Not primitive," corrected Neffie. "Just less technological, which really isn't a bad thing if you ask me. In fact, I wish Earth had less technology. Our technology messes up so many things."

Gwenlie shook her head and again laughed. "The primitives of Fastness. That's what we are."

"I'll tell you one thing I haven't figured out," Neffie said, ignoring Gwenlie's joking. "It's how you light your streets at night without, you know, any streetlights. It feels almost magical to me, the way there's light without any visible lights."

"Now you're saying we're magical," Gwenlie said, her eyes twinkling.

"I didn't mean literally magical. I'm just saying making light without lights seems kinda magical to me," Neffie answered.

"Ah," said Gwenlie, growing serious. "Tell me, have you noticed other seemingly magical things?"

"Well," said Neffie, "now that you ask, you also have these zabbatons that grow when you flick them even though I don't see any . . . what's the word?" Neffie thought for a moment. "Joints. And when we were running with Rem earlier, this door opened and closed in the cliff out of nowhere. That was pretty magical looking."

"Good!" exclaimed Gwenlie. "What else?"

Neffie laughed. "There's this giant blue cat with pink eyes and golden feathers on its neck. Believe me, that cat is straight out of some fantasy movie. Not to mention those garffles. And the munchkins walking around everywhere."

While Neffie went through her list, Gwenlie tried to maintain a serious expression, but she was unable to pull it off. When Neffie finished, she burst into laughter.

"Oh my," she cried. "My lady, do you really think our zabbatons are magical? Great Gessen! Don't you humans have microchips on your planet? According to Rem, you are a rather advanced world in some ways."

"Of course we have microchips," Neffie muttered.

"And mini-computers? Solar power? Efficient batteries?"

"Yes, yes, of course. We have all those things."

"And it hasn't occurred to you there's a microchip in our zabbatons controlling their functions? Powered artificially?"

When Gwenlie gave another good-humored laugh, this time Neffie grinned back. She had been kinda stupid, she suddenly realized. Or perhaps overly influenced by the fantasy movies she liked to watch.

"I really thought your zabbatons might be magical," she confessed, giving Gwenlie a sheepish grin.

"No, my lady, digitally controlled."

"But they make magical sounds and get bigger without any moving parts. You know, like a tree branch growing in super-fast motion."

"The sounds are from digital recordings, my lady, and the growth comes from implanted gene accelerators in the wood. All very simple stuff here on our primitive world of Fastness."

"Okay, I get it. Fastness isn't some kind of magical place like Middle Earth."

"No, my lady. Not magical, and assuredly it's not Earth."

"I didn't say Earth. *Middle Earth.*"

Gwenlie looked perplexed.

"You know, where Gandalf is from. Where the hobbits live. Along with good and evil wizards."

"Ah, I know what wizards are. You're talking about a child's tale," Gwenlie said. "Yes, my lady, we have those kinds of stories here, too. Ancient tales of wondrous events. Sadly, we're in no tale of wonder now."

Sighing, Neffie looked around with new eyes, and instantly it became obvious to her that the blue light illuminating the alley had faint but discernible points of origin along the tops of the buildings. *Not magic at all,* she now realized, just ordinary lights—albeit well-hidden ones. Another question popped into her head.

"There's one thing I've been wondering. How do you guys speak our language? You know, English?"

Gwenlie chortled. "Your question should really be the opposite. How is it humans can speak one of the languages of Fastness?"

This answer again surprised Neffie. She thought about it for a second and decided she wasn't yet ready to go there. But another question came to mind, this one rather intriguing.

"Say, does my zabbaton grow and shrink like yours?"

Gwenlie smiled. "I wondered why you were keeping yours extended. I thought perhaps it had been damaged. Apologies, my lady, I didn't realize you've never been shown how it works."

"No problem. Just tell me how I make it open and close."

"It's quite easy, my lady. Let us start with the basic move, shall we?"

"Please," Neffie agreed.

Gwenlie held out her zabbaton to demonstrate. "To retract it, you simply start with one end, either end, pointed downward, and then you press your thumb hard into the wood while quickly flicking the zabbaton upward. The motion must be very quick to work. To open it, you simply do the opposite. Here, watch."

With a smooth but very quick movement downward, Gwenlie extended her zabbaton. Bells tinkled and the zabbaton grew to its full length. With a nod to Neffie, she then retracted it in the manner she had just described, by flicking it rapidly upward. There was another tinkling as the thing shortened. Nodding, Neffie got ready.

"Like this?" she muttered, summoning all her strength to copy Gwenlie.

Neffie swung her arm out and up as fast as she could, and the zabbaton flashed with such extraordinary speed that it practically disappeared. To Neffie's dismay, the bells failed to tinkle and the zabbaton failed to shrink. Gwenlie gasped.

"Much, much more slowly, my lady," she advised. "The zabbaton's inner controls are not designed for so profoundly speedy a movement. Try doing it like this."

Gwenlie held out her own zabbaton and demonstrated again, first extending it and then retracting it. Her movements were fast but fluid—certainly not the explosion of speed Neffie generated in her first attempt.

"Got it," said Neffie, nodding.

Concentrating, Neffie made a conscious effort to match the speed of her arm to what she had just seen from Gwenlie. To her delight, bells tinkled and her zabbaton shrank when she flicked it upward, its length reducing by more than two-thirds.

"Nice," Neffie remarked as she tucked the much smaller zabbaton into her belt. "Now explain about tracking."

"It is certainly not being done electronically," Gwenlie said. "That would be too crude a use of technology, my lady, as I have just explained."

"Then what?"

"The best way to put it is to say every light guardian has his or her own *skilsheths*. We now shorten the ancient word simply to *skilths*, which is different from your more ordinary word, *skill*. The most powerful light guardians possess several skilths. One skilth some very talented light guardians possess is that of *tracker*."

"Tracking is a skilth?"

"Yes. And once a tracker has been in contact with another person's light, he or she is able to hold the connection over distances. It's not always a precise skilth, and some trackers possess more of this skilth than others, but a good tracker can hold and follow the connection over great distances. This depends to some extent on the strength of the connection between tracker and prey."

"How is the connection made?" asked Neffie. "From looking into someone's eyes?"

"No, my lady, with a tracker it requires physical contact. The longer the contact, the better the connection. Which is why I must ask you, my lady, have you been in physical contact with anyone for more than a passing touch?"

Neffie thought for a moment. "Um, Rem shook hands with me when we first met. That's the only time I can think of, except for hugging my grandfather."

"Your grandfather?" queried Gwenlie, her eyes widening. "You mean Gannen Sargie Vong? My lady, he is one of the best trackers of our Tymes."

Neffie cringed. She didn't exactly have warm feelings for the old man, but he was her grandfather, one of only a few people on Fastness she might hope to trust. Neffie felt compelled to defend her grandfather even if the defense was half-hearted.

"What are you saying?" she asked.

Gwenlie shrugged. "Only that he is a renowned tracker, my lady. I wasn't suggesting anything more."

*Sure you were*, Neffie thought.

# CHAPTER 18

# TRADING IDENTITIES

Neffie took time to quell her emotions. It troubled her that her grandfather might be the one tracking her. But there was no way to know for sure. Who was tracking her seemed less important than how she was being tracked and that it was obviously being done for Maggus Jonesy.

"What do we do about it?" Neffie asked.

"We need to break or at least weaken the connection."

"How do we do that?"

"We might try swapping clothing."

"Do what?"

"My lady," Gwenlie explained, "one's light is the totality of you. Your clothing is a part of your totality; it's part of your light. By switching clothing, we might confuse any tracker who is following a connection to your light. In theory, the tracker may be fooled into following the clothing rather than the rest of your light—at least for a while, anyway."

"It doesn't sound like you're sure."

"Oh, I am decidedly not sure, my lady, but it might work, that's all I can say. Fortunately, we are close enough to the same size to give it a try. It is therefore my humble suggestion we turn our backs, undress and trade clothing. Agreed?"

Without another word, Gwenlie turned her back and began stripping off her tunic followed by her shirt. That they were standing in the middle of a city square made Neffie feel a little weird about undressing, but Gwenlie had already removed her shirt and was starting on her trousers.

Taking a deep breath, Neffie turned her back and nervously began undressing, her fingers trembling. After she had removed her sweater, shirt, boots and jeans, dropping them in a pile at her feet, an embarrassing question suddenly arose.

"Um," she asked, "by clothing, do you mean everything?"

"Yes, my lady. It is the only way."

"Oh my gosh, I can't do that," Neffie cried. "We can't trade underwear. No way!"

"All right, my lady," Gwenlie agreed. "I suppose they're trivial in size and therefore we might reasonably take the chance of leaving them on."

"It's a chance I'm definitely taking," said Neffie. Still, Neffie impishly wondered what the average female of Fastness wore for underwear beneath the drab and masculine outer clothing. She was a little tempted to peek behind her but decided against it.

"I'm leaving my socks on, too," she told Gwenlie.

"As will I," Gwenlie agreed.

After dropping the last item of clothing on top of her pile, Neffie used her heel to nudge the pile backward. A second later, Neffie found a neat stack of clothing beside her. Curiously, she pulled Gwenlie's shirt from the stack. Its fabric was soft and sleek. She slipped on the shirt, which fit pretty well.

Gwenlie's loose-fitting, cottony trousers had a five-button fly and two smaller buttons to hold the waist closed. Her calf-length boots were made of a soft material that didn't feel exactly like shoe leather and smelled more like hay. The boots were a size too large, and so they pulled on easily, the lining soft and comfy.

Next, Neffie slipped the tunic over the shirt. It hung below her waist to about mid-hip and had a V-neck that plunged almost to the waist and was held closed by long buttons. On the left side of the V was a long inner pocket obviously designed to hold Gwenlie's zabbaton. Neffie slipped her own zabbaton neatly into this useful pocket.

Gwenlie's garments fit pretty well. The woman was a little wider in the shoulders and stouter of torso, so everything was a bit too large on Neffie but not a terrible fit. As a final touch, Neffie put on Gwenlie's wide-brimmed hat, which was too large for her head even with the large volume of frizzy hair Neffie stuffed inside it. Adjusting the hat as best she could, Neffie finally turned to check on Gwenlie, who was fully dressed.

"Your trousers are very strange, my lady," remarked a confused-looking Gwenlie. "Perhaps you could help."

Neffie looked down. Her tight-fitting jeans were obviously too small for Gwenlie, who had wider hips and thicker thighs. And yet, somehow Gwenlie had managed to squeeze into them. That was not the problem. With a start, Neffie realized Gwenlie's zipper was completely open.

Laughing, she cried, "Oh my gosh, you don't know how a zipper works, do you?"

"A what?"

"That thingy with the little metal teeth in front there," she said, pointing generally in the direction of Gwenlie's pelvis. "It's what closes your fly."

Looking down, Gwenlie remarked, "I thought maybe it was some kind of decoration and I was wondering where the buttons had gone."

"No, no," Neffie laughed, "no buttons. You need to grab the little tab near the bottom." Pointing again, she explained, "See that little thing at the bottom of the zipper there? You need to grab it and pull it up."

Gwenlie bent down to examine the zipper more closely. After a few seconds, she looked up with an expression of total confusion on her face.

"The what? My lady, I don't see what you mean. Please, will you do it for me?"

Gwenlie asked the question with such complete innocence that Neffie had to smile.

"Oh, Gwenlie," she answered, "trust me, you don't want to hear the word girls in my school would call me if I did that. No, no, just find the little tab and pull it up. It's not all that complicated, believe me."

Nodding gamely, Gwenlie fumbled a bit with her fingers, searching for the zipper's little tab. To Neffie's relief, she finally managed to find the tab and get the zipper closed. With the jeans as tight as they were, it was a struggle. Once finished, she looked up and grinned at Neffie.

"You wear your trousers awfully tight, my lady," she remarked, squirming uncomfortably.

That was undeniably true. Back on Earth, Neffie liked her jeans form-fitting. Unfortunately, on the wider-hipped Gwenlie, they were positively skin-tight. Now that Gwenlie was no longer hidden underneath her loose-fitting trousers, Neffie noticed she had pretty nice curves.

"We call them jeans," Neffie said. "And with your figure, you wearing jeans that tight would have all the boys in my school for sure calling you *hot*."

"*Hot?*"

"You know, cute. Super cute, really."

"That doesn't sound bad."

Neffie grinned. "Not where I come from." Then she grew curious. "Um, how do I look?" she asked, striking a model's pose for fun.

"*Hot.*"

Neffie laughed. It was a nice compliment even if she really didn't believe it. Back in Iowa, there was no way she'd be caught dead going to school in an outfit as loose and baggy as Gwenlie's clothing.

Gwenlie now pointed to her feet. Neffie's favorite shoes, her high, gray boots with the dark-brown laces, were still untied.

"I have no idea how these strings work," Gwenlie confessed to Neffie.

Unlike the zipper, Neffie had no problem helping with the laces.

"Here, let me," she offered, kneeling in front of Gwenlie.

When she had finished threading and tying the shoelaces, she stood and gave Gwenlie a final looking-over. The woman had put her sweater on backwards, but otherwise everything appeared to be arranged correctly.

"You don't look bad," Neffie pronounced. "Not bad at all."

"You don't look bad, either," said Gwenlie.

"What's next?" Neffie asked. She had enjoyed the moment of fun, but fun never seemed to last very long on Fastness.

Gwenlie's smile quickly dissolved as she answered. "Here's where it gets difficult, my lady. I'm thinking the best way to keep you safe is for us to split up and hope my wearing of your clothing will fool any tracker into following me instead of you."

This took Neffie by surprise. She hadn't thought past the trading of clothes, but of course it wouldn't do them any good if she stayed with Gwenlie.

*Duh,* she thought. "I'm not thrilled about us splitting up."

"It is unarguably necessary, my lady," said Gwenlie. "You must move in the opposite direction of your clothing."

"But how?" Neffie asked. "If I may say the obvious, I'm a total stranger here. I don't know your city."

Gwenlie pointed into the sky toward a bluish star twinkling brightly about halfway between the top of a distant roof and a cluster of more reddish stars in the sky directly above it.

"Do you see that bright blue star under the red ones?" she asked.

"I do," Neffie answered.

"Yes, I think this is the best way. You must go inside this building here. Find a staircase and climb. When you get to the top of the stairs, there will be a door that opens onto the roof. Go out and then head toward that blue star. Understand?"

Grimacing, Neffie gave a reluctant nod. "Keep going."

"We call that blue star *Hensis.* It will be your guide, my lady. Keep the star in front of you until you reach the fifth building. Then turn to your right and travel three more buildings. Then turn to your left and aim for the star once again. When you reach the third building, stop and wait for me. Do you have all of that?"

"Yes," answered Neffie. "I go five buildings toward the blue star, turn right and travel for three buildings, then turn left toward the star for three more buildings. Then I stop and wait. Correct?"

"Oh yes, quite correct, my lady. Your memory is admirable."

Neffie suddenly decided she liked Gwenlie.

"I wish you'd stop calling me *my lady*," she said. "I know it's some kinda custom here, but I don't feel like a lady. Where I come from, I'm just Neffie."

"Neffie?"

"Yeah, Neffie."

Nodding, Gwenlie put a hand on Neffie's shoulder. "We should get started . . . Lady Neffie."

Neffie laughed. "Not *Lady Neffie*, just *Neffie*."

"One piece of advice," Gwenlie added. "Once you stop, be sure to keep out of sight. Sometime tomorrow, I will come for you. Do not leave the rooftop under any circumstances and do not speak with anyone. Stay where you are no matter what because I will come. Do you understand?"

"Yes, yes," agreed Neffie. "Just promise you're going to take me to Rem."

"It will be my storied honor," answered Gwenlie.

To seal the promise, Gwenlie performed an honorium with great formality. As soon as she was done, Neffie performed her less-practiced but well-intentioned version.

"I thank you, Gwenlie," she replied, doing her best to follow the customs of Fastness, "and your pledge of service is gratefully accepted."

With an appreciative smile, Gwenlie moved to a nearby door. There was a small black circle in the center of the door but no visible doorknob or keyhole. Giving Neffie a wink, Gwenlie took her zabbaton out and pressed its wooden surface in several places with her thumb and index finger. One end of the zabbaton began glowing with a pale, green light. As the light intensified, Gwenlie moved the glowing end against the small circle in the center of the door. Instantly, there was an audible click. Gwenlie then placed her hand on the door and pushed. The door swung open on invisible side hinges.

Turning, Gwenlie whispered, "Good luck, Neffie."

"Thanks," replied Neffie. "You be careful, too," she added when it suddenly occurred to her that Gwenlie might well be putting herself in danger by traveling in her clothing.

With a quick wink, Gwenlie said, "I am always careful. Now let us each get going."

Nodding, Neffie stepped through the doorway into a dim hallway. The air inside the building was dry and cold. She was about to start down the hallway when Gwenlie called quietly after her.

"Want to hear something funny?"

Looking back, Neffie asked, "What?"

"I can't remember anything about it, but I used to live on Earth, too," she said. "And I probably wore clothes much like these. Funny, huh?"

Then she closed the door, shutting Neffie inside the building.

Alone, Neffie's mood changed quickly. It had been nice to joke and tease a little with Gwenlie, but now that the woman was gone, Neffie quickly felt the absence of both Jessica and Gwenlie. It was time to concentrate on the task of getting her back, no matter what the cost, and so she pushed Gwenlie's last little piece of information out of her mind. Still, the words tugged at the back of her consciousness. *Gwenlie. Earth.* The two words were suddenly linked together.

Taking a shallow breath, Neffie peered ahead to get her bearings. To her relief, a staircase was immediately visible at the other end of the hallway. Taking soft steps, she headed toward it.

*Please, no one be there,* she thought as she closed the distance, moving quietly through a building that was as silent as a cemetery in the depths of a windless, soulless night.

# CHAPTER 19

# ALL ALONE

**N**effie mounted the stairs on her tiptoes, hoping with all her heart to pass through the building undetected. She heard and saw nothing. At each landing, a dim, bluish light with no discernible point of origin illuminated her way.

Just as Gwenlie had predicted, when Neffie reached the top of the stairs there was a door. Cautiously, she pushed, and it was unlocked. Opening it, she stepped onto a large rooftop with a grassy surface stretching ahead of her under a sky full of twinkling stars. Being so high up instantly made Neffie feel dizzy, and she looked down at her feet until the dizziness passed. Neffie decided the safest course was to travel quickly and keep her eyes fixed on the roof in front of her. Her hope was *maybe, just maybe,* this would keep the dizziness away. Or not.

All she knew for certain was she was standing all alone on an unfamiliar rooftop on a strange world and about to go running blindly from building to building. Talk about scary. And yet, the woodpecker in her chest kept oddly silent.

She took a deep breath to ready herself for the task in front of her.

Shifting to face Gwenlie's blue star, Neffie set off, accelerating so quickly she reached the end of the first roof in virtually no time. She closed her eyes and hurled herself up and out. She flew across the empty space between buildings, landing gracefully on the next rooftop. There was no time to reflect on this extraordinary feat. Neffie raced across the rooftops, thrilled by the sensation of her hair flowing behind her, her speed so great her eyes watered and her face stung.

*Amazing,* Neffie thought.

When she reached the fifth building, she didn't slow down. Turning on a dime, she crossed the rooftop at a right angle, and just before she reached the end, Neffie decided to experiment. Instead of aiming her jump merely to reach the next roof's edge, she instead threw all her strength into the leap to see how far she might carry. To her delight, Neffie soared over the next rooftop for a good twenty feet or more, and in spite of the crazy distance she traveled, her landing was smooth and easy.

In no time, she reached the third roof, and with a leftward veer, in a remarkably short time she found herself flying over the last alleyway and landing gracefully on the final rooftop of her journey. Only slightly out of breath, Neffie came to a stop and glanced around.

Like all the other rooftops, the surface of this one had a grassy feel. Little trees shaped like skinny question marks sprouted here and there in small clusters, creating tiny groves. Circling the trunks were tulip-like blooms on tall, slender stems. It was all very garden-like.

Neffie walked slowly forward, all her senses alert.

In the center of the roof was a small wooden shed with a roof sloping like a lean-to and made of the same grass-like material as the rest of the rooftop. Punctuating the tallest wall of this shed were three waist-high, slatted doors. Behind the left and middle doors, Neffie heard the sound of fans humming with little noise. There was no sound behind the far right door, and so Neffie peered between its upper slats. The inside was dark, and Neffie had no sense of any movement or sound, only the impression of a small, empty space.

When Neffie tried the door's little handle, it turned easily. Sucking in a slow breath, she pulled the door open. Immediately starlight flooded the space, casting enough light to reveal a small room that must have housed a fan at one time, though where the fan once rested were now only the empty channels for its axle.

Neffie decided this was as good a place as any to hide while she waited for Gwenlie. Ducking her head, she slipped through the doorway. Inside, the space had a pleasant smell like freshly cut grass. When Neffie placed her hand on the floor, she discovered it was strewn with soft grass, as if someone had intentionally spread the material to make a natural bedding.

With the welcoming material under her palm, Neffie instantly felt a tsunami of exhaustion wash over her. How long had it been since she last enjoyed a decent sleep? For a girl who treasured her eight hours, too long.

*Baby, you need sleep,* Neffie told herself.

She had never been fussy about where she slept, and this place was more than adequate. Yawning, Neffie was about to pull the door closed when a shadow flashed just on the edge of her vision. Startled, she swiveled her head to see what was there. Her hand went instinctively to the lapel pocket of Gwenlie's tunic where her zabbaton was now tucked.

Whatever was out there, it moved again. Neffie squinted and tried to make out the thing through the darkness. Something very large and powerful-looking slowly turned and moved steadily toward her. Neffie's hand tightened on the zabbaton. Then she heard a familiar cooing sound.

"Nobila," she cried, "is that you?"

Indeed it was. To Neffie's delight, the giant cat-like creature continued her friendly cooing as she padded up to Neffie and lowered her head to rub a cheek gently against Neffie's leg.

"Hey there, what are you doing here, pretty kitty?" Neffie purred, reaching a hand to scratch the top of Nobila's head.

The creature's fur was as soft as the fuzz of an old dandelion. As she stroked the fuzz, the giant cat looked up and yawned.

"Oh, so you're tired, too," Neffie whispered. "Well, I'm exhausted and I'm going to sleep. Want to join me?" Neffie made room in the doorway for the creature to pass. "Well? It's your choice."

Having already had a small but memorable taste of Nobila's stubbornness, Neffie had no great hopes, and therefore it was a delightful surprise when Nobila moved to the doorway and sniffed cautiously. Apparently deciding the place was acceptable, the creature crouched and moved inside, curling herself on the floor at the back of the little space. Happy to have a friend, Neffie pulled the door shut behind her and then curled up on the floor beside Nobila.

Although tired, Neffie wasn't quite ready to sleep. Her mind spun as she tried to digest this strange planet and her station in it. Sarge's odd story first told to her back in her kitchen was real. Neffie had lived her whole life on Earth, and yet she really was from a different world. *This world.*

*No, that isn't right,* Neffie quickly corrected. Her mother was obviously human and from Earth, which meant it was her never-met father who was from this other world. She was therefore a stranger in a strange land, like a character from an old sci-fi movie.

*So what am I?* Neffie wondered.

Curious, she held up one of her hands. In the darkness of the shed, she imagined the familiar, long fingers and the long nails with their pinkish hue. All pretty normal-looking. Neffie moved her hand to her head and ran her fingertips lightly along the funny ridge of bone in the center of her forehead. It was the feature she had always hated so much. There had been a similar ridge on Sarge's forehead, she reminded herself. And on Rem's. *What does that mean?* Neffie suddenly remembered a classic line from a TV cartoon.

"I am what I am and that's all that I am," she muttered aloud. Funny words that suddenly made a weird kind of sense.

As quickly as the moment of enlightenment had come, it now left. Neffie was growing too tired to think intelligently. Closing her eyes, she told herself to sleep, and before she had taken ten breaths, she was indeed sound asleep.

Her sleep was dreamless until the early morning when a string of strange, nightmarish images flooded her mind, disturbing the peacefulness of her rest. The first few were of real things. The evil fangs of garffles. The cruel beating of Mr. Planck. The shocking beating of Jessica.

After these, the images became less real. In the last one, a pair of large, saucer-shaped eyes gleamed at her while she slept. They were eyes that might have belonged to a wild animal of some sort—not sweet Nobila, but not a garffle, either. The eyes belonged to something much worse, something terribly mean and nasty. Neffie finished her night's sleep with her body twitching, unable to pull out of this frightening nightmare.

What finally saved Neffie were the streams of sunlight filtering between the slats of the door in the early morning. One of the shafts played on Neffie's eyelids, and the brightness woke her. Stirring, Neffie shifted out of her curled position, being quiet so as not to wake Nobila, who was still asleep behind her. Scooting along the floor to the door, she peered between two slats.

Instantly, she froze, horrified.

The evil eyes from her nightmare were right there, on the other side of the door, staring nastily at her. With a gasp, Neffie fell backward, and her old woodpecker instantly awoke, thumping on her sternum. With hands trembling, Neffie reached instinctively for the zabbaton inside her tunic.

"Who is in there?" a child's voice called.

"Is that you, Gliddie?" another young voice called.

The first voice sounded like a boy's. The second one probably belonged to a girl, Neffie decided. Hearing the soft sweetness of children's voices calmed Neffie's nerves.

"No, not Gliddie," she called out.

"Who then?" the owner of the second voice asked.

"Just a sec. I'm coming out."

Sucking in a breath, Neffie pushed open the door and stuck out her head. Four stocky kids, two boys and two girls, each of them with dark-brown hair almost as frizzy as Neffie's and faces covered in deep-brown skin, stared wide-eyed at her. Now that Neffie was over her first shock, the kids' eyes were nothing like the eyes of her nightmare—not nasty at all, just darting and curious.

Giving the four youngsters a smile, Neffie crawled slowly through the door's low opening, her muscles stiff from sleeping too many hours in the same position. Taking care not to make any sudden movements that might startle them, Neffie knelt and gave another friendly smile. She was about to say hi when one of the boys suddenly cried out in surprise.

"Great Gessen," he shouted, "a light guardian!"

Instantly, the other kids cried their versions of "Oh my" as they scattered in all directions, leaving Neffie kneeling alone, facing an empty rooftop.

*Well, that's great,* she thought. *Seems we agree about light guardians.*

Sighing, she reached inside the doorway and found her hat. Nobila was still asleep against the back wall. Pulling the hat on, Neffie stood and took a couple of steps away from the shed, feeling alone. She stretched one arm over her head and then the other to get out the night's kinks. Yawning, she looked around.

To her right, the low morning sun was red and warm. The sky overhead was turning a pretty shade of orange halfway between a partially ripened pumpkin and one ready to pick. Tipping her hat back, Neffie tilted her chin to let the bright sunshine warm her face. The temptation to wander around the roof and explore tugged at her, but it was no doubt better to heed Gwenlie's warning about staying out of sight and avoiding being seen by anyone.

*Of course, I've already been seen by a bunch of kids.* Cute as they appeared to be, Neffie knew she shouldn't trust impressions. Not on this crazy planet.

Sighing, she shuffled back to her little hideaway and sat just outside the doorway, her back against the wall. Closing her eyes to savor the warmth of the sun, Neffie was just starting to feel sleepy when the sound of a door opening startled her out of her languor. Before Neffie could open her eyes to look, she heard the trilling of a child's anxious voice, followed by a quick, emphatic shushing. The voice doing the shushing was low-toned and decidedly adult.

*Oh man!* thought Neffie, her eyes popping open.

She rolled onto her knees and hurriedly crawled into her little den. Unfortunately, it was too late to hide. Before Neffie could close the door, several taller figures marched into view, followed by the four kids from earlier.

*Courage,* she told herself as she crawled back outside and climbed to her feet, pulling down the brim of her hat to hide her face as much as possible.

# CHAPTER 20

# TRIAL AND JUDGMENT

There were four adults in the group, all short and dressed in hooded jackets like the ones worn by those who had beaten poor Jessica with their clubs. They walked purposefully toward Neffie led by a man with a face hidden deep inside his hood. To Neffie's relief, his hands were empty. He halted when Neffie raised her head and looked him in the eyes.

*Act tough,* Neffie told herself, figuring the arrogant style displayed by Maggus Jonesy was perhaps her best and only protection.

"The childrenses were right," the lead man said. "She is most incontestably a light guardian. Welcome, lady. My name is Warkel, proudly of the Grinnder clan. This woman beside me is my wife-consort, Nairria, formerly of the Shregger clan. We are humbly at your service."

"Ask her!" the woman named Nairria hissed at her husband.

"*Sshhh,*" Warkel hissed back, "not now, Nairy, not yet."

"If he shan't ask, then I shall!" called out the woman standing behind Nairria. "My lady, my name is—"

"Be quiet, Laggy," the lead man insisted. "This is most definitely not the proper moment!"

"No, I will speak," Laggy protested, tossing her head defiantly, "so you be quiet!" Taking a step forward, she performed an honorium before addressing Neffie.

"My lady, my name is Laggilie, of the clan of Shooshers. I am wife-consort to Clackker, my husband-consort standing beside me. I humbly beseech you to settle a grievance. These two liars and thieves, Warkel and Nairria, claim they know how to do carpentry, but really they know nary a thing."

"We can carpenter better than you can shoes-make," Nairria shot back indignantly. "How dare you dissemble so dishonorably to this finesome lady, upon whose judgment we will most confidently rely."

Before Neffie could speak, Warkel jumped to his wife's support, exclaiming, "And, lady, believe me, you will quickly judge my Nairria and I are not liars."

"Don't listen to either of them, my lady," Laggy cried. "They are the ones who are most definitely liars and cheats, not Clackker and me!"

"Liar back!" Warkel cried angrily.

"You two are the liars," countered Clackker, glaring angrily at Nairria and Warkel.

"No, you are!"

"Are not!"

"Liar!"

"Disassembler!"

Neffie stood silently, watching this bizarre, angry exchange between the two couples, whose shouting and squawking quickly grew so nasally and high-pitched they reminded Neffie of the munchkins of Oz, which made her giggle.

Hearing the giggle, Warkel pointed at his two adversaries and shouted, "See! She is laughing at the two of you. Laughing at how absurd you are!"

"Idiot, she is laughing at you," retorted Clackker, his face reddening.

"You're the idiot," Nairria screamed at Clackker.

"Not *half* as much as you," Clackker shouted back.

Suddenly, Nairria pulled a club from her cloak. Immediately, Laggilie pulled a club from hers. Her eyes bulged and her face grew crimson red.

"Swindler!" she screamed at Nairria.

"Thief!" Nairria screamed back.

"Who are you calling thief?"

"The one who is a thief."

The sight of the clubs sickened Neffie. She had seen enough of violence on this planet. It took her a few seconds to react, but then her disdain and disgust took hold of her.

"Hey, all of you," Neffie shouted, her voice almost cracking, "let's all just calm down, shall we?"

Her words had no effect. After a pause, the bickering between the couples only grew fiercer.

"Pathetic excuse for a carpenter!"

"Heel of a shoemaker!"

"Hammer head!"

"Flat foot!"

Neffie couldn't stand another second of this idiotic name-calling. Summoning all her strength, she screamed two words at the top of her lungs.

"*Shut up!*"

The four of them froze, Warkel with mouth wide open, Clackker with one arm raised angrily, his hand balled into a fist. Nairria held a finger in front of Laggilie's face and Laggilie stood with a white-knuckled grip on her club. After an awkward moment of silence, they all shifted uncomfortably from foot to foot. Clackker lowered his arm. Warkel closed his mouth. The two women each took a deep breath. Calm seemed restored, at least for the moment.

"There," remarked Neffie. "Isn't that much better?"

"Er, my lady," said Warkel, his words tentative and even more abnormally drawn out than before, "as you must know, we don't really want to calm down. We—"

"Why not?" Neffie interrupted him.

"Er, why not, my lady?" Warkel looked awkward and confused, but Neffie didn't care.

"Yes, that's what I just asked. Why not?"

"Well, because, my lady," Warkel answered uncomfortably, "as you know, we must prove to you that our quarrel has grown so irreconcilable it is in danger of becoming unacceptably violent."

Neffie laughed at that one. "If one of you punching the other in the eye is what you mean by unacceptably violent, then definitely yes, you have proven it."

For some reason, this answer seemed to please Warkel and the others.

"That is the thing we have all craved but never believed possible, my lady," he continued, "to have a light guardian willing to judge our quarrel *dangerous* enough to allow a low challenge between our women."

"What do you mean, *challenge*?"

Warkel slowly answered. "We being all of us too poor to hire champions to act for us, we had hoped to settle our dispute groober to groober." He looked around at the others. "Hadn't we?"

When the others nodded, Neffie had an obvious next question to ask.

"Groober, is that what you are?"

Warkel looked shocked.

"Yes, my lady, we are all groobers. You know, laboring folk from the many clans of the laboring classes. Labor lifters we are also called." Then he added, "Certainly not fit to champion unless you judge us permitted to do so."

"Well, it's an ugly word, groober," Neffie said. "I don't like it . . . and I don't like challenges."

Warkel glanced nervously at the others. Neffie noticed he had started to perspire. She was in no mood to mince words. She glared at the couples, causing Warkel to smack his lips noisily while a bead of sweat ran down his nose, dripping off the end.

"Our profoundest apologies, my lady," he said. "And if we have offended you, we do all apologize profoundly. Don't we?" When the others said nothing, Warkel raised his voice and repeated himself. "Well, don't we?"

The others gave uncertain nods, all the while looking as terribly unhappy as Warkel.

Neffie was about to accept their apology when a sudden gust of wind puffed up, and before she could react, it caught the brim of her hat and blew it off her head. Flipping once in the air, the hat landed unceremoniously upside down at her feet.

Neffie was about to bend to retrieve it when she noticed the four of them staring at her in awe. Gasping, Warkel dropped to one knee, his head lowered reverentially. The other man, Clackker, quickly followed. The two women each performed an elaborate ritual with her hand, one Neffie had never before seen.

"Stars in the sky," Nairria murmured in awed amazement, her eyes lowered, "to be blessed by the presence of a bearer of true light."

Hearing this, the four youngsters behind the adults immediately began to whimper and then, bizarrely, to sing. While the children crooned what sounded to Neffie like a short, simple ditty, the two women turned to face the four singing children, arms outstretched and palms up while they swayed back and forth.

Neffie had no idea how to react. This was the craziest thing. Before she could decide what to say or do, Warkel stepped forward. Bowing, he performed a long, impressively respectful honorium.

"Now we understand why you were so angered by the idea of a challenge, sovereign lady. We humbly beseech you please to forgive us, for truly we did not know who or what you are."

"That's all right," Neffie answered. "No offense taken."

"Then, if I may presume to speak," continued Warkel, "we beg and beseech you to judge our dispute not through a low challenge, which you rightfully and now understandably find objectionable, but in the perfect way of a bearer of true light, as faithfully told in the much storied and very ancient tales so proudly kept by our clans, the many proud clans of labor lifters."

Neffie really didn't know what Warkel was talking about. Clearly a challenge was out, which was a good thing. But as to the rest, not wanting to admit her ignorance, she decided to wing it.

"Um, okay. I am willing to judge your dispute in the old way," she agreed.

Warkel gave another deep, very formal honorium. "Thank you, sovereign lady," he murmured. "May I therefore presume to present my case to you?"

His words made it clear to Neffie they wanted her to be some kind of judge.

*What the heck,* she thought. Straightening her back and shoulders, she did her best to mimic the actor Cate Blanchett from her movie about Queen Elizabeth of England, striking the kind of regal pose she did so perfectly in the movie. This seemed to please Warkel, who now walked up and gave her another deep honorium. Then the man surprised Neffie by lifting his face and opening his eyes wide for Neffie's examination.

*Is this what he means?* she wondered.

"Um, you sure you want me to do this?" she asked. "I thought it was against the rules."

Warkel answered, "Labor lifters are traditionalists, sovereign lady. Whatever the modern ways teach us, your lofty presence here justifies returning to the old ways. I am ready to proceed."

Neffie decided it would be best to play along.

"Everyone agrees with Warkel here?" she called to the others. When there was a murmuring of *yeses,* Neffie decided, *Might as well.* Bending a little at the waist, she gazed deeply into Warkel's eyes. "All right, Mr. Warkel, tell me your side of things."

Warkel started talking freely, presenting a more or less chronological case for damages from the shoes-makers, Laggy and Clackker, for selling

Nairria and him each a bad pair of boots. As Neffie listened to the man's story, she was amazed to discover she could read all his thoughts and emotions, every truth, every exaggeration and every little lie. At the same time, she could also sense and understand the murkier emotions the man was feeling—his twitters of doubt, twinges of nervousness, and twangs of indignation.

Unlike her earlier experience with Mallaine, whose mind had been full of subtleties and complexities, and with Gwenlie, whose mind had been a swirl of uncertainties and conflicts, Warkel's mind was pretty much an open book. The thing most surprising to Neffie was the utter certainty she sensed from Warkel about how he was supposed to behave, even down to the petty dispute he was now describing. Neffie never knew life could be so simple.

When Warkel finished, ending with a demand for two new pairs of boots to replace the defective ones, Neffie knew exactly what recovery he deserved. Nevertheless, she held her tongue, waving the man away and gesturing for Clackker to stand before her.

"Let's hear from you," she commanded.

When Clackker opened his eyes to hers and began telling his side of things, his mind was just as easy to read. He told his sad tale of a wall cabinet paid for with all the savings remaining from his wife-consort's dowry. It was the cabinet they had always wanted, it seemed, except the doors didn't close properly and there was an unsightly stain on one side. Clackker concluded his tale by demanding all their money back, plus a brand-new cabinet delivered to his wife-consort and him free of charge.

As soon as he had finished, Neffie waved him away. Her judgment seemed obvious, and she just hoped she was right.

"Mr. Warkel, I have heard your story," she said, "and it has some truth to it, though not everything you say is true. But as I understand things, the boots have not kept their shine nor repelled water as well as you'd have wanted from decently made boots. Yes?"

Warkel simply nodded.

"Mr. Clackker," she continued, "I have also heard your story and it has some truth to it, though not all of it sounds completely true to me. But as I understand it, the two lower doors of your cabinet do not close as you would wish. The stain bothers you, but it is not so important. Yes?"

Clackker nodded humbly.

"Then this is what I have decided. It seems ridiculous for me to order Mr. Clackker and . . . um, what's the name of your wife?"

"I am Laggilie, sovereign lady," the woman answered, bowing.

"Right. It seems ridiculous for me to order Clackker and Laggilie here to make completely new boots when the old ones are pretty much okay, so I order the two of you must polish the boots whenever they need polishing for the next year. But only when they really do need polishing. Do you understand?"

"Yes, sovereign lady, we most certainly understand," Clackker answered respectfully.

"And it seems ridiculous to me to replace a cabinet that is perfectly good in most ways just because two doors are a little out of whack. Therefore, I order Warkel and Nairria here to fix the two bottom doors and to do it quickly, like, in the next three days. And for the next year, if the doors ever need fixing again, and I mean if they really and honestly need fixing, Warkel and Nairria will fix them right away. How's that, Mr. Clackker?"

"I am most gratefully satisfied, sovereign lady," the man murmured, bowing.

"Good. Now get off the roof and go back to your business, all of you. I am tired and I need some rest."

Neffie gave an impatient wave of her hand and each bowed and left. Neffie noticed they were chattering in a friendly way as they crossed the roof and disappeared through the door. When they were gone, she sighed. She did indeed feel tired, and she was looking forward to a nap. Turning, she was about to start back to her little hideaway when she got the shock of her life.

Gwenlie was on the roof above her, sitting cross-legged with a man Neffie instantly recognized.

"Rem!" she exclaimed.

She was so happy she almost cried.

# CHAPTER 21

# A HAPPY REUNION

Rem called to her with a big grin. "I am profoundly impressed. A most wise and judicious verdict, my lady."

Neffie grinned back. "I'm way too happy seeing you to mind your teasing."

"I am decidedly not teasing," Rem shot back. "Do you have any idea what a mythically storyworthy moment you've just created? Groobers will storytell this event for generations."

"Stop it."

"No, I mean it," Rem said, hopping off the roof and walking over to Neffie. He peered into her eyes. "Take the measure of my eyes, my lady. I'm telling you quite seriously you just did something that hasn't been done for countless generations. Am I not right, Gwenlie?"

Behind him, Gwenlie smiled. "Not for many lifetimes. It is a profoundly storied moment, my lady."

Rem laughed again and reassured her. "I'll explain everything later. Right now, we need to get you someplace safe. Come, Lady Neffatira, follow Gwenlie and me and we'll take you where we can all relax and talk easily until we run out of things to say."

Without another word, Rem turned and sped off, moving at the pace of a loping thoroughbred racehorse across the roof and then leaping over the alleyway to the next building. Neffie took off after him, and as she followed Rem, matching his speed and agility roof to roof, she again kept her eyes focused on the rooftop in front of her, resisting the urge to steal a glimpse at the panorama around her.

Once again, it was wonderful to run on the grassy roofs. As Neffie raced over the soft, natural material, she wondered why the roofs on Earth weren't all made of grass. They were so much more pleasant to look at, and they didn't get unbearably hot in the sun the way tar and asphalt roofs of her native Iowa did.

With daytime arriving, Neffie now discovered another benefit of grassy roofs; their soft coverings turned them into sweet little parks. Everywhere, children of Fastness had emerged to play and adults to work or relax. Some children played tag while others kicked a ball slightly larger than a basketball in the manner of soccer players. On one roof, a man was hanging laundry, and on another two women drank from mugs. Others lounged in chairs and on stools. Crossing another rooftop, she spotted a woman trimming low plants and a child sitting on a stool playing what looked like a tiny, three-string cello.

As the trio hurried along, Neffie occasionally observed a startled look. Other times, her ears picked up a few words, usually the beginning of a long, slowly spoken phase doubtlessly conveying amazement or surprise.

After they had traveled maybe a dozen rooftops, a particularly tall structure emerged, looming in the distance. Neffie wasn't sure exactly what it was since she couldn't risk lifting her eyes to look, but she assumed it was one of the birdhouses. As they traversed one, two, and then three more rooftops, the shadow of the distant structure grew larger until its shape so filled the sky in front of Neffie it obscured the sun.

Rem finally halted, giving Neffie a friendly smile as he pointed at the structure. Sure enough, it was one of those birdhouse-shaped buildings on slender columns. This building, though, was much larger than the others Neffie had seen, with perhaps eight or ten stories atop its thick columns rather than the usual three or four.

"Our destination," Rem said to her. "The storied main compound of all the blood-clans of light guardians with ugly green eyes and blotchy cheeks, as Maggus Jonesy would put it."

Neffie sucked in a breath. "You mean the enemies I'm supposed to fear and distrust?"

Laughing, Rem quickly answered, "Nothing is that simple here. Yes, the blood-clan of the Charmaines. Don't worry, you're with Gwenlie and me, so you'll be completely safe in there."

Neffie trusted Rem, but he was talking about the sworn enemies of her clan.

"Promise?"

Putting a hand on her shoulder, Rem answered. "Sure, though I can't promise you won't get some strange looks."

Neffie almost said she was used to strange looks from her days in school. Instead she said, "What kind of looks?"

Rem laughed. "You know, hostile, angry, untrusting, and maybe even downright hating."

With a more serious tone, Gwenlie chimed, "My lady, while Rem is making a joke of it, you must be forewarned, and not lightly should you make the decision to enter as you are most noticeably a yellow-eye and all within are green-eyes."

"Believe me, I get the difference. If Rem and you say it's okay, I'll go."

"So, you are willing to enter the compound of your blood-clan's sworn enemies?" asked Rem.

Nodding again, she agreed. "Whatever you say, Rem."

"All right, then here we go."

Without another word, Rem turned and exploded into a sprint toward the building. The nearest column was perhaps twenty or twenty-five feet from the edge of the roof, but the distance didn't deter Rem. Just before he reached the end, he hurled himself into the air. His body easily carried the distance to the column. Unfortunately, Rem was going too fast to manage a graceful landing. Instead, his chest banged hard against its curved surface and he began sliding down. Pawing with his hands to get a grip on something—anything—Rem slid maybe a half dozen feet before he finally managed to catch hold of a ladder rung and stop himself. It took Rem another moment to recover his poise before scrambling the distance to the top of the column where he disappeared through a hatchway.

Neffie gave Gwenlie a dubious look.

"Does he seriously want me to do that?" she asked.

"Yes, because he knows you can."

"Um, if you don't mind, you can go first."

Gwenlie shook her head.

"No, my lady—I mean, Neffie. I have other tasks taking me elsewhere. While you go with Rem, I will walk in quite ordinary fashion on the streets."

Walking ordinary on the streets sounded pretty good to Neffie.

"How about I come with you?" she suggested to Gwenlie.

It was meant to be a joke, but Gwenlie answered seriously.

"No, your way is with Rem," she said, gesturing toward the column. "Don't worry, you are quite capable."

"Rem didn't exactly make it look like a piece of cake."

"A piece of cake?"

"An expression from home."

"I don't see what cake—" Gwenlie started.

"Never mind," Neffie said. "Here I go."

Neffie exploded into action. Reaching the end of the rooftop, she threw her body into what was certainly not her first long jump in these Tymes but definitely the farthest, aiming for the same spot on the column where Rem had landed. Her body carried the distance effortlessly and she landed as gracefully as a mountain lion, her hands catching a ladder rung, her feet gripping the sides of the pillar, and her arms and legs absorbing the shock of the landing like springs. She scrambled up the pillar and through the hatchway. Rem was waiting inside for her.

His eyes twinkling, he muttered, "That was easy, yes?"

"Oh my gosh, I can't believe I did it."

Rem laughed. "Girl, you have no idea what you are capable of."

"That's funny."

"What's funny?"

"You just called me *girl*. Since I got here, all I hear is *my lady* this, *your lady* that, which makes me feel, like, totally weird."

"Sorry, an Earthly slip of the tongue."

"No, no, it's all right," Neffie quickly answered. "I liked it."

Neffie felt herself blushing, so she lowered her eyes to avoid Rem's radiant green gaze.

"We should get going," Rem suggested, changing subjects. "You'll need to face Maggus Sanguina before I find you a place where you can relax and even get some sleep."

"And where I can also get some food?" asked Neffie. "It has been profoundly and uncomfortably a long time since your noble lady, Neffatira of the storied Vongs, last ate any real food."

Rem laughed.

"Absolutely, we must do something about my lady's acute hunger," he agreed.

Neffie liked hearing Rem's laugh, and she enjoyed joking with him. "Thank you, most kind sir," she said. "This lady really appreciates you taking my hunger so profoundly seriously."

"It is my honor to serve," said Rem, performing a formal honorium.

In reply, Neffie murmured, "And it is my honor to be served by you."

She was about to return the honorium when Rem frowned.

"As I mentioned," he said, "we will need to make an obligatory visit to Maggus Sanguina before I can find you food and a place to stay. Don't expect the conversation to be easy."

"Why do you say that?"

"I'm afraid you're going to find out for yourself," Rem replied ominously, and then he turned to lead her into the compound.

"Hey!" she cried, putting a hand on Rem's shoulder to stop him.

"What?" He turned to face her.

"I seriously need to know something."

"Yes?" replied Rem, his eyebrow raising.

"Seriously, it's about all that running you did when the sky exploded—plus, why did you suddenly disappear and leave Jessica and me alone in those caves?"

Rem gave Neffie a funny look. Neffie got the impression he didn't want to answer.

"As you now know," he slowly explained, "those caves are the caves of the Vongs where we green-eyes aren't exactly welcome. I needed somewhere safe and they came to mind because they were nearby and safe for you, if not me."

"You could have said something before disappearing."

"Lady Neffie, I didn't exactly have time to think. Believe me, there are forces out there even light guardians fear; that's all I can say for now."

"I need more than that," she complained.

Shaking his head, Rem could only mumble, "It's way too complicated, and you've got other things to worry about. Just know, when a hole opens in the sky it means run like crazy."

"Run from what?" she cried. "You're totally not giving me anything."

"I know," answered Rem, his face reddening. "Listen, I'll explain more later, I promise. Right now, we need to talk with Maggus Sanguina. She already knows you're here, and trust me, she's waiting impatiently for us to come. We really shouldn't keep her waiting."

Before Neffie could object, Rem turned and headed into the compound. Sighing, Neffie followed. After all, what else could she do?

With Rem leading, they hurried through the compound's lower levels, which were very much like the lower levels of Maggus Jonesy's compound in most aspects, only everything was quite a bit larger. Otherwise, there were the same polished wooden floors, the same paneled wooden walls, the long hallways and the narrow staircases—all with a notable scarceness of furniture.

Rem eventually led Neffie through a set of unguarded double doors that opened onto what must have been Maggus Sanguina's main chamber. Neffie looked around curiously. The chamber was bright and cheery. A narrow shelf ran along three of the four walls at about shoulder-height. Along the length of the shelf were arrayed numerous vases holding flowers that reminded Neffie of marigolds only with taller stems and blooms in shades of blueberry and green grape. Like Jonesy's chamber, the entire room was windowless except for a huge opening on the back wall. This opening was completely uncovered, allowing raw sunlight to stream into the room. Outside the opening, a quilt-like pattern of buildings and streets stretched to the horizon.

Neffie made the mistake of allowing her gaze to linger on the view. She immediately grew dizzy and had to look away. Luckily, her thing didn't start. After taking a few deep breaths to calm herself, she returned to her examination of the room. In the center was a simple wooden chair resting on the floor, which was made of polished stone.

In front of the chair stood a middle-aged woman dressed entirely in a green so dark it was almost black, with her tunic, pants, gloves, boots, and wide-brimmed hat all trimmed in varying, lighter shades of the same color. In her right hand, the woman held a long zabbaton colored metallic blue with pale-green tips. Her face might have been Jonesy's face except the wrinkles were fewer and her eyes blazed not with yellow fire but with the same brilliant shade of green as Rem's. Her cheeks were each marked with four long, irregular freckles, and there was a green tattoo of a half-moon and two stars on her forehead.

Turning her head in Neffie's direction, Maggus Sanguina gave a smile that appeared friendly enough, though the words that followed were rather less so.

"Seeing you here, old Jonesy would pitch a heart-stopping fit. I like that."

Rem spoke. "Maggus Sanguina, I am most honored to present to you Lady Neffatira of the Sargie blood-clan, those storied light guardians and producers of great Tymes benders who are also reputed to have produced the last known bearer of true light. Indeed, I feel profoundly fortunate to be making such a storyworthy presentation of such an esteemed lady as this one here," Rem said.

"Is that so?" said Maggus Sanguina. "We usually save the word *esteemed* for our own clan."

Raising his chin, Rem countered, "We don't have a monopoly on the past."

Maggus Sanguina emitted a shallow laugh before facing Neffie. "Lass, you must forgive Kerem here. The lad has his own ideas about the past, and now it seems he is ready to make his arguments for his controversial positions anywhere and anytime. Or am I incorrect to object to your introduction, lad?"

"My apologies, Maggus," muttered Rem, giving a quick bow. "I didn't mean to offend."

"Your apologies are not accepted since they are not sincere. I am well aware of your feelings and I will at least concede you're passionate about them, if not diplomatic."

"Then I must repeat my apologies, Maggus," said Rem.

Maggus Sanguina shifted her gaze back to Neffie.

"Well, what do you say, lass?" she asked.

Neffie was already finding it hard to like this woman, though she quickly reminded herself not to trust first impressions. After all, they were seldom reliable in this strange place.

"I've experienced some of Rem's teasing," she answered cautiously, giving Maggus Sanguina a small smile, "and it's not too bad once you get used to it."

Maggus Sanguina's next words were so direct and to the point, so unlike the customarily veiled speech on Fastness, they took Neffie by surprise.

"We have heard you can transport a human across the Tymes," remarked Maggus Sanguina, studying Neffie closely. "Is this true?"

All Neffie could do was answer honestly. "I don't know. When it happened, I didn't even know we were bending the Tymes. When I started floating, my friend grabbed onto me and wouldn't let go, and when I landed here, she was still hanging on."

It felt good to speak the plain truth for once. She glanced at Rem, who didn't look so pleased.

"Excellent answer, lass," she said. "Spoken plainly enough. You sounded much more like a Charmaine than one of those obfuscating Vongs. Hearing such an exceedingly honest answer, I almost like you. Your Vong blood aside, you have a wholesome style that does you credit."

Maggus Sanguina's last remark sounded as likely to be an insult as a compliment. No, she was not liking this woman, not at all. Apparently, it was back to game-playing. *Whatever,* she thought.

"Kerem," said Maggus Sanguina, turning to face him when Neffie didn't speak, "why don't we find the lass here something to eat. Let's put our newest servant to the task, shall we? Go find Planck in the lower halls and have him escort the lass to a private room. Then he can fetch her some food."

*Planck!* Neffie hid her excitement and instead nodded. "Thank you, Maggus Sanguina. I am really hungry and I could definitely use some rest."

"Then go, both of you. You are excused."

With Planck back in Neffie's thoughts, she felt a twinge of doubt about Gwenlie. Was she really a friend? And what about Rem? *Heck,* she told herself, *what am I supposed to think about anything here?*

With these thoughts troubling her mind, Neffie gave Maggus Sanguina an insincere and rather mechanical honorium and then hurried after Rem, who was already leaving. Once they were out the door and alone, Neffie couldn't contain herself.

"Mr. Planck! Oh my gosh! Is he all right? Can I see him?"

"You will see him soon enough," Rem answered. "I can assure you, he is fully healed and doing quite well."

"Are you sure? They beat him pretty badly!"

"Yes," Rem assured Neffie, "Mr. Planck is in good health. Now, let's get you to the food."

"No, wait!"

"You're worrying about Jessica, aren't you?" Rem asked, reading her mind.

"Oh my gosh, yes."

"I have no news of her, I'm afraid," answered Rem, giving Neffie a sympathetic look, "but I promise you, we'll go after her as soon as we can. And we will surely get her back."

"For sure?"

"Absolutely. But if we're going to get Jessica back, first I need to explain some things to you. Things you're not going to like, though you must hear them. Then we'll discuss how to get her back."

"That's all I want to hear!" cried Neffie, suddenly tired of all the twists and turns, lies and manipulations of these Tymes.

"We are most definitely going to get her back," Rem assured. "But first, you really do need to hear what I have to say. It's important. All right?"

"I guess."

"Good. Now, while I go looking for Planck, you wait here."

"I want to go with you," Neffie quickly objected, less than thrilled with the idea of being left alone.

To her dismay, Rem shook his head. "No, it's better you not be seen by too many Charmaines, if we can avoid it. Once I find Planck, I'll send him back for you. Stay close to him, look no one in the eyes and try not to say anything."

"What about you?" she asked.

"I'll join you later after I take care of a few matters," he answered. "You eat and rest and I'll join you very soon. Okay?"

"All right," Neffie reluctantly agreed, not liking the idea of waiting but seeing no other choice.

Rem nodded goodbye and then turned and headed out, leaving Neffie standing alone in the hallway. Tired and discouraged, she leaned against the wall, trying not to think, though her mind refused to shut off. She sighed. Rem had said she wasn't going to like the things she needed to hear. That didn't sound good. In fact, it sounded downright bad.

*So what's new?* she thought gloomily.

# CHAPTER 22

# THE AWFUL TRUTH

Neffie waited for a long time, and fortunately, no worrisome strangers came by. Rem finally showed up, not Planck. For some reason, he had been unable to find Planck, and he was a little grumpy about it.

To make him feel better, Neffie pointed out, "I'd rather be with you."

Rem heaved a big sigh before leading her away. At an uncharacteristically slow pace, they traveled through the compound, climbing up two stairways and traveling down a maze of hallways. Only once did they pass anyone. Two tall women came their way laughing and talking as they walked. The second they saw Rem and Neffie, they grew silent. Taking Rem's advice, Neffie lowered her eyes and said nothing. Once they were past, Neffie heard urgent whispers and noticed the women didn't resume their cheery conversation.

Finally, Rem stopped in front of an ornate door with a brass-like handle. With a wink to Neffie, he grabbed the handle and pushed open the door. The room on the other side was large, and although its one window was shuttered, a soft, bluish light shining from an invisible source in the ceiling gave the space a nice glow. In the middle of the room stood a small table with a chair on either side.

"Our private dining room," Rem explained.

Neffie felt her eyes drawn irresistibly to the large, wooden platter of food in the middle of the table, and as if on cue, her stomach grumbled. Piled on the platter were a bunch of lime-colored grapes, a hunk of what looked like soft, white cheese, and half a loaf of thick-crusted, black bread. Set in front of the two chairs were two small plates with a knife laid beside each one. There was also a teapot-shaped vessel on the table and two filled mugs. How the food and drink had gotten there, Rem didn't explain and Neffie didn't care.

Closing the door behind them, Rem sat on the far side of the table in the chair facing the door and gestured for Neffie to seat herself in the other chair, which she did. Lifting the knife beside his plate, Rem cut a piece of cheese and handed it to Neffie. Taking a small nibble, Neffie immediately liked the flavor.

"Good," she proclaimed. "My dad likes a cheese from Sweden much like this."

Rem gave her a funny look.

"I like to imagine there are cheeses like this in Turkey, too," he mumbled. Sighing, he cut and handed Neffie another small piece from the hunk. She popped it eagerly into her mouth.

"Will I get to see Mr. Planck?" she asked.

"No, it would be unwise."

"Why's that?"

"That's a difficult question. You might not like the answer."

Neffie popped a grape into her mouth and then took a sip of the cool liquid, which tasted a lot like apricot juice, though less tart.

"Go ahead, try me," she said. "I'm getting used to unpleasant answers."

"Mr. Planck cannot be trusted."

"What do you mean, cannot be trusted?"

"Neffie, it is highly likely Planck is a spy for your blood-clan."

"Well, he's married to a Vong," she muttered.

"Indeed," Rem agreed.

Eating another grape, Neffie decided it was time to face whatever it was Rem wanted to tell her.

"Okay," she said, "let's get to the stuff you said I need to hear."

"Right. Let's start with you. Have you guessed it?" asked Rem, his voice soft and gentle.

This question took Neffie by surprise. Back on Earth, she had always been the school freak. On Fastness, she was not as much a freak in a world where light guardians looked like her but not exactly normal, either.

Thinking aloud, she said, "Is this about my showing up unexpected? That seems to be a big deal with everyone."

"Kind of," Rem said. "Gwenlie was the first, you know."

"The first what?" she asked.

"Before I answer, I need to explain to you some things about these Tymes."

Neffie had heard nearly the same words once before. "My grandfather said much the same," she remarked. "I mean, back in Iowa when we first met."

"I'm nothing like your grandfather," answered Rem, his face reddening. "You must never think that."

She muttered, "He's my family, isn't he?"

"Neffie, nothing here is at it seems, Sarge included. Surely, you've learned this by now."

"I hope you're what you seem."

"It should be obvious to you that I'm a vile gangly. You've heard that word before, right?"

"I've heard it. It sounds really bad and I don't like using bad words."

"Gangly is ancient slang for the ugly green your face turns after eating something horrible. How's that for bad?"

"Totally."

"Well, guess what we ganglies call your kind."

"I know you call us stuff like ugly yellow-eyes."

"That's one of the nicer names. Try *puzzer*, another slang word, this one for the ugly, yellow fluid that oozes from infected cuts."

"That's gross."

"In private, the fine nobles of both clans say much worse about the other side."

"I already get that the blood-clans don't like each other," Neffie said.

"It's more than that. Many a challenge has started because a puzzer called someone a gangly. Or vice versa. This has been going on for countless generations."

"Personally, I hate challenges. They're violent and mean," Neffie said.

"Yes, but no one dies from a challenge. That's the point. For all its generations of hatred and rivalry, somehow Fastness managed to figure out how to keep the hatred and rivalries under control."

"You're not telling me challenges are good?"

Leaning forward, Rem flicked his forefinger against the handle of the knife lying beside the plate of cheese. "It's hard to believe it now," he said, "but far in the past, the blood-clans of the light guardians were fighting and killing each other until one of them, Great Gessen is his name, came up with challenges as a better, bloodless way to settle disputes."

"Okay, so challenges stopped the killing, but they're still violent and end in good people getting beaten and kidnapped."

"I repeat, no one dies anymore."

"So, all is good?" Neffie couldn't keep the sarcasm out of her voice. The loss of Jessica still hurt terribly.

"I'm not saying that," replied Rem. "They ended the killing, but they didn't end the hatred."

"Is there a point to this?"

"Yes," answered Rem with a frown. "It's where Gwenlie comes in. She was the first."

"First what?"

"First offspring of a light guardian bred with a human to produce a super-champion."

This was a big piece of news, but for some reason, Neffie wasn't really all that surprised. Deep inside her, it seemed she had already guessed it. Nodding, Neffie asked, "And me?"

Neffie already knew the answer to this. She just wanted to hear it from Rem.

"Actually, I came next," replied Rem.

"Then you're also—"

Quickly interrupting, Rem explained, "I'm not exactly the same as Gwenlie and you. Only females may act as champions here, but yes, they went to Earth and bred me. Unfortunately for them, they messed up and got a boy. They brought me back to Fastness anyway because there's always a use for someone like me. They also learned from each new experiment, and after Gwenlie, they realized they could do better." Pausing, Rem locked his vividly green eyes on Neffie's. "Which brings us to you."

"Super-champion number two, right?" Neffie muttered.

"Indeed. But then there was another mess-up. To everyone's surprise, you arrived here on your own before you had received your training. In fact, it was before you had even reached the right age for training. It's an unexpected wrinkle, and believe me, it has been driving the Vongs crazy. But not as crazy as the other thing that happened."

"You mean Jessica? I've noticed she's a big deal."

"You have no idea," said Rem. "Creating half-human super-champions grew into a crazy race between the blood-clans. Being the first to master the process could potentially create all kinds of advantages—not to mention dangers. But Jessica's arrival is something else."

"What do you mean?" she asked.

Sighing, Rem shook his head. "I think we've talked enough for now," he suggested. "Let's do it one step at a time, okay?"

"Oh, no," cried Neffie. "You can't start and leave me like this."

"We'd be getting into seriously frightening stuff," Rem warned.

"I need to hear it all," insisted Neffie.

Rem didn't give an immediate reply. Instead, he picked up the knife and handed it to Neffie.

"Take a look at this thing," he suggested, pointing to the knife. "In these Tymes, it is just a table tool, has been for many generations. Thanks to the Great Gessen's success, to take a life on Fastness is now utterly taboo. It's like humans eating other humans, practically unimaginable. But what about half humans? Everyone imagines the instincts of a light guardian would be a check on more violent instincts. But what if the bitter feelings between blood-clans drove one side to start importing full humans? What if it were possible to bring many?"

Neffie didn't like where Rem was going, but she knew she had to go with him.

"You're really talking about me, aren't you?"

"Yes, you showed them a power they didn't know super-champions could possess."

Neffie held up the knife and peered at its deadly blade. *They wouldn't,* she thought.

"I don't care about your stupid blood-clans here," she huffed. "All I want is to get Jessica back."

Rem laughed. "Spoken like a true friend. I promised I'd help, and I will keep my promise. I just wanted you to know what we face. The arrival of Jessica has a lot of crazy minds thinking crazy ideas. Dangerous ideas. Maggus Jonesy wants Jessica all to herself because really the stakes have gone from who will win the most challenges to life-and-death considerations."

"What are they going to do to her?" Neffie asked.

"Not hurt her," reassured Rem, "though I do worry about the experimenting some might want to do on her. For most light guardians, humans are of less worth than groobers."

This answer was not to Neffie's liking.

"If they hurt her . . ." Neffie's voice trailed off. She was gripping the knife tightly, and suddenly she detested the thing. With a shudder, she dropped it on the table.

"You don't have to worry," said Rem. "She's too valuable."

"What's next?" she asked.

"Cut yourself some cheese and a slice of bread and eat up. Then we should go to Maggus Sanguina. This is her problem, too, and she's the only one who can help us."

Neffie wrinkled her nose. Her first impression of Maggus Sanguina had not been good.

"You sure?" she asked.

"No," Rem answered honestly, "but this is out of our league."

*Great,* thought Neffie.

# CHAPTER 23

# FACING THE MAGGUS

After finishing their small meal, Rem and Neffie left the sleeping chamber, and Rem again led the way through the maze of hallways and stairs. As they moved closer and closer to Maggus Sanguina's chamber, Neffie's nerves tingled. It seemed so long ago that Jessica and she had been standing together in the little mechanical room in their school, waiting for her odd convulsions to start, clueless about the torrent of events they were about to unleash. Little time had passed since then, and yet Neffie felt like a different person. Still, as she walked through the compound with Rem, her old, familiar woodpecker friend stirred in her chest.

When they finally reached Maggus Sanguina's main chamber and Rem pushed open the door, the woman was there, standing with her back to them, talking to a group of three light guardians. Each wore a wide-brimmed hat and looked dignified but somber in both dress and attitude. In the back of the room, another group of light guardians, five or six of them, were arguing.

As soon as Rem and Neffie came into the room, all conversations ceased. There were hushed whispers that sounded like *puzzer*, along with some angry *hmmph*s and a couple of displeased *hah*s. The light guardian nearest Maggus Sanguina glared hostilely at Neffie.

"Courage," Rem whispered to Neffie.

He nudged her to walk ahead of him. Going first was not to Neffie's liking, but this was not the time or place to stop trusting Rem. As they moved into the chamber, Maggus Sanguina pivoted to face them with a sinister smile.

"I see the lad and lass have returned," Maggus Sanguina said. "All fed? Rested?"

Not wasting time, Rem performed an honorium and came straight to the point.

"Maggus Sanguina, I am here because I have made a promise to Lady Neffatira on which I have pledged my honor. Because I am bound, the blood-clan is bound as well."

"Pray tell, lad, what promise might that be?" queried Maggus Sanguina.

"I have promised to retrieve her maidservant for her."

The tall woman cackled. "Well, dear lad, I am all for fetching the maidservant here; that would be quite the coup. But precisely how would you propose accomplishing such a mightily impossible task?"

Rem answered slowly, "It is my great hope, Maggus Sanguina, that in your wisdom and experience, you might suggest a possible means. As you say, it would be a storyworthy coup for the Charmaines."

Maggus Sanguina shifted her gaze from Rem to Neffie, who met the woman's eyes squarely but politely. "What about you, lass?" she asked. "Is it your intention, too, to flatter old Sanguina with the notion she can help?"

Neffie wasn't exactly sure what she should say, so she decided to follow Rem's lead and employ his tactic of appealing to honor.

"I'm here because Jessica is my maidservant. I want her back and Rem pledged his honor to help." Pausing, she added, "It's true, isn't it, that honor is of utmost importance to the Charmaines here on Fastness?"

Neffie was gambling, she knew, but she really had no choice but to take a chance. Maggus Sanguina's eyes bore fiercely into hers. Neffie stared back. Finally, the woman chuckled.

"I'll give you credit, lass," she observed. "You're a fast learner. Much smarter than your average Vong. I can see why Rem likes you."

Rem now spoke up, pressing the woman by saying, "Maggus Sanguina, are you going to do your duty as a Charmaine and as a light guardian? You know I don't have the rank to act on my own, but my pledge of honor is equally binding on the blood-clan as that of any light guardian."

Maggus Sanguina sighed before replying. "Your pledge of honor was recklessly made. I don't see any way to fetch back the maidservant. She is now bound to the Vongs as the prize of a challenge, and only a challenge could get her back. Maggus Jonesy may be a Vong, but she's still too smart to put the human in a place and position where she might become the prize of a challenge. Don't be a fool, lad. It's hopeless."

"Perhaps you're right," he muttered, reluctantly agreeing.

Was it possible he was just being polite before trying another approach? Neffie knew she should wait and see, but she was tired of the long, slow, deviously indirect ways of these Tymes. For all she knew, Rem did have another approach, but it would take a day or two for the right time to come to propose it. Perhaps that was the custom of Fastness, but she was from Earth, a human girl, and she wanted faster action.

Her fists tightening, Neffie said, "I have a thought. We could challenge Maggus Jonesy herself for Jessica."

There was a moment of silence. Then Maggus Sanguina whooped loudly. Other light guardians in the room snickered or laughed. Undaunted, Neffie pressed.

"What's wrong with my idea? My impression of Maggus Jonesy is she is too arrogant to say no. She thinks she's unbeatable."

Her eyes narrowing, Maggus Sanguina studied Neffie closely. Then she closed her eyes and thought for a moment. While she did, the rest of the light guardians grew equally silent as they waited for their maggus to respond.

Finally, Maggus Sanguina opened her eyes and slowly answered. "I'll again give you credit, lass. You're a quick learner—and smart, to boot. Yes, yes, old Jonesy is proud enough she would have a hard time turning down the unusual challenge you're suggesting. Except—and this is a big exception—for the challenge to be storyworthy enough for her to accept it, she would require a most worthy challenger and a prize in return at least equal to the human you want her to put up as her prize. That is quite impossible, I fear."

"Obviously, you must offer me," Neffie said.

Shaking her head, Maggus Sanguina responded firmly. "There is no way I'm offering you, lass. Having the human girl, Jessica, in her possession here on Fastness may be quite exciting for old Jonesy, but she'd risk five humans for a chance to possess you. And I'd do the same if roles were reversed. It would not be a wise challenge."

It was more or less the answer Neffie expected. Taking a gamble, she decided to push the honor point with the maggus.

"It is a risk I'm willing to take so Rem can keep his promise. I know how important it is for him to do his duty."

There was another moment of silence while Maggus Sanguina again closed her eyes to think.

Finally, she opened them and observed drily, "To challenge would be a most foolhardy risk with Maggus Jonesy herself sure to act as champion. Lass, you have no idea what you're saying."

Rem now joined Neffie, arguing, "It's a great risk, yes, but Maggus Jonesy is not unbeatable. And think about what we'd gain."

Shifting her gaze to eye the young man, Maggus Sanguina asked, "And just whom would you put up as our champion?"

When Rem answered, his words were carefully chosen. "I say Gwenlie because she would have an excellent chance of beating her if the style of fighting were favorable to Gwenlie," he suggested. "She is well trained in one particular style old Jonesy has not used in a long time, if ever she used it."

Maggus Sanguina shook her head.

"I know of what you speak and I must point out the style is forbidden."

Rem pressed his point. "Given the prize we would be offering and the temptation old Jonesy will suffer when we challenge, this might just be the perfect time to demand its use. In ancient times, it was reserved for only the most storied challenges, after all."

Maggus Sanguina waved a hand impatiently. "Even assuming it were possible," she reminded Rem, "as the one being challenged, Maggus Jonesy would have the choice of styles. Stop being foolish, lad."

"That might normally be true," replied Rem, speaking slowly and politely, "but we could frame the challenge in such a way that it is a conditional one, with the condition being the style of fighting is our choice, which we will not name until the challenge is accepted. Conditional challenges have been done before. They are proper under the ancient customs, and given the prizes are not strictly equal, under the same ancient ways it would be within our rights to make the challenge conditional."

"And why would Maggus Jonesy acquiesce to your conditional challenge?"

"I'm not sure she would," Rem said. "However, if we sweetened the prize to make it irresistible to—"

"I don't know if I want to hear," she muttered.

This didn't deter Rem.

"How could she resist if the prize were both Lady Neffatira and me? I suggest we offer two for two. If we win, we get the maidservant and Lattiana. Old Planck would like that. And we offer Lady Neffatira and me. I believe it would be impossible for Maggus Jonesy to refuse such a challenge."

"Well," Maggus Sanguina mused, "you are certainly correct in your belief, lad, because the maker of such a challenge would have to be a complete idiot to risk so much for so little. Are you utterly mad?"

Sighing, Rem replied, "Perhaps I am, but I must claim my right as a member of the Charmaine clan. Your honor is bound to mine, and not to help me keep my honor-bound promise, solemnly made, would be unbefitting a maggus of the Charmaines."

Maggus Sanguina gave Rem a frosty look.

"So, you presume to remind me of my obligations as maggus, do you?"

"I presume only to invoke my right to expect your help," Rem answered. "You obviously know your duty and so I would not presume to tell it to you."

Maggus Sanguina laughed. "Like the lass here, it seems you have learned the customs of this blood-clan well, but you have not been with us long enough to make a demand such as this. In spite of your markings, you are and will remain half human, and your light is not fully of these Tymes."

"When is a Charmaine not a Charmaine?" Rem retorted, and then he let his gaze fall on the others in the room. Raising his voice, he called out, "I ask all of you here in this chamber, when is a Charmaine not a Charmaine? If a crisis called for my sacrifice, would I not be asked to make it for the sake of the Charmaines? If a human's powers were needed, would I not be called upon as a Charmaine?" Rem scanned the faces. "Think about it. When you needed someone to fetch this lass to the compound to keep her from being misused by the Vongs, was I not then a Charmaine? Having served my blood-clan, do I not have as much right as any Charmaine to claim your help?"

Pausing, Rem waited for an answer from the light guardians in the room. When no one spoke up, Maggus Sanguina's lips curled into a grin and her face grew bright with a sense of victory. She opened her mouth to speak, but one of the light guardians behind her, an elderly man with a wrinkled face, spoke first.

"The lad is right, Maggus," he suggested. "He may be young and he may be newly with us, but no one can dispute he is a member of our blood-clan. His long lineage is most storied and mightily storyworthy."

Maggus Sanguina's face tightened. "Do you not understand what he is proposing? Do you not understand the recklessness of it?"

"Does it matter?" the wrinkled man answered, shrugging.

"Hargwiddie has a point," another light guardian observed. "Honor is honor and even more so when the dangers are great and the consequences are dire."

"Well said," remarked Hargwiddie. "Such is the truest test of honor—to face a dangerous demand and meet it."

Maggus Sanguina waved her hand impatiently.

"I must point out your storyworthy but dangerous senses of duty to honor could cost us everything. Are you so willing to risk the future of the Charmaines?"

"I say it is the nature of honor," Hargwiddie answered. "That the lad's promise is difficult to keep doesn't make it any less binding on the honor of the Charmaines."

Giving a deep sigh, Maggus Sanguina suddenly relented, though only halfway, Neffie noticed.

"Oh, very well. Admittedly the lad has the right, but let's not be silly. Why not think on it some more? Obviously, his plan is hastily made and exceedingly dangerous. I propose we take the time to do more thinking and come up with a better plan, one that meets our duty without risking so much. With a better plan made, we can then come to the aid of the lad's honor with full heart and willing hand and yet with less risk to the Charmaines."

There were murmurs of assent from other light guardians in the room. For his part, after a moment of hesitation, Hargwiddie had to agree.

"Maggus Sanguina is making a good suggestion, lad," he said to Rem. "Why not think some more on it and come up with a better plan? Put our collective wisdom to work. Why be hasty?"

"No way!" Neffie immediately interjected. "Rem made his promise to me and I expect it honored now. We are not going to sit around and twiddle our thumbs while they have Jessica. No way!"

Maggus Sanguina's eyes flashed angrily at Neffie.

"The lad may be a Charmaine, but you are decidedly not. How dare you talk of honor. You are a puzzer, nothing more, and what right does a puzzer have to demand honor from the Charmaines?"

Neffie didn't have an immediate answer. Maggus Sanguina must have sensed the swing of the pendulum in her favor. Pressing her advantage, she looked over her shoulder at the other light guardians in the room and appealed to them.

"Some of you may disagree, but I will say what most of you are now thinking. Yellow-eyes are not worthy of the honor of a Charmaine. The lad is young and just learning our ways, so I don't blame him. But a promise made to a yellow-eye—and not just to any yellow-eye, but to a half human who is not even fully a light guardian—is not one we should feel bound to support."

There was ominous silence. As Neffie glanced from face to face, searching among the light guardians behind Maggus Sanguina for a sympathetic expression, she saw none to give her hope. One of the light guardians in the back stepped forward, his head bobbing up and down in support of Maggus Sanguina. *Oh no,* Neffie thought as he opened his mouth to speak. She felt all hope slipping away. *What to do?*

An idea popped into her head. Drawing herself into her most imperious Queen Elizabeth pose, Neffie glided forward as regally as she could manage and came to a halt directly in front of Maggus Sanguina. This sudden movement stopped the other light guardian from speaking.

"Maggus Sanguina," she said, "how dare you? I am most certainly a light guardian worthy of honor. I am Lady Neffatira Akou Sargie of the profoundly storied blood-clan of the Sargies, granddaughter of a tracker of the highest skilth. More than that, I am a bearer of true light, with six marks of distinction for all to see. My friend Rem, who is a member of your own mightily storied blood-clan, has pledged his honor, and now I expect and demand you uphold his pledge."

Maggus Sanguina glared at her. Determined not to back down, Neffie stared back, and as their eyes locked, she felt the woman's fierce resistance, her anger and distaste at having yellow eyes so near hers, and also, buried under the layers of defiance, a small kernel of uncertainty. As Neffie concentrated all her energies on that tiny shred of weakness, the uncertainty grew.

Neffie shifted her gaze, her eyes now sweeping back and forth across the light guardians. While she eyed them defiantly, their expressions grew uncertain. Then Maggus Sanguina cackled loudly.

"Light guardian or not," she cried, "bearer of true light or not, you have courage, lass, I'll give you that. But you are still a puzzer."

One of the light guardians laughed. But old Hargwiddie took a step forward and spoke as if for everyone.

"She deserves our honor," he pronounced. "Now is the time to help her."

To Neffie's surprise, there was a chorus of yeses from most of the others.

"Wow," Rem whispered to Neffie.

Refusing to give up, Maggus Sanguina again cackled loudly before addressing Neffie in an intentionally haughty and sarcastic tone of voice.

"Oh, you must be quite impressed with yourself, Lady Neffatira of the puzzers," she mocked before turning to Hargwiddie to ask, "Are you all so willing to risk all for one such as this?"

Hargwiddie answered for everyone, speaking not to the maggus but to Neffie and saying most respectfully, "Lady, it will be our most storied honor to serve Rem's promise and thereby serve you."

When he then performed a most formal honorium, Neffie practically cried. "Oh, thank you." Bowing, she added, "I am most grateful."

Then her eyes did mist with tears. She was about to say thank you again and to extend her good feelings to all the light guardians in the room when Maggus Sanguina raised a hand to stop her.

"Honor expects no expressions of gratitude from one such as you."

"But I am grateful," replied Neffie.

Giving a stern look, Maggus Sanguina warned, "Do not believe duty is being served to you beyond the simple reason that Charmaines are honorable and thus we are bound." When Neffie opened her mouth to answer, the woman shook her head and commanded, "You should now go before we change our minds. We have preparations to make, and since our duty is to Rem, not you, you're no longer needed here."

"But I'd like to stay."

Maggus Sanguina shook her head sternly. "Lass, let us find you a sleeping chamber and while we are making our preparations, my servant will bring food and whatever else you need. We will summon you when the time is right."

"Go," whispered Rem to Neffie.

Neffie didn't argue. Win or lose the challenge, at least she'd be back with Jessica. For now, this was all she needed to know.

# CHAPTER 24

# AWAITING THE CHALLENGE

While Neffie made her way through the compound, Rem lingered in the main chamber to be part of the planning. Although she was not thrilled to be separated from Rem, Neffie had no choice but to follow the servant, allowing him to lead her silently. As she walked, fear collected in her stomach and formed a giant knot. Before long, the silence in the compound was more than she could endure, and she had to say something—anything—to keep from going crazy.

"What's your name?" she asked the tall, thin man in front of her.

He looked to be in his late twenties or early thirties, Neffie guessed—not that she had any idea how long a year lasted on Fastness or how age showed itself on the people here.

"My lady, my name is Gled."

Neffie took note of Gled's polite tone. Lady or not, she was of the Vong blood-clan—a puzzer—and so she hadn't expected any politeness. On the other hand, servants appeared to be frequent prizes in challenges, meaning for all she knew Gled was a Vong.

"Gled, how long have you been a servant here?"

"Since birth, my lady."

That answered the question of clan loyalties.

"I'm surprised you call me *lady*," she remarked. "I don't exactly have your favorite eye color in this compound."

"My lady, blood-clan rivalries are no reason to be impolite. Your rank demands my respect."

*Interesting,* Neffie thought.

"Well, this lady appreciates both your politeness and your respect."

"It's a storyworthy moment for me to escort a lady bearing six marks. Most storyworthy."

As the two of them continued in silence, the emptiness of the compound surprised Neffie. She wondered more than once, *Where is everyone?* She was curious, of course, but she felt she had pried enough.

Finally, they reached the sleeping chamber assigned to Neffie, and Gled bowed and left, promising to bring food. Then he closed the door behind him and Neffie took a moment to examine her room. It was much like the sleeping chamber in the compound of the Vongs—large, comfortably furnished and decorated in bright colors.

Sighing, Neffie plopped in one of the room's two cushioned armchairs. She felt tired. Back in Iowa, Neffie had always hated being her school's biggest freak, but being royalty in Fastness had even greater stresses.

Soon Gled reappeared, carrying a tray with a pitcher of water and some simple foods: a round fruit the size of a grapefruit with a rough, red skin sliced open to show a soft, pink meat inside; a dark loaf of heavy bread; a square hunk of soft, yellowy cheese; a bowl holding soup with a jumble of perfectly round noodles of different sizes floating on top. He arranged them on a small table, bowed, and left. Once he was gone, the door shutting behind him, Neffie used a sharp knife to cut a piece of cheese from the hunk. Holding the knife made her shudder as her conversation with Rem came back to her.

"Don't," she muttered aloud. "Don't think, Neff."

It was hard to take her own advice. Rem had talked of violence returning to Fastness for the first time in countless generations because of humans like Jessica and half humans like Neffie.

*Why are we so violent all the time?* she wondered. *And why did the blood-clans ever think of using half humans to grab power? Didn't they realize it was a dangerous idea?* Maybe, in their hunger to get on top, they just hadn't cared.

Neffie shuddered again. The wait for word on the challenge was going to be long and hard. Suddenly, she didn't feel much like eating and she no longer felt tired enough to sleep, even though she had slept hardly a wink since arriving on Fastness. And so she waited impatiently.

During the long wait, Neffie discovered she had left her timepiece in the clothing she gave to Gwenlie. *Of course, what good is a clock?* Time was still a mystery here. How long did a Fastness hour last? Since her arrival on the strange planet, Neffie had lost all sense of day and night, hours and minutes.

While fretting about these things, somehow Neffie fell asleep. When she awoke, she had no idea how long she had slept. She did know she felt a bit rested—and now hungry. Tearing an uneven piece of bread from the loaf, she dunked it in the soup, which had gone cold, and ate it.

A knock on the door startled Neffie.

"May I come in?" Rem asked, opening the door.

"Oh, yes," cried Neffie, relieved to see him. Rem took a seat at the table. Neffie went over to the bed and perched on the edge of the mattress.

"Well," said Rem, "did you sleep?"

"Who cares about that?" replied Neffie. "What's happening with the challenge?"

"The formal challenge has been made. Every detail—hour, term, condition—has been specified, each one carefully formulated with the goal of maximizing our chances. I have to say, Maggus Sanguina did a pretty good job."

"So, what now?"

"What now?" echoed Rem. "Why, we wait, of course."

That was not the answer Neffie wanted to hear. "Wait? All I do on this planet is wait."

Rem chuckled. "As you've no doubt noticed, nothing moves quickly here. And everything has endless formalities."

"I know, I know," Neffie agreed impatiently. "So, what are we waiting for this time?"

"The Vongs must formulate their formal response."

"How long will that take?"

"Ours is an unusual challenge. I suspect we might manage a nice, long vacation while Maggus Jonesy digests this one. Maybe visit the lakes region above Galleyton or take in the mountains."

"Please don't joke!"

"I may not be joking," warned Rem, his voice somber.

"Oh my gosh, you think it could take that long?"

"Who knows? It's not the kind of challenge you rush to accept. On the other hand, the prize being offered is pretty enticing. Maybe the Vongs will feel the need to act quickly."

"You don't sound like you believe it."

Shaking his head, Rem said, "We must do our best to be patient. I'll check back when I know something."

When Rem stood and turned to leave, Neffie cried, "You're not leaving me here to wait by myself!"

"I can stay for a bit more if you'd like."

"Oh, I do like!" cried Neffie, blushing.

"As I say," Rem muttered, "all we can do is wait and hope the wait isn't too long."

"There's still cheese," offered Neffie, pointing to the tray on the table. "Have a little."

"No, thank you. Maybe you should sleep."

"Thank you, Dad, but I have been sleeping," laughed Neffie. "I'd rather talk."

"Talking with you usually means getting an excessive number of questions," Rem remarked drily.

"You're not the first to say that," Neffie agreed. "In Iowa, I'm famous for it."

"Well, go ahead and ask one."

Neffie thought for a second. "You sure?"

"Is that your question?"

Neffie had to laugh.

"No, but I mean it," she said, grinning. "You really want me to ask a question?"

"Yes, but only one, okay?"

"Okay."

"Now ask."

"Tell me about light. You know, as in light guardians and opening your light and bearer of true light."

"Good question," Rem nodded. "Light is maybe the most important notion on Fastness. It's a little like the idea of human soul on Earth—or the sum of your genes and environmental influences if you're scientific—but it's also different."

"Meaning?"

"On Fastness, folks believe light is in everyone and in every living thing. Even those who don't follow the ancient ways still kinda believe in it. They say one's light comes from *Esh*, the giant sun existing at the beginning of all Tymes. When Esh exploded, sending its parts hurtling everywhere and launching the universes, Esh became a part of every living thing."

To Neffie, this sounded like many of the ancient stories from her own world.

"You're telling a story of creation, aren't you?"

"Maybe," murmured Rem, staring into space before resuming. "Whether or not you believe Esh was the beginning of all things, everyone on Fastness believes, at least to some degree, there's something called light animating the living substances of the universes. In the past, light guardians were the protectors of every kind of light on Fastness because all light was considered sacred. And then there was the story of the bearer of true light. They say the bearer was . . . is—"

"You're afraid to say it, aren't you?"

"I am," Rem answered, his eyes locking on Neffie's. "You're not ready to hear it. You haven't been here long enough."

"I once asked Gwenlie if this place was magical and she laughed at me."

"Magic is only an explanation for what can't be explained. Like bending across Tymes. Some might say it's magic and others say it's the power of Esh. Let me give you one last thought and then I suggest we stop talking of such things."

Chuckling, Neffie said, "I warned you I'm the queen of questions."

"You certainly did," agreed Rem, the corners of his mouth twitching.

"What's your thought?"

Nodding, Rem said, "If the ancients are right that the light of Esh is what fires all life in the universes, what would it mean if someone could control that light?"

"Are you playing with my mind, Mr. Light Guardian?"

Rem grinned. "Don't you like pondering great imponderables?"

Neffie grabbed a pillow off the bed and threw it playfully at Rem's head. Rem caught it, and with a quick motion of his hand, he fired it back at Neffie, who caught it just as easily.

Neffie complained, "I'm the one supposed to be asking the questions, not you."

"Totally guilty," agreed Rem.

Their joking made Neffie feel a little better, but still she faced what could be a very long wait for the Vongs to reply to the challenge.

*Gotta do something,* she thought. Suddenly she had an idea.

"Can you train me?" she said to Rem.

"What?" said Rem, startled.

"I keep getting told I lack training, so why don't I train?"

Rem blushed. "You don't know what you're asking, Neffie."

"Yes, I do," Neffie responded. "It's all about challenges here on this crazy planet, so I want to train so I can fight them."

"Neffie, trust me, it can't be done."

"Why not?"

"For one thing, you're too young. Custom requires you to be sixteen."

"I wasn't supposed to bend the Tymes, either, but I did."

Rem took a moment to think about this. "Okay, maybe age isn't an issue. But the training must be by a member of your own blood-clan, and I am definitely not a Vong."

"That excuse is pretty lame considering you're not supposed to be helping me with anything, really, but it sure hasn't stopped you."

"The thing is," he finally admitted, "I've never been trained, either."

"Why not?"

Laughing, Rem answered, "Let's definitely save our discussion of gender bias for another time."

"Then I'm going to train myself." Before Rem could voice another objection, she pointed to the table and chair in the middle of her chamber. "Here, help me move these."

Rem didn't look thrilled, but after a second or two of hesitation, he nodded, and they quickly carried table and chair to the wall. Then Neffie moved to the center of the chamber. Looking at Rem, she tightened her lips and pulled her zabbaton from her belt. Following the instructions from Gwenlie, she flicked her wrist downward, extending the instrument to its full length.

"Here we go," she muttered to Rem.

"Do you have any idea what you're doing?" he asked.

"Well, I have watched two challenges," she pointed out. Taking a moment to think, she decided she might as well start close to home. "Lattiana and Gwenlie agreed to fight in the style of the Sargies," she recalled. "I like the name of that one."

Taking the zabbaton by its middle with one hand, she slipped her other hand behind her back, flexed her knees slightly and began oscillating the instrument's two ends up and down, as she had seen Gwenlie and Lattiana do. Then she started moving her body slowly in a small circle. Every once in a while, she flicked an end of the zabbaton at some imaginary target and, in her mind, always hit it perfectly. After repeating this exercise a few times, she quickly used her oscillating zabbaton to parry an opponent's imaginary strike.

It was remarkable to Neffie how easily she could control her zabbaton. The thing's balance was perfect. Before long, her blows and parries were lightning fast, no more than a blur. While she worked, Rem watched silently with an amused grin. As Neffie continued to improve, his expression changed to one of surprise and admiration.

"You are seriously fast," he finally remarked when Neffie paused to catch her breath.

"You think?"

"Totally. Maybe the stories are true."

"Stories?" asked Neffie. She resumed her challenge position, flexing her knees and again grasping her zabbaton by its middle.

"That's for another time," said Rem with a laugh. "Here, let me help."

Going to the table, he picked up the knife. Moving in front of Neffie, he faced her and pointed the tip of the knife in her direction.

"Pretend this is a zabbaton," he said. "Whenever I go at you with it, knock it away. Not hard—I don't want to get hurt. Just flick a little to work your reflexes."

"I'm not sure I want you stabbing at me with a knife," remarked Neffie, eying the sharp blade.

"Even with zabbatons, challenges can be dangerous," Rem pointed out. "It's not exactly a soft toy you're flashing at your opponent."

"All right," Neffie agreed. "Just don't kill me."

Resuming her challenging stance, Neffie oscillated her zabbaton in front of her. As she had seen Gwenlie doing, Neffie began swaying her torso forward and backward in compact, fluid movements. While she did this, Rem matched her movements, waving the knife's blade back and forth in sync with her oscillations, his own torso following the dance of hers.

Suddenly, he stabbed the knife at her. With a speedy movement, she shifted the end of her zabbaton to meet the attack. Her zabbaton parried so quickly, the force of the blow nearly knocked the knife out of Rem's hand.

"Good!" he cried. "But not so hard. Remember, we're working on your reflexes."

Taking up her position again, Neffie started her dance, and Rem followed her movements. They danced and swayed and circled, and then suddenly Rem stabbed the knife at Neffie's chest. Reacting instantly, she flicked the zabbaton and easily batted away the knife. Then Rem surprised her by stabbing at her shoulder. Reacting without thinking, Neffie whirled and parried the blow with the other end of her zabbaton.

"How did you do that?" cried Rem.

"What?"

"Spin so quickly. I could barely see you, it was so fast."

Neffie laughed. "I'm a bearer of true light, remember?"

A somber expression on his face, Rem said, "Seriously, I think you are."

"Or not," laughed Neffie. "Come on, let's keep going."

Just then, there was a knock at the door. Rem signaled Neffie to wait while he hurried over.

"Yes?" he called through the wood.

"An emissary of the Vongs has arrived with a reply to the challenge," said the man on the other side. Neffie didn't recognize the voice. "You are therefore summoned."

Giving Neffie a quick wink, Rem said, "We will come to Maggus Sanguina's chamber immediately. You need not wait for us."

After a brief moment of silence, Neffie heard the sound of the man's footsteps leaving. Rem pointed at Neffie's zabbaton.

"Stow that away," he said to her. "Let's get going; it's showtime."

# CHAPTER 25

# WORD FROM THE VONGS

**N**effie quickly retracted her zabbaton and slipped it into her tunic. With Rem leading, they hurried through the compound. When they arrived at the door to Maggus Sanguina's main chamber, a formally attired servant ushered them silently into the room. As before, Maggus Sanguina stood in front of her chair, dressed in fine black clothing with her extended zabbaton in her right hand. Standing in a half circle behind her was a throng of light guardians of the Charmaines, all of them finely dressed.

Rem whispered to Neffie, "Go wherever the servant leads you."

Then he moved to take his place in the circle, standing a few paces behind Maggus Sanguina. The servant gestured for Neffie to follow him, and he placed her to the left of—and a little behind—the circle of light guardians.

Other light guardians entered through a small back door, doubtlessly coming to hear the Vongs' response to what must now be a much-discussed challenge. None spoke or seemed nervous

Before long, a good many light guardians, perhaps four dozen of them, had assembled to watch the storyworthy event. Hargwiddie, the old man who had first supported Neffie, stood toward the middle of the first circle.

*Good,* she thought.

When Maggus Jonesy's emissary finally strode into the room, Neffie observed she was very tall, with three prominent pink spots on each cheek. Her clothing was more flamboyant than the typical light guardian, with a knee-length cloak of a snowy white material shot through with shimmery green flecks that reminded Neffie of new spring leaves. Beneath her cloak, she wore charcoal-gray trousers and black boots with gold toes. On her head, a very wide-brimmed hat matched the green flecks of her cloak.

Striding confidently through the chamber's double door, the emissary halted about five paces from the maggus and bowed. Her voice was strong and sure, yet its tone was only respectful enough to avoid sounding discourteous. Neffie was certain none of the Charmaines present in the chamber missed the tinge of arrogance.

"Maggus Sanguina, my name is Serrianna of the profoundly storyworthy Vong blood-clan," the emissary declared. "On behalf of Maggus Jonesy, also of the gloriously storied and storyworthy Vong blood-clan, a blood-clan allied by marriage, blood and common interests for countless generations to the equally storied Sargie blood-clan, it is my honorable charge to report the acceptance of your challenge precisely as issued, to be answered only by one worthy of answering so storyworthy a challenge, a light guardian of the highest rank and most storyworthy honor."

There were several murmurs in the room.

Taking a determined step forward, Maggus Sanguina performed an elegant honorium before replying, "Excellent. I am most profoundly pleased to hear this news."

The emissary gave a brief half bow before continuing. "Indeed, it is a storyworthy moment in the history of all our blood-clans. I have also been charged to inquire on behalf of my maggus as to your choice of styles for this challenge between champions, that I may return the information so that proper preparations can be made."

Maggus Sanguina gave Serrianna, a long, probing stare. "Ma'am, as maggus of the mightily storied and gloriously storyworthy Charmaine blood-clan, I must first thank you for giving such a rightful and courteous answer to our challenge. May I correctly presume from your words thus spoken that the honorable Maggus Jonesy herself is going to act as champion for her alliance in this challenge?"

The emissary smirked. "Maggus Jonesy has indeed elected to put aside the burdensome duties of her office to act once again as champion on behalf of her blood-clan's alliance."

"I see," Maggus Sanguina replied, speaking coolly. "Then you may tell your honorable Maggus Jonesy, who is so nobly setting aside her important duties as maggus to serve as champion of the Vongs, that our own profoundly respected champion, the most worthy and honorable Gwenlie of the Charmaine blood-clan, has indicated the challenge shall be fought in one of the most mightily venerable and mythically storied styles of the ancients—that is to say, in the historic style known as the Posts of Eighteen."

There were gasps throughout the chamber, and the emissary's jaw dropped.

"The terms are understood," she said, recovering her poise. "I shall convey your champion's rather startling selection to my honorable Maggus Jonesy. When shall the challenge take place?"

Neffie prayed it would be soon. *Please, please,* she thought.

Fortunately, her wish came true.

"The challenge shall be in two hours," Maggus Sanguina said. "As dictated by ancient tradition, nine light guardians shall accompany each champion to the challenge, which shall take place on the Great Roof as specified in the original challenge. Maggus Jonesy shall bring Mr. Jedd Planck and the maidservant, of course, who will stand beside Lady Neffatira and Mr. Kerem Alp in the prize circle. The choice of the nine to accompany each champion shall be in accordance with the ancient ways as understood by our storied blood-clans. All must be in keeping with our champion's choice of such an ancient style. These are our terms and they are unconditional."

Nodding, Serrianna answered, "Your terms are understood and they shall be communicated and followed. Is there anything else that needs deciding?"

"No."

Maggus Sanguina's one-word answer was so perfunctory and unembellished, so icy and unfriendly, so outside the customs of the Tymes, it was shocking. Maggus Jonesy's emissary was visibly taken aback, and she stood awkwardly for a second or two, unsure what to say or do next. Not finding appropriate words, she bowed slightly; then she backed out of the room. The second she was gone, the light guardians gathered in the chamber burst into chatter. Curious, Neffie turned to watch.

"The Posts of Eighteen!" exclaimed a female light guardian with red hair, starting things off. "Why on Seramonia would we want to choose that style?"

"It will certainly take old Jonesy by surprise," suggested another light guardian, this one a burly man with white hair matching his white eyebrows.

"Yes, but will it gain us any advantage?" the first speaker replied. "Most disturbingly, I think not."

"Certainly Gwenlie is more recently trained," a younger light guardian on the far right of the group pointed out, "and therefore she will have had more recent experience with this style."

"And it's quite possible old Jonesy has never trained in the style of the Eighteens," an older guardian added, "and even if ever she did, it was generations ago. She will be rusty."

"All that may be true," another countered, "but I profoundly doubt Maggus Jonesy ever forgets her training. In fact, when did she last lose a challenge? Who here remembers when she last lost a challenge?"

"That is an easy question to answer," replied the red-haired woman who had started the discussion. "There is no one who can remember such a thing."

Hearing this, Neffie found it impossible to hold her tongue.

"What do you mean, no one can remember?" she cried.

A stony silence followed.

Finally, the white-haired light guardian spoke up in a quiet voice. "No one can remember because Maggus Jonesy has not lost a challenge in a hundred contests or more. The truth may be she has never lost a challenge. Not in her entire life."

Neffie gasped. "Never?"

"Never," muttered Maggus Sanguina.

# CHAPTER 26

# READYING FOR THE CHALLENGE

Neffie couldn't believe it. *Why did no one say Maggus Jonesy is unbeatable?* When Rem gestured for her to follow him out of the chamber, Neffie trailed a few feet behind as if she were sleepwalking in a dream, her mind fogged and her thoughts jumbled.

"Keep up," Rem called. "It is imperative we help Gwenlie."

"How do we help?" she asked.

"First off," Rem answered, "by looking as confident as we can. Gwenlie will be carrying a heavy burden. She can't have anyone or anything planting an unnecessary seed of doubt."

Neffie tightened her lips. Rem was right. It was time to summon all her strength and hope for the best. Nodding, she said, "What now?"

"Even before the emissary arrived, our nine had been selected. We must join them and then wait for Gwenlie."

"Okay, fine," agreed Neffie.

Rem led her down a long hallway that ended in another double door, this one somewhat smaller than the pair opening into the maggus's main chamber. Pulling back the doors, they entered a large, unfurnished room with a high ceiling, a polished wooden floor, and blank, pale-yellow walls. Nine light guardians waited quietly inside.

"The Chamber of Gathering," Rem whispered to Neffie. "During the ancient wars, this is where the champions waited while the armies assembled below. Every battle started with a challenge between champions."

At that moment, Gwenlie arrived in the room, splendidly dressed and looking cool and calm. She flashed Neffie a confident smile.

*Time to focus,* Neffie told herself. *The challenge is all that matters.*

One of the nine called to Gwenlie, "Ready?"

"Of course," the woman answered in a firm voice.

Wordlessly, she moved to the center of the gathering room. The nine formed a circle around her. While they took their places, Rem steered Neffie to the side.

Once all the light guardians were in place, Hargwiddie, who appeared to be the oldest in the group, slipped onto his knees. Immediately, the others fell to their knees, leaving Gwenlie standing in the middle. Gwenlie turned to face Hargwiddie, who raised his hands, palms up, in front of his chest.

"For safeguarding the honor of the Charmaines," he declared, "you have my light."

Gwenlie responded by performing an elaborate honorium in front of Hargwiddie, and then she answered, "I accept the gift of your light and I thank you profoundly."

Next, the guardian immediately to Hargwiddie's left—the same red-haired woman who had spoken earlier in Maggus Sanguina's main chamber—raised her hands, palms up, and declared, "For safeguarding the honor of the Charmaines, you have my light."

The ritual repeated until all the light guardians had offered their light and Gwenlie had accepted their gifts. Sometime during the ritual, Neffie suddenly found herself wanting to offer Gwenlie her light, but considering she was not a Charmaine but a detested Sargie of the Vong Alliance, she decided it would be best to refrain.

Once the ritual was over, Gwenlie and her escorts gathered together and stood, waiting for the next step. No one spoke. A long time passed, and Neffie couldn't believe how quiet everyone remained. Finally, there was a single knock at the door.

"Time," a voice called, and there was an echo of receding footsteps.

Gwenlie walked past her escorts, heading for the double doors. One of the nine hurried ahead to open the doors for her. Rem and Neffie followed the procession as they made their way silently through the compound, moving down hallways and stairways that were oddly empty of onlookers.

When the party finally descended from the compound, large crowds of ordinary people awaited, filling the streets. Word of the challenge had spread like an Iowa prairie fire through the streets and houses of Galleyton High Main.

Neffie studied the crowds. Everyone's hoods were up, making it impossible for Neffie to see faces, but their short statures marked all the onlookers as groobers of one kind or another. For the first time since her arrival in the Tymes, she became aware that for the most part people gathered with others wearing the same color clothing. It suddenly occurred to her that the color of one's cloak or jacket might have meaning, perhaps denoting a family or clan connection. In fact, now that she thought about it, each of the two couples whose dispute she had judged wore matching colors, one pair a dark brown and the other a light yellow.

It must have been late in the afternoon because the reddish sun was low in the sky. Without a word, the Charmaines' challenge party wove through the crowd, heading toward the site of the great challenge that would decide the fate of Planck, Jessica, Neffie and Rem. Neffie's heart beat a bit too fast, and she was aware of a tightening of the muscles in her stomach. Strangely, despite the dangers ahead, Neffie's woodpecker was quiet.

Neffie glanced at Rem, who was walking silently beside her. He gave her a smile meant to communicate confidence. She smiled back. Slowing, she allowed the line of Charmaines to get a few feet ahead of them.

"If Gwenlie loses," she finally whispered, "is that the end of our hopes?"

"Not the end," Rem whispered back, his forehead furrowing, "but a terrible beginning."

"At least we'll be with Jessica," Neffie muttered.

"Oh, I can hardly wait for our life with the Vongs," Rem remarked coldly. "Such a clever blood-clan they are."

"If Gwenlie wins, what will the Charmaines do to her and me?"

"Jessica and you will eventually get to go home, I suppose."

"You think?"

Rem again paused before answering, "Let's not talk about it now. The first step is to get Jessica back."

"Right," muttered Neffie.

When the nine-plus-two finally reached their destination, Neffie faced a sprawling, ten-story superstructure that stood on twelve widely spaced columns of stone. Unlike the typical compounds of the light guardians, which denied access except to those with the physical ability to shinny up a tall column, this building offered public access via a corkscrew ramp that curled up from the ground to a huge triple door on its fifth floor.

"Here we go," Rem whispered to her.

Neffie and the others climbed the long ramp and entered through the triple doors. Once inside, they mounted a long, ornamental staircase with marble-like steps winding through the top five floors to a doorway opening onto the roof. From the doorway, Neffie looked onto a beautiful park covering roughly half the roof, with row upon row of flowers stretching in long beds in every direction. Among the rows of flowers were crisscrossing walkways lined with blooming fruit trees. Along the outer edges of the roof, a series of fountains running the entire length of the parapet walls tinkled musically as they spurted little bursts of water rhythmically into the air.

*Wow,* thought Neffie.

Beyond the park, at the other end of the roof, a long, skinny grandstand with four rows had been erected. Each row held about fifty individuals all dressed in long cloaks with narrow-brimmed hats. The cloaks were of a silvery material that reflected the sunlight in bright flashes.

"Those are the sages and the high sages," Rem explained. "They've come to watch the challenge."

Neffie had no idea what a sage was. "Is that good or bad?" she asked.

"I don't know. But it's seriously storyworthy they're here to watch."

In front of the grandstand stood eighteen posts, each of them slightly taller than Neffie and laid out in uneven rows forming an intricate pattern. All the posts were white, and they varied slightly in shape and thickness, though they all appeared to be supple and soft, reminding Neffie of the river willows she loved back in Iowa.

On top of each post was a small, bronze-colored bell suspended from a slender, S-shaped bracket, each rusted and very old. At two of the four corners of the post area, a star was painted on the roof's surface. Two triangles were painted at the opposite corners. The stars were gold and the triangles silver.

The contingent of light guardians from the Vongs waited silently on the other side of the roof. Neffie anxiously searched among them until she found Jessica standing in the middle, flanked by two guardians who towered a whole head above her. To Neffie's relief, Jessica looked unharmed.

Neffie didn't hesitate. Without a word to anyone, she took off toward her friend. Rem tried putting a hand on her shoulder to stop her, but she brushed it off. As Jessica stepped out of the contingent of Vongs to meet her, Neffie hurried to hug her.

"Oh my gosh," she whispered, "I'm so glad to see you."

"Me too, you," Jessica answered, her mouth so close Neffie felt the warmth of her breath.

Her eyes growing misty, Neffie asked, "Are you all right?"

"I'm fine, though I have to say, you have one freaky, weird family."

I mean it; they make our leaders back on Earth look normal."

"Tell me about it," Neffie chortled as a tear trickled from one eye.

"Now it's my turn to ask. You all right?"

"I am now," answered Neffie.

"What's going on?"

This question surprised Neffie. It hadn't occurred to her Jessica might be out of the information loop. On the other hand, she was a mere maidservant, not a noble. If Neffie had learned nothing else during her time on Fastness, she certainly understood there were ironclad rules and traditions dictating most behaviors.

"No time to explain," she answered. "Just do whatever I tell you, all right?"

Rem walked over and gave Neffie an accusatory look. "You just have to do your own thing, don't you?"

"I guess."

Then he turned to give Jessica a friendly grin. "How are you, maidservant? Did they treat you well?"

"Just peachy."

"Excellent. Now come with me, you two," he said, turning to lead them away.

"Take this other one, too," the Vong light guardian closest to Jessica called. A red-faced Mr. Planck came stumbling out of the nine and hurried over.

"Oh, Mr. Planck," cried Neffie, "it's good to see you."

Planck bowed. "My heartfelt thanks, my lady," he mumbled, looking embarrassed.

"Come," urged Rem, "all of you follow me." Rem led them to a platform and climbed onto it. "This is where we prizes wait," he said.

"What gives?" Jessica whispered.

"This challenge has four prizes," Rem said. "It's winner take all."

"What idiot made that bet?" asked Jessica, frowning. "Let me guess."

"*Ssh*," Rem said. "They're about to start. There's Gwenlie, our champion."

Tall, athletic Gwenlie did indeed look like a champion. She was splendidly dressed in a velvety, maroon tunic-cloak cinched at the waist by a gold sash. Her wide-brimmed hat was the same color as her tunic, and her elegant, beige trousers reminded Neffie of the horse-riding breeches worn by the heroic girl in the old movie *National Velvet*, with the pant legs tucked into the tops of high, shiny black boots.

Gwenlie carried the longest zabbaton Neffie had ever seen, chin-high if you were to place one gold-tipped end on the ground and hold the thing straight. Gwenlie held the zabbaton in her right hand. In her left hand she clutched a piece of cottony white cloth shot through with golden specks. Her face was resolute and calm as she took her place at one of the corners of the Posts of Eighteen, standing on the gold star painted just in front of the prize platform.

On the other side of the Posts of Eighteen, Maggus Jonesy emerged from behind the Vongs. She was as resplendently garbed as Gwenlie, wearing a tunic-cloak of vivid sapphire with a matching hat and a sash of silver. In her right hand, she held a similarly long black zabbaton with tips of matching silver. In her left hand, she carried a long length of white cloth with silver specks. She silently took her place on a silver triangle painted on the roof diagonally across from Gwenlie.

"Are you here as champion of the Charmaines?" Maggus Jonesy called to Gwenlie. "For I am here to answer the challenge of Maggus Sanguina and to act as champion of the Vongs."

"I am champion on behalf of Maggus Sanguina and all the Charmaines," Gwenlie called back, "and I demand your name."

"I am Jonesy, maggus of the most storied blood-clan of the Vongs and their champion in this challenge."

"And I am Gwenlie, a humble lass here, unworthy to act on behalf of so mightily storied a blood-clan as the Charmaine yet nonetheless their chosen champion."

"Who is your secondus?" Jonesy demanded.

"It shall be Lady Neffatira of the mightily storied Sargie blood-clan who will stand as my secondus," Gwenlie responded.

Cries of anger and dismay came from the light guardians on the Vong side, who apparently didn't like the idea of a Sargie serving as secondus to the champion of the Charmaines. Neffie was surprised; Rem hadn't mentioned anything to her about this. *What is a secondus?* she wondered.

Unfortunately, there was no time to ask Rem.

"And who is your secondus?" Gwenlie called to Maggus Jonesy.

"Mine is Lattiana, storied champion of many challenges on behalf of the honorable and profoundly storyworthy Vong blood-clan."

"How shall we fight?" the older woman called to Gwenlie.

"In the manner proposed," Gwenlie replied, "following strictly and reverently the ancient ways. Are you agreed?"

"I am," Maggus Jonesy answered calmly, with a hint of arrogance. "Prepare yourself and let the victor claim the prizes."

Turning, Gwenlie walked slowly to the platform where Neffie stood. The young woman's face was tightly drawn, Neffie observed, with her eyes narrowed, her lips taut, and her forehead creased with small wrinkles. A vein pulsed in her neck, hinting at the stress she was feeling.

Gwenlie said to Neffie, "Will you do the honor, my lady, of acting as my secondus?"

"I will do anything you ask," answered Neffie.

Giving a nod of gratitude, Gwenlie proffered to Neffie her piece of gold-specked cloth. Then she gave a little wink and whispered in a hushed, excited voice, "It is time to put Rem's plan into action, my lady. Are you ready?"

Neffie had no idea what this meant. Rem hadn't said anything to her. But it was too late to back down.

"I'm ready," she said.

"Excellent," Gwenlie muttered. "Now look into my eyes as I open myself to your light."

This took Neffie by surprise. Before, Gwenlie had suffered greatly from being exposed. Now she offered herself willingly.

Rem leaned her way and whispered, "Just play along. I had a last-minute idea, but it's a great one. Trust me."

Neffie stared at Rem. He gave her an encouraging smile and nodded. *Trust him?*

"Please, my lady," Gwenlie urged. "I believe Rem's idea will help."

Taking a deep breath, Neffie looked deeply into Gwenlie's eyes, probing for the woman's light. She found it quickly and was pleased to discover a willful determination mastering and controlling Gwenlie's nervousness and keeping her from succumbing to fear. Once Neffie was in full touch with Gwenlie's light, she relaxed and opened her own light to the woman, allowing a deep connection to be made. She sensed all of Gwenlie's emotions, her wants and fears, her hopes and doubts. The connection between the two women gradually deepened until they were virtually one person sharing the thoughts of two.

Inside their deep connection, Gwenlie hastily told Neffie the role she had to play. Then Neffie pulled back, severing the physical connection. Giving Neffie a quick wink, Gwenlie removed her hat. Now aware of what needed to be done, Neffie stretched Gwenlie's gold-flecked cloth in her hands and slipped it over the woman's eyes, blindfolding her.

"The cloth must be wrapped thrice," Gwenlie told her.

Nodding, Neffie wrapped the cloth three times around Gwenlie's head before tying the ends behind her. Once the woman was fully blindfolded, Neffie took Gwenlie by her shoulders and guided her back to the star marking her starting point. Taking a deep breath, Gwenlie slipped her hat back on her head as she took up her challenge position.

"Wish me luck," she said to Neffie in a solemn voice.

"Luck."

On the other side, Lattiana guided a blindfolded Maggus Jonesy to her place on a corner of the Posts of Eighteen. Neffie backed away from Gwenlie and returned to her place with the other prizes. As soon as Maggus Jonesy was on her triangle, Lattiana rejoined the other Vongs.

"Ready?" Rem whispered to Neffie.

Neffie could only give a tiny, quick jerk of her chin. She was too nervous to say or do anything more.

"Remember what you learned from Gwenlie's light," Rem whispered. "It's going to be your combat as much as it is hers. Concentrate!"

"I will," Neffie answered. "Now shut up!"

"Concentrate."

"I said shut up."

# CHAPTER 27

# A DREADFUL CHALLENGE

One of the high sages in the grandstand stepped down and moved toward the Posts of Eighteen. He was a very tall and slender man with white hair and a small, blondish goatee on his chin that looked rather silly to Neffie. He took up a position in one of the corners not occupied by either champion, striking a formal pose on the empty triangle. Another high sage, this one with black hair matching a long, black goatee, moved from the grandstand to stand in the last empty corner, positioning himself on the painted star there. Neffie got the impression they were going to stay there throughout the whole challenge.

*Referees,* she guessed.

"Is the champion of the Vongs ready?" the blond-bearded referee called.

"I am," cried Maggus Jonesy.

"Is the champion of the Charmaines ready?" the other referee called.

"I am," cried Gwenlie.

"Then the challenge may begin," they both declared in unison.

Neffie forgot to breathe as she stood silently on the prizes platform, waiting and watching without any idea what to expect. Then Gwenlie took the first step, starting to her left and eventually slipping inside the first post. She held her long zabbaton in front of her with both hands wrapped around the near end and the far end pointed high in the sky and tipped forward.

Moving on the balls of her feet, her heels raised off the ground either to keep silent or because it was the required custom, Gwenlie gradually eased into an open space defined by the first four posts, carefully guiding the end of her zabbaton to avoid hitting any of the posts. On the other side, Maggus Jonesy remained motionless, her long zabbaton also gripped at one end in both her hands, but with the leading tip angled downward rather than upward.

"I hear your breathing, Gwenlie," she taunted, "and for such a young lass, you have mightily heavy feet!"

As Neffie watched, Gwenlie stood silently, doubtlessly planning her next move. Then she slowly bent at the waist. Extending one arm as far as she could manage, she shifted her zabbaton to hold it with the tips of her fingers, and by doing so, she managed to stretch her arm just far enough for the leading end of her zabbaton to reach a distant post. Carefully, Gwenlie touched the end of her zabbaton lightly against the post and gave it a little push, causing the bell mounted atop the post to tinkle slightly. Though blindfolded, Maggus Jonesy instantly turned her head in the direction of the sound and then grinned.

"Clever lass," she called. "But you'd better think of something cleverer if you wish to fool an old hand like Jonesy."

In the next instant, Maggus Jonesy exploded off her star, racing obliquely in Gwenlie's direction down the open aisle between the first two rows of posts, her zabbaton leveled in front of her as she charged. Gwenlie must have understood her adversary's plan because she quickly darted down an aisle parallel to Maggus Jonesy's line of charge and took refuge behind a distant post.

How both women could move so quickly while blindfolded without bumping into any of the posts was beyond Neffie.

Gwenlie's escape plan failed. As soon as Maggus Jonesy passed the post dead in the middle of the formation, she veered abruptly to her right, zigzagging through posts toward the corner where Gwenlie now stood. Hearing her adversary's change of direction, Gwenlie quickly retraced her steps, taking long, measured strides to get herself back near her starting point.

The two women came even with each other on their separate routes, with only two rows of posts between them. Maggus Jonesy slowed as she neared Gwenlie, her zabbaton extended in front of her like the sword of a fencer. She took a noisy step to the left, causing Gwenlie to counter the move by sliding to her left, keeping two posts between them.

Suddenly, Maggus Jonesy burst into action, quickly covering the distance between the two women. Feigning left, the charging maggus made an abrupt move that brought her to the right side of a post with an open line to Gwenlie. With a grunt, Maggus Jonesy stabbed her zabbaton at Gwenlie with such speed that it was only a blur. Just in time, Neffie remembered that she was supposed to be helping.

*Dodge to your right,* her mind screamed at Gwenlie.

Gwenlie threw herself right and barely managed to avoid getting struck by Maggus Jonesy's thrusting zabbaton. Emitting a gasp of surprise, Maggus Jonesy pressed her attack, circling quickly around the post now separating Gwenlie from her.

*Keep going right,* Neffie's mind shouted at Gwenlie.

Gwenlie raced to the right.

*Now split the two posts in front of you!*

To Neffie's relief, Gwenlie did exactly as told, which put some distance between Jonesy and her.

*Go right again,* Neffie told her. *Now through the posts.*

Maggus Jonesy was on the move, too, matching Gwenlie's movements but keeping her distance. How she could know what Gwenlie was doing was again beyond Neffie. Instinct? Training? Luck?

Or did her obvious talents somehow have to do with Maggus Jonesy's light? Neffie suspected the answer was a combination of all these factors.

*Now turn and go forward,* Neffie told Gwenlie.

Following Neffie's directions quickly and precisely, Gwenlie maneuvered deftly through the posts, never actually putting any distance between Maggus Jonesy and her but keeping her opponent safely away. At Neffie's next command, she pivoted and came to a halt, leveling her zabbaton in front of her and standing at the ready, poised in perfect fencing position, her knees slightly bent, her feet in the classic *L* of the sport, with front toe pointed forward, back foot at right angles.

Maggus Jonesy now changed tactics to move very slowly and very silently, sidling to her left, her body facing roughly in the direction of Gwenlie. Watching her, Neffie couldn't believe the woman. It was as if Maggus Jonesy was not wearing a blindfold, so sure was she of every post's location and of exactly where Gwenlie stood in relation to her.

*She doesn't need her eyes to see,* Gwenlie whispered to Neffie.

*Stop thinking,* Neffie told herself. *Focus.*

*Yes, please,* Gwenlie agreed.

*Okay, I will. Now move to your right, behind the next post. Jonesy's moving that way about three posts from you.*

Gwenlie sidestepped to her right, perfectly mirroring Maggus Jonesy's movement while angling toward her.

*Take another step to your right,* Neffie thought. *You're closing on her and it doesn't look like she knows. That's it!* Neffie watched Gwenlie glide smoothly through the pattern of posts. *Almost there,* she thought. *Two more posts. Wait, watch the post in front of you! Your zabbaton is—*

To Neffie's horror, the end of Gwenlie's zabbaton brushed ever so lightly against the left side of the post, producing an audible click of wood against wood and a tiny tinkling of the bell mounted on the post. Maggus Jonesy reacted instantly, throwing herself to the ground in a long forward roll over one shoulder and then bringing her zabbaton up from below toward Gwenlie's stomach as she completed the roll.

Shocked, Neffie watched as the sudden, vicious attack unfolded, her mind freezing in the moment of crisis. With a post in the way, a blocking parry was impossible and there was no way for Gwenlie to dodge the blow.

*Jump,* Neffie's mind finally screamed, after she had wasted an agonizingly long second deciding what to do.

Fortunately, Gwenlie was a young, very athletic half human. Her body exploded off the ground, lifting high into the air.

Rising out of her forward roll and nimbly springing to her feet, Maggus Jonesy adjusted the thrust of her zabbaton, sweeping up with the tip of her weapon. Meanwhile, Gwenlie's body continued to rise like a space rocket launching off its pad. For one glorious moment, it looked like Gwenlie was going to lift out of range of the thrusting zabbaton in time to avoid Maggus Jonesy's blow.

But then, Maggus Jonesy pitched her body forward, and with this last desperate effort to extend her thrust, the leading end of her zabbaton cracked against Gwenlie's knee, knocking her askew and causing her body to spin out of control. The young woman cried out in pain, and as she twisted in the air, reeling from the blow, she threw out her arms to regain her balance but lost all sense of the posts around her. Her right hand slapped hard against a nearby post, causing the bell to clang noisily. In the next second, she crashed to the ground, landing on her knees, her shoulders hunched, her head slumped forward, defeated.

Maggus Jonesy reached up and ripped off her blindfold. "Victory!" she cackled. "To the Vongs, victory!"

*Plan B,* thought Neffie. There was no time to feel sorry for Gwenlie. She had only seconds to act.

"Come quickly," she whispered to Jessica.

Neffie knew she was about to break every rule of the blood-clans, but neither Jessica nor she belonged to these Tymes. They were from Earth, and this planet's customs were not their customs. Jessica and she had every right to get home.

Grabbing Jessica by the arm, Neffie yanked her friend forward, averting her face as she passed a startled Rem, not wanting to see the shocked, disapproving look that was undoubtedly spreading across his face. Accelerating to a sprint with Jessica in tow behind her, Neffie raced past the grandstand, heading for the nearest end of the rooftop, her muscles tightening for the leap to the next building.

In seconds, they were rushing past the gaping mouths and wide eyes of the sages and high sages arrayed in the grandstand. They were about to take the last ten or twelve strides that would bring them to the end of the roof when Gwenlie's voice screamed in Neffie's mind.

*Stop! You must stop!*

*No,* she answered back.

*You'll never get away,* Gwenlie warned. *Wherever you go, they'll find you.*

Inexorably, Neffie found herself slowing, frightened by the certainty in Gwenlie's thought, which was too persuasive to ignore.

*Yes, now please stop,* Gwenlie urged.

Reluctantly, Neffie halted, her chest heaving, all hope fading as she gave up on making a run for it.

*We'll find another way, I promise,* Gwenlie told her.

Sighing mightily, Neffie turned and looked back at Gwenlie, who stood awkwardly on one leg, the knee of the other leg shattered. Maggus Jonesy stood off to the side with an arrogant smirk on her face, flush with the excitement of her victory.

*What way can there be?* Neffie thought gloomily.

Before Gwenlie could send another thought her way, Neffie had a flash of inspiration.

*I've got it,* she told Gwenlie.

*You can't,* the woman answered.

*It'll work,* Neffie thought. *I'm sure of it.*

Taking a deep breath, Neffie drew herself into her best Queen Elizabeth pose—*no, my Lady Neffatira pose,* she told herself—and then she walked slowly back to the arena, taking calm, measured steps in Maggus Jonesy's direction.

When she was within reach of the nearest post, she called out, "I am Neffatira Akou Sargie of the profoundly and mightily storied blood-clan of the Sargies. I am Lady Neffatira, both from this side of the Tymes and from Earth on the other side, both human and light guardian. On behalf of my friend, Jessica, who should be home where she belongs, and not here, I challenge you, Maggus Jonesy, for the prize of her."

"Lady, you may not challenge. Have you forgotten? You are the prize," Maggus Jonesy laughed.

"I may be the prize," she responded, "but I am not merely some maidservant, nor am I a mere labor lifter. I am a storied Sargie and a light guardian and, as such, my rights and honor may not be lost through a challenge. Is this not true?"

"That is highly debatable," Maggus Jonesy answered, "considering that the challengers proposed the prizes and the challenge was accepted on those terms."

"No, it is indisputably true," Gwenlie cried, coming to Neffie's support. "A light guardian of the lady's stature has never been a prize. Never."

Maggus Jonesy shot Gwenlie a hateful look. "It may perhaps arguably be true," she countered, "but as everyone here well knows, the lass is too young to make such a challenge."

"That would be true," responded Neffie, playing another of her hunches, "except I am also a bearer of true light, and as such, age matters not."

"Oh, is that so?" replied Maggus Jonesy, snorting. "You may be marked by six spots, but that alone doesn't make you a bearer of true light."

Neffie summoned all her spirit to gaze fiercely into Maggus Jonesy's eyes. She imagined her own eyes flashing majestically, but there didn't seem to be any great effect on the woman. Then, out of the crowd of Vongs who had been inching slowly forward to witness this exchange between the two women, Mallaine suddenly spoke up.

"I can vouch for her. She has looked into my light and I can assure everyone here that Lady Neffatira is indeed a bearer of true light."

Neffie hadn't noticed Mallaine before, but now she turned her head to regard the young woman, who gave a small, encouraging smile. Maggus Jonesy spun and shouted venomously at Mallaine, her face contorting with rage.

"How dare you side with this one. Traitor!"

"I am within my rights," Mallaine retorted calmly. "Speaking the truth is never dis-honorable."

"That is so," spoke up Lattiana from the crowd, suddenly and unexpectedly voicing her agreement. "Mallaine is an honored light guardian of the Vong blood-clan, and as such, she has the right to speak, and she certainly has the right to vouch for Lady Neffatira if it is indeed the truth."

To Neffie's relief, there were a few cautious nods of agreement among the throng of Vongs standing near Lattiana. Maggus Jonesy was undeterred, however.

"Whether she is a bearer of true light or not," she argued, "a Sargie challenging a Vong just isn't proper; it is against the customs of our blood-clan and it is decidedly against the principles of our Alliance."

This, too, drew nods from the Vongs. Lattiana tightened her lips and said no more. When Gwenlie also failed to speak up, Neffie searched her mind, sifting through all she had seen and heard since her arrival in these Tymes, desperately looking for the proper answer. An idea came to her.

She called out, "As a bearer of true light, I reject the modern ways and draw on the traditions of our past to challenge in the ancient ways, back to the days when light guardians were champions without alliances, back when light champions of the same blood-clans challenged each other. It is my right as bearer of true light to claim the old ways."

Neffie glanced at Gwenlie, whose eyes had widened considerably. Then she gave Neffie an encouraging wink.

"So," Maggus Jonesy cried in a mocking tone, "we have here a bearer of true light. This is indeed a storied moment that we can witness such a challenge. Very well, I accept your challenge, issued according to the old ways. Take Gwenlie's binding cloth and her zabbaton and choose your secondus if you dare to continue this ridiculous challenge as if there were any hope you can defeat the great Maggus Jonesy."

Neffie glanced from Gwenlie to Mallaine and then back to Gwenlie. When their eyes met, Gwenlie gave a small, sad shake of her head.

*My knee makes me unfit to act as your secondus,* she told Neffie.

Quickly, Neffie made her decision.

"My secondus shall be Kerem Alp, honorable lad of the mightily and profoundly storyworthy Charmaine blood-clan, and like me, both human and a light guardian."

Maggus Jonesy's face immediately showed her disgust at the prospect of a despised Charmaine acting as secondus to a Sargie, even if the Sargie were her opponent in the challenge.

"Very well," she said. "Loyal Lattiana shall remain my secondus. Let us get started so I can finish this up quickly."

Neffie now walked over to the platform where Rem had stood watching. He regarded her silently with a most unhappy expression on his face that didn't change when she tried to give him a brave smile.

"What are you doing?" he asked.

"I'm being a bearer of true light."

"I can see that," he agreed gloomily, "and I repeat, what the heck are you doing?"

Having committed to this course of action, Neffie now refused to display any doubts. And she needed Rem on her side.

"Don't you believe in me?" she asked.

"Of course I believe in you. And you may indeed be a bearer of true light, but do you have any idea what that means?"

"Like, totally no, so tell me," said Neffie. "Please," she added, "I need help."

Sighing, Rem answered, "I'm afraid I can't tell you much. It's complicated and hard to explain. All I can say is, don't think about anything when you're out there. Empty your mind of all thoughts. It's the only way."

Limping awkwardly, Gwenlie now joined them on the platform. With a brave smile meant to be supportive, she handed her blinding cloth to Rem, Neffie's chosen secondus, who took it solemnly and stretched it between his hands. Before tying it around Neffie's head, Rem winked and flashed an encouraging grin.

"All right," he said to her as Gwenlie slipped her long zabbaton into Neffie's hands, "I do believe in you, and if you believe who you are, you can win this."

"I have to believe," replied Neffie.

She took off her hat, the hat that had belonged to Gwenlie before they traded outfits, and faced Rem. With three wraps, the young man bound her head thoroughly, covering her eyes and submerging her in darkness. Then he took the hat out of Neffie's hands and slipped it back onto her head, adjusting it for her.

"Ready?" he whispered.

"Yes."

Neffie felt Rem's hand on her shoulder as he gently nudged her toward her star in one corner of the Posts of Eighteen. Across from them, Lattiana was no doubt guiding Maggus Jonesy to her starting triangle and the two referees were taking their places. Neffie could almost picture the arrogant upturn of Maggus Jonesy's lips. She gripped the end of her zabbaton tightly with both hands, extending the length of it in front of her, with one end tipped upward as Gwenlie had done earlier.

*Maybe I should try pointing it down,* she thought. After all, down had worked for Maggus Jonesy.

She took another step, and then Rem brought her to a halt. To her dismay, his hand lifted from her shoulder. No doubt she was now standing on her star and therefore Rem was leaving.

*Up,* she decided, raising the tip of her zabbaton a little higher.

Neffie took a long, deep breath and waited. There was a painful moment of silence when nothing happened, and then a voice punctured the silence.

"Is the champion of the Vongs ready?" the blond-bearded referee called.

"I am ready," answered Maggus Jonesy.

"Is the champion of the Sargies ready?" the other referee asked.

"I am," Neffie affirmed, trying to sound confident.

"Then the challenge may begin," the two referees declared.

# CHAPTER 28

# BEARER OF TRUE LIGHT

Neffie had no idea what to do first, so she decided to mimic Maggus Jonesy from the previous challenge and do nothing. Standing dead still on her star, she breathed slowly and shallowly to be as quiet as possible, listening intently, following Rem's advice and trying her best to empty her mind. How many times over the years had her teachers reprimanded her for not concentrating?

*All the time,* Neffie thought. *Stop thinking. Concentrate!*

Neffie sucked in a breath and held it, hoping for one little sound from Maggus Jonesy that would give her away. Unfortunately, the woman was silent. Behind her, there was a hacking cough, likely from one of the sages in the grandstand. Then Neffie heard Jonesy because Jonesy wanted to be heard.

"You breathe more loudly than poor Gwenlie did," the woman taunted. "Pathetic!"

Neffie decided this was an empty boast because she wasn't taking any breaths for Maggus Jonesy to hear. Not that she could hold her breath much longer. Her lungs ached, and if she went on, she would become light-headed. Slowly and quietly, Neffie exhaled and then drew in a short, shallow breath. The fresh air felt good.

All of a sudden, she heard Maggus Jonesy coming slowly in her direction, though not directly at her. Neffie guessed that she was creeping along the far line of posts, zigzagging between the posts in a way that would gradually close the distance between them.

*What hope do I have of beating this unbeatable woman? . . . Stop it. Listen to Rem. Empty your mind.*

Neffie thought she heard the tiniest scrape of a boot heel on sand not too far from her, but she couldn't be sure. All of a sudden, she had an idea. Turning her head to feel the wind on her cheek, she gauged its direction.

*Okay,* she thought, *let's see what this does.*

She quietly removed her hat and took it by the brim. With a flick of her wrist, she sent the hat floating on the wind, Frisbee-style. A few seconds later, a bell tinkled somewhere near the middle of the posts.

Immediately, a heel did indeed scrape sand as Maggus Jonesy reacted to the sound. Neffie's best guess was that the woman was about ten or twelve feet away and a little to her right. Neffie's instinct was to move away from the woman, but in the next breath, she grew unsure. Jonesy obviously liked to make sudden, fierce attacks, so perhaps the best tactic would be to turn the tables on her by making the same kind of wild charge. But how could Neffie avoid the posts? She hadn't been trained to know their locations.

The alternative tactic was to move slowly and try to circle around the woman. Neffie didn't feel good about this choice, either. Jonesy seemed able to see without needing to see. Poor Gwenlie hadn't taken one step without the other woman sensing exactly where she was and what she was doing.

All of a sudden, Maggus Jonesy made the choice for her. Out of nowhere, she came blasting at Neffie, running full tilt, her long zabbaton preceding her like a lance. Blindfolded, Neffie couldn't see any of it, but somehow she knew exactly what was coming at her.

She wasn't ready to fence with the more experienced woman, and so she dove headfirst to her right, aiming for a space between two posts. Taking a page from Maggus Jonesy, she tried performing a neat shoulder roll, but her left shoulder smacked squarely into a post, and Neffie found herself sprawling to the ground on her stomach and sliding several feet before bumping into another post and coming to an abrupt stop.

Climbing quickly to her feet, Neffie shuffled past the post and took two steps back before coming to a stop, out of breath and panting, her zabbaton held in front of her, readying herself for the attack that was sure to come. To Neffie's surprise, however, no attack came.

*Is Maggus Jonesy playing with me? Enjoying herself at my expense?*

Drawing in a breath and holding it, Neffie stood as silently as possible, but even with that, she was unable to detect any sound from Maggus Jonesy. Exhaling, Neffie took three small, quiet steps backward and to her left, hoping to put a little distance between her and Maggus Jonesy. To her relief, she didn't hit any more posts, and the woman didn't come charging at her.

Then a bell tinkled somewhere to her right. Neffie strained to detect any sound from her adversary, but the only sound was the gradual fading of the bell.

*Where is she?* Neffie wondered. *How can she be so quiet?*

She needed another trick. But what? No great idea came to her. Then a voice interrupted Neffie's thoughts.

*My lady,* thought Gwenlie.

*Gwenlie. I need help,* Neffie signaled.

*Rem says to empty your mind, but it doesn't seem you can manage it. I've been trying.*

*Let me try helping you,* said Gwenlie. *Maybe we can beat her together.* The woman obviously didn't believe Neffie could win.

*Thanks, but it's no good,* Neffie replied as she took two cautious steps to her left. *You can't think fast enough.*

*Then empty your mind. Rem says it's the only way. Trust him!*

*I do trust him, but I can't do it.*

*You can,* answered Gwenlie.

Maggus Jonesy didn't give Neffie any time to try. There was another explosion of movement as the woman launched a powerful attack. Before Neffie could react, Maggus Jonesy rapidly closed the distance between them, galloping across the space like a cheetah after its prey.

*I'm dead,* Neffie thought as she desperately threw herself backward, certain it was too late to get away but trying nonetheless. Suddenly, there was a wild, animal-like scream near Neffie, not from the attacking Maggus Jonesy but from something or someone leaping between Jonesy and her.

"Get that felinx out of there!" one of the referees shouted.

"Nobila, how dare you?" cried Maggus Jonesy.

A huge commotion followed as the referees rushed into the posts to shoo away the creature. Neffie took advantage of the chaos to back slowly away, her zabbaton held protectively in front of her, her ears straining for any sound of her adversary.

*Thank you, Nobila,* she thought. *Thank you.*

After a few steps, Neffie came to a stop and waited silently, her zabbaton at the ready.

"Will both champions please stay standing where you are," an agitated referee commanded, "while we confer."

Nodding, Neffie gripped her zabbaton tightly and stood her ground. Several moments passed with painful slowness. Neffie heard the referees whispering in the distance. There was a bit of noise outside the Posts of Eighteen, and then the noise gradually faded.

"The felinx has now been restrained and so we may continue," one of the referees said. "Is the champion of the Vongs ready?"

"I am," Maggus Jonesy answered, her voice slightly agitated.

To Neffie's relief, she didn't sound nearby.

"Is the champion of the Sargies ready?" the other referee called.

"I am," Neffie answered calmly.

"Then the challenge may resume," they pronounced.

*Remember, empty your mind,* Gwenlie urged.

Inside the fabric of her blindfold, Neffie squeezed her eyes as tightly shut as she could manage. A bead of sweat trickled down her cheek.

*Don't think about the sweat,* she told herself, *don't think about anything.*

Neffie stared into the deep darkness of her eyelids. The black nothingness slowly engulfed her. Her mind went blank as she sank into a thoughtless state much like what happened just before falling asleep. Surrendering to the blackness, Neffie no longer listened for sounds of Maggus Jonesy. The woman no longer mattered to her. She was fading, sinking, emptying.

All grew as dark and as empty as death.

Then, to her surprise, everything suddenly became light, and Neffie found herself in a different world, a world where she could see without her eyes. Maggus Jonesy stood a mere three posts away from her, the woman's tall body partly turned in Neffie's direction. Maggus Jonesy was bareheaded, her hat no doubt having blown from her head during her fierce charge. Beyond Maggus Jonesy, the contingent of Vongs watched anxiously. Neffie noticed that Mallaine had taken Lattiana's hand and was squeezing it tightly.

Neffie turned her attention back to Maggus Jonesy. She sensed the woman's fierceness, mixed with such supreme confidence it frightened Neffie. Then she sensed other emotions running through Maggus Jonesy. Her dark hatred of all her enemies on Fastness. Her desire for power. Her anger at Neffie for betraying her blood-clan. And above all, her burning need to hurt Neffie. There were some other, less clear emotions in the mix, not in the forefront of the woman's light but tucked in the back, among them her doubt that she could be the clever leader her blood-clan needed and her sadness at the loss of her only daughter.

Neffie suddenly felt a great pity for the woman, and she found herself wishing with all her heart that she could just end this challenge and go home. Her wish for an ending grew stronger, and as it did, a strange thing happened.

Neffie began to tremble.

*Oh no,* she thought as the familiar dizziness crept over her. Helpless, she felt the force of her condition taking hold. Her hands quaked and her knees shook, and soon her whole body was awash in wave after wave of convulsions. Neffie grew light-headed and sensed she was about to black out.

*No, no,* she thought, *not now. Please, not now!*

She didn't want to fly away; she didn't want to bend alone, leaving Jessica behind, and so she concentrated all her thoughts on the ground just behind Maggus Jonesy and imagined herself there instead of flying across the Tymes. She imagined herself surprising Maggus Jonesy with a sudden blow of her zabbaton.

Suddenly, a giant crackle like thunder exploded above her, and in the next second, Neffie was standing directly behind Maggus Jonesy, no more than three feet away. The sky shimmered weirdly, and there was electricity in the air. Maggus Jonesy whirled, and Neffie flicked her wrists and neatly tapped the woman on the side of her head with the tip of her zabbaton. Then she thrust up the end of her zabbaton faster than the eye could follow and easily blocked Maggus Jonesy's hasty blow, which swept fiercely toward her head.

Before Maggus Jonesy could recover to aim another blow at her, Neffie jumped back out of range of the woman's zabbaton. Overdoing the jump slightly, Neffie banged against a post and fell to her knees. Sensing an advantage, Maggus Jonesy drove forward with blinding speed, tightening her grip on her zabbaton and aiming the weapon at Neffie's head. Out of nowhere, a loud voice boomed a sharp command.

"Stop!" the blond-bearded referee cried out. "I command you to stop!"

Taken by surprise, Maggus Jonesy froze, her arms half extended to strike at Neffie.

"A blow has been struck," the other referee cried. "The challenge is done."

"I concur," the blond-bearded referee shouted. "Neffatira of the Sargies is the victor."

Shocked, Neffie ripped off her blindfold and took a step back, anxious to get away from Maggus Jonesy and unable to believe the challenge was over. Not far from Neffie, Maggus Jonesy stood frozen in place, her jaw dropped, and Neffie saw that her hands were trembling. Then she loosened her grip on the zabbaton and it fell to the ground.

Slowly, Maggus Jonesy reached up and pulled the blindfold from her eyes. She stared in shock at Neffie, who felt compelled to return her gaze. Their eyes locked, and Neffie penetrated the maggus's light. At first, she could sense only puzzlement, but then a slow, burning hatred began to grow.

Frightened, Neffie broke the connection.

Neffie looked around. Every eye on the rooftop was on her. For a long moment, the whole world seemed frozen and unreal. Then one of the male light guardians in the Vong group dropped to one knee. Another followed. Mallaine began performing the Ritual of the Hand. Soon, all the women were performing the Ritual of the Hand and all the men had fallen on one knee.

Neffie turned slowly around. A handful of the sages and the high sages payed her homage by dropping to one knee or gesturing with a hand, but most of them were slipping uncomfortably from the grandstand and hurrying to leave via the door at the end of the roof. Neffie returned her gaze to Maggus Jonesy, who was still standing in the same place but now regarded her with eyes ablaze with hatred. Neffie wasn't afraid anymore, and so she returned the maggus's gaze calmly, almost compassionately.

*I'm sorry for you,* she thought.

Maggus Jonesy's face appeared to soften, but then the ugly scowl returned. In the next moment, Maggus Jonesy reached down and grabbed her zabbaton. With a fierce cry, she charged at Neffie, but before she could close the small distance, Rem was suddenly beside Neffie, having hurried from the prizes platform to come to her aid. Grabbing Neffie by the shoulders, Rem thrust her out of the way just in time to save her from being struck by the zabbaton.

Adjusting her aim, Maggus Jonesy swept her zabbaton through the air and smacked Rem on his shoulder, causing the lad to cry out in pain. He threw himself to the ground and rolled away from the attacking woman.

"Run!" he cried to Neffie as he rolled. "Run!"

Maggus Jonesy whirled to attack her, but by this time, one of the light guardians of the Charmaines had inserted herself between the hate-filled Maggus Jonesy and Neffie.

"Run!" she cried, repeating Rem's advice. "It is my fight now."

Neffie didn't linger to watch. Heeding the advice of her two allies, she spun and ran. She spotted Jessica to her left, and quickly she waved to her friend to come. Jessica didn't hesitate. With an explosion of speed only possible on Fastness, Jessica took off and quickly closed the distance, joining Neffie in her sprint across the roof. Around them erupted the sounds of zabbatons striking zabbatons. There were cries of anger and pain. As they sped past the battling light guardians, Neffie glimpsed a face red with blood and spotted an arm cocked as if it had been broken.

A war had just erupted on the rooftop, but there was no time to think about what this meant. In no time, the two girls reached the edge of the roof and without hesitating hurled themselves into space. Unfortunately, the nearest building was farther away than Neffie had remembered—the full width of a wide boulevard, at least—putting its roof clearly out of their reach. Neffie felt herself falling. She screamed. Behind her, Jessica screamed, too.

*This is the end*, Neffie realized. She closed her eyes and waited— waited for the crushing impact of her body hitting the pavement of the boulevard ten stories below.

# CHAPTER 29

# PRESENT AND FUTURE

When Neffie awoke, she was lying on the unreachably distant rooftop of the building across the boulevard. She had blacked out during the fall, and how she managed to reach the rooftop was beyond her.

A group of labor lifters in a mix of purple jackets and purple sweaters stood around her. They stared silently. There was a groan. Neffie looked toward the sound and found Jessica beside her. A trickle of blood ran out of her nose and into her mouth.

"Jess, you all right?" whispered Neffie.

Eyes popping open, Jessica quickly answered, "Peachy."

Neffie shifted her gaze back to the crowd around her, and this time she saw that Rem was among them. With a grin, he stepped forward and knelt beside her.

"Well, that was a mightily and profoundly storyworthy moment."

"What was?" Neffie mumbled, confused.

"Both the event on the roof back there," he remarked, pointing across the boulevard, "and your flight to this one. Seriously amazing," he confirmed.

Rem's eyes were so full of frank admiration Neffie suddenly grew very shy. Lowering her eyes, she looked briefly at her feet at the end of her long legs stretched along the rooftop, but then she felt enormously stupid for doing this and so she looked up to peer again into Rem's bright-green eyes.

"I have no idea what just happened," she said.

"Come here," said Rem, grabbing Neffie's hand to pull her up and then leading her away from the curious onlookers. Neffie instantly noticed the warmth of his hand. "You too," he added, waving for Jessica to join them.

"What about them?" asked Jessica, glancing across the boulevard. "It looked like World War III is starting over there."

"Don't worry about them," said Rem. "It's truly not your fight."

Rem led Neffie and Jessica to the far edge of the rooftop where they would be out of earshot of the labor lifters, who, of course, chose politely not to follow them. Rem was about to speak when suddenly there was a long rumble above them. Neffie looked up. High in the sky, a hole was opening above the rooftop where the Vongs and the Charmaines battled each other.

The sun turned blood red, and with this sudden darkening of the world there came cries of surprise and fear from the light guardians on the distant rooftop. Another rumble shook the sky, causing the rivals to cease their fighting and flee into the building.

Hooking a finger in the direction of the yawing hole, Rem said, "Seems you got their attention, Lady Neffatira." Oddly, he sounded calm and unafraid.

"Shouldn't we be worried about that hole?"

"No, this time we're in no danger," Rem said. "It seems your lady has gotten their attention, but now that you're no longer on that roof, it will take them a little while to find you."

"They? Who's they?"

"We need to talk," said Rem, "and talk quickly. It seems our last moment together isn't going to be long."

"What do you mean, last moment?"

"You know."

In fact, Neffie did know.

"There's so much I still want to say," she muttered. "I have so many questions."

Waving a hand at the sky above the distant rooftop, Rem answered, "It's good they're more curious than angry, but you can see their hole is growing and spreading in our direction."

"You still haven't said who they are," Jessica said.

"That is for another day," said Rem. "All I can say is, for once, the danger they bring might be less important. Those light guardians they've chased away will soon start thinking as they lick their wounds, and when they do . . ."

Rem's voice trailed off. Neffie didn't need him to finish his thought. The fighting on the rooftop had broken an ancient truce preventing war. Also, her defeat of Maggus Jonesy had perhaps proven once and for all that she was a bearer of true light. Whatever that meant, a new element had been added into the rivalries between the blood-clans. This frightened Neffie but also made her curious. In her short time on Fastness, the place with all its strange ways had become a home that somehow felt more like a real home than Iowa did.

"Everything is happening so fast," Neffie complained. "I want to stay longer."

"No," replied Rem. "This is the moment."

The sky rumbled again, this time closer and louder.

"Well, I'm ready," said Jessica, eyeing the sky. "Come on, Neff, it's time."

Rem agreed. "We need to say our goodbyes."

Facing Jessica, he locked his eyes on hers. "It has been seriously an honor to meet you, Jessica of Iowa, and I am profoundly privileged to have shared your light."

"Don't make me blush." Jessica smiled. "For a long time, I wasn't sure about you, but you're all right and I will miss you."

Laughing, Rem took Jessica's hand, raised it and then kissed it while staring into the girl's eyes. Then he turned to Neffie. Taking her by the arm, he drew her a few feet away from Jessica where they could speak privately.

"You need to know, your time on Earth won't last. They won't let it."

"I figured," Neffie answered, "and I hope it's you who comes for me."

"I can't promise that," said Rem. "Be careful. The first to come could be a friend. Or it could be something else."

"Let's not think about it," said Neffie, a lump forming in her throat. "Let's just say goodbye."

Nodding, Rem raised Neffie's hand and kissed it. His lips were soft and warm.

"Goodbye, Lady Neffatira Akou Sargie, goodbye," he whispered, his voice catching on the last word.

"Oh, goodbye," cried Neffie, pulling away her hand and throwing her arms around Rem.

Sighing heavily, Rem wrapped his arms around her in a tight embrace. Another long rumbling sounded in the distance, causing them to break apart.

"Um, so just how do we get back?" asked Jessica.

"Neffie, take my hands," said Rem, holding out both his hands for her. Nodding, Neffie gripped Rem's warm hands tightly. "Now, Jessica, you hang onto Neffie's waist," Rem instructed. "Hold tight, just as you did on your first bending."

When Jessica took hold, Rem gave Neffie a little wink.

"Did I ever mention my particular skilth is an ability to bend precisely across the Tymes? Just like your grandfather is supremely able to do?"

"No, you never did."

"It is one of the purposes for which I was bred and eventually trained. To be an escort, of sorts."

"So you've done this before?"

"Gwenlie was my first. You were supposed to be my second."

"Really?"

Laughing, Rem said, "Yes, part of a most clever plot conceived by the Charmaines, who have spies everywhere on Earth. I have to admit, bending a human across the Tymes as only you have done was not something they trained me for."

"Great," muttered Jessica. "You sure about this?"

"With Neffie and me acting together, I think we can manage it. Are you two ready?"

Neffie nodded. She liked the idea of working as partners with Rem.

"Ready," Jessica answered for them.

Pointing into the sky, Rem said, "Do you see those two evening stars just appearing on the horizon?"

"Uh-huh," said Neffie.

"Okay, take a good look at the one on the right, the red one. After you have it fixed in your mind, close your eyes and keep the image of that star before you. When we get going, hang onto my hands tightly and, Jessica, you keep a tight hold of Neffie. When I tell the two of you to let go, you must both let go immediately. Understood?"

"Got it," said Jessica.

Neffie didn't answer. She wasn't scared. She only felt sad because she knew what letting go of Rem would mean.

"Ready?" Rem asked.

"Yes, ready," said Jessica.

Neffie recalled the first time Jessica and she had done this. It seemed now to have been such a very long time ago, almost like an adventure from a different lifetime.

"Yes, ready," echoed Neffie.

Neffie picked out the pretty red star above the horizon, stared at it for a good, long moment and then closed her eyes. Immediately, her body shuddered as the blackness took hold. She became dizzy. Her body convulsed.

Then there was a drumroll of thunder overhead—not the rumble of the mysterious *they*, but a crackling of a different kind: the sound of force bending the Tymes. In the next instant, the three of them vanished.

# WANT A PREVIEW OF LADY NEFFATIRA'S NEXT ADVENTURE ACROSS THE TYMES?

Send you name and email address to **tom@eshmagick.com** and right away, author Tom Xavier will send you a sampling of unfinished first chapters from his next book in the Light Guardian series—plus a brief preview of what's likely to happen to Neffie and her friends.

**Warning!** With this sampling, you'll be getting a glimpse of Tom Xavier's work while he is writing it. What you receive could change in big ways as the story gets revised and edited, but here's a chance to see how Tom Xavier gets going at creating one of Neffatira's fantasy adventures.